A selection of recent titles by Judith Cutler

A Matthew Rowsley mystery

THE WAGES OF SIN *

The Lina Townend series

DRAWING THE LINE
SILVER GUILT *
RING OF GUILT *
GUILTY PLEASURES *
GUILT TRIP *
GUILT EDGED *
GUILTY AS SIN *

The Fran Harman series

LIFE SENTENCE
COLD PURSUIT
STILL WATERS
BURYING THE PAST *
DOUBLE FAULT *
GREEN AND PLEASANT LAND *

The Jodie Welsh series

DEATH IN ELYSIUM *

* available from Severn House

THE WAGES OF SI

THE WAGES OF SIN

Judith Cutler

This first world edition published 2019
in Great Britain and 2020 in the USA by
SEVERN HOUSE PUBLISHERS LTD of
Eardley House, 4 Uxbridge Street, London W8 7SY.
Trade paperback edition first published
in Great Britain and the USA 2020 by
SEVERN HOUSE PUBLISHERS LTD.

British Library Cataloguing in Publication Data
A CIP catalogue record for this title is available from the British Library.

ISBN-13: 978-0-7278-8938-6 (cased)
ISBN-13: 978-1-78029-654-8 (trade paper)
ISBN-13: 978-1-4483-0352-6 (e-book)

All Severn House titles are printed on acid-free paper.

Severn House Publishers support the Forest Stewardship Council™ [FSC™],
the leading international forest certification organisation.
All our titles that are printed on FSC certified paper carry the FSC logo.

Typeset by Palimpsest Book Production Ltd.,
Falkirk, Stirlingshire, Scotland.
Printed and bound in Great Britain by
TJ International, Padstow, Cornwall.

ACKNOWLEDGEMENTS

The biggest influence in this book was Cutler family folklore: my great-grandmother, a daughter of the estate's gate-keeper, was made pregnant by the youngest son of one of Shropshire's richest landowners. Noblesse clearly not obliging, she was despatched from the estate with the warning that if she did not go quietly, her family – her parents and all their siblings – would lose their employment and their tied accommodation. She survived, as did her daughter, Granny Cutler, a redoubtable woman who by the time I knew her was more to be feared than to be loved, having raised a large family in absolute poverty.

Apart from having spent a lifetime visiting National Trust properties, where the areas behind the green baize door seem to me tell more about life than the glossy, front-of-house rooms, I turned to several invaluable books: *The Rise and Fall of the Victorian Servant* by Pamela Horn; *Keeping Their Place* by Pamela Sambrook; *The Victorian Kitchen* by Jennifer Davies; and Norah Lofts' *Domestic Life in England*. My thanks to all these women whose deep knowledge puts mine to shame. My good friend John Marshall gave invaluable advice about the clergy of the time.

Any mistakes? Mine. Apologies.

To the women running and supported by Gloucestershire Domestic Abuse Support Service

ONE

There were days when my responsibilities running Lord Croft's estate weighed heavily on me. I might be responsible for increasing – and spending! – my employer's fortune, but I had to ensure his people were treated fairly too. After nearly two months in the post, I was all too aware that most of the glances they exchanged as I approached were suspicious or even actively hostile. Who could be surprised, when only last week I had to tell a tenant that his farm was in such poor heart he would have to leave come Candlemas. Before that it was a dairyman watering milk. I had no natural allies in the household as yet; both Mr Bowman, the butler, and Mrs Faulkner, the housekeeper, had every reason to doubt me too: a man younger than they suddenly descending on their realm, a real live *deus ex machina*.

So it was a great pleasure to ride on my own in the early morning sunshine hoping to find a few white-skinned mushrooms, their gills a delicate oyster-brown, for my solitary breakfast in a house almost embarrassingly bigger and better appointed than any other on the estate. But having gathered my harvest and remounted Esau, I saw that someone else was stirring, had indeed already finished one of his daily tasks. A portly gentleman carrying a medical bag was emerging from the Kentons' cottage, with an expression of satisfaction on his worthy face at odds with its weariness: Dr Page. Silas Kenton was more than simply seeing him out, he was practically dancing round him, pressing on him what looked like newly picked peas, in, of all things, a cricket cap. Obviously Mrs Kenton had successfully been delivered of her latest child.

'I gather congratulations are in order,' I called, dismounting and looping Esau's reins over the fence. 'Good morning, doctor; good morning, Kenton.'

Page shook my hand; Kenton tugged his forelock. ''Tis another boy, Mr Rowsley.'

'And a very fine, lusty fellow too,' Page agreed. 'But I've been telling young Kenton here not to think of going in for a whole team of cricketing sons. His sixth already! He's got a beautiful wife, and he doesn't want to wear her out with childbearing.'

'No, indeed.' How on earth did they all fit in the cottage, by no means the largest on the estate? Impulsively I passed the young father the clutch of mushrooms, trying not to laugh at his bemused disbelief. 'An easy breakfast for you, Kenton, and your good wife. Now, I can see your garden is doing well, and that you will not lack for food. But I'm sure her ladyship or Mrs Faulkner will be sending down beef tea and everything else that women consider needful in these circumstances.' This time I pressed a couple of guineas into Kenton's hand, closing his fingers round them. I added, overriding his stuttered thanks, 'But if Dr Page considers that your wife needs anything in particular, you are to use that to purchase it. Understand?'

Another tug of the forelock, with more stammering and a deep blush; he had just realized I had given him twice what he might have expected.

'The chickens are laying all right, sir.' Did he sound defensive? Perhaps I had been too generous and he felt patronized. 'We've still got a scrap of that old porker we killed; one of the litter he sired is doing nicely.'

I followed his gaze. Yes, penned in a so far untamed corner of the garden it was chewing its way through the scrub with every appearance of enjoyment. 'I don't like the way it's eyeing your hat,' I told Page, with a laugh.

'Indeed, after all those brambles and nettles, straw would be an epicurean feast. Now, good day to you, Kenton – and don't forget what I said.' Dr Page took my arm, propelling me towards his trap. Once out of earshot, he said, 'You won't have to do anything about that animal, will you, Rowsley?'

'Do anything?' I repeated stupidly.

'Blakemore – the last land agent – was very much against tenants keeping any sort of livestock, even the odd hen, for goodness' sake.'

'Did he give any reason?'

'Said his lordship – his *late* lordship, of course – didn't want his land turned into a menagerie. Personally I think it was the man's own prejudice.'

'I trust his son has more sense.' At least in public I did. In private was entirely a different matter. 'And to be sure, well-fed workers should be better workers, shouldn't they? Purely in terms of self-interest Lord Croft should encourage such activity.' But might not, I conceded silently, if he actually knew about it.

Page clapped me on the shoulder: 'It's clear *his agent* has more sense, at any rate! Of course it's right that people should eat adequately. How a family can sustain itself on bread soaked in tea to taste like meat, I cannot imagine. But I have been idle long enough,' Page said quickly, almost as if he wished to dissociate himself from any criticism of my employer that his words might have implied. 'Good day to you.' He waited until I was on horseback before he waved and set off.

I could have waylaid one of the lads dredging the lake, telling him to take to the household staff the news of Mrs Kenton's safe delivery. But I decided to go myself, taking a circuitous route back to the House to see how his lordship's other 'improvements' were progressing. No! I must not allow irony to enter my thoughts, let alone my voice, when I spoke of them. In truth, there was much urgent work needed to preserve the house and the Capability Brown estate. The house in particular needed attention. The original must have been Tudor, perhaps earlier, in a sort of capital E shape. Since then there had been many additions, not all of them aesthetically pleasing – perhaps the worst being a grand entrance hall, which strove hard to be impressive, but sat uneasily on a frontage that would have preferred Georgian restraint. Much of his land, not just here in Shropshire but in other counties across the country, was in bad heart too. But it was hard, very hard, to make his lordship invest in anything that would not bring an immediate return of pleasure or financial benefit. I was becoming accomplished in delivering half-truths, if not outright lies.

Leaving Esau to the care of the stable lad, I chose to enter the House through the servants' entrance, though I was sure that Mr Bowman would have preferred to see me bowed and scraped through the imposing entrance hall into the corridor leading to my office. What must these men and women, through whose territory I passed, make of my habit? Some might have suspected me of spying on the menial staff – from the latest terrified tweenie who pressed into the shadows as I walked past, to the occasional pot-valiant footman. In fact I did it in honour of my father, once a country clergyman. In his time he had experienced the humiliation of being turned from the front door as one too lowly to use it. When he became an archdeacon, of course, this was no longer the case; perversely he would often insist on using the below-stairs route, greeting his old friends as he did so.

By now I was learning to know the staff and their functions, though the standard liveries on tall young footmen with impassive faces and the desperately unflattering caps on the young women in their ugly grey dresses made the task harder. And there were so many of them – there were some twenty-eight permanent indoor servants. To all of them I was always 'Sir', or to the dozens of outdoor workers 'Gaffer'. At the moment, the only reason I had for my authority was my role. A land agent was a man to be feared because of his ability to take away livelihoods at a stroke. What I wanted was to be respected for the breadth and depth of my knowledge. I wanted to be admired for my human decency and my sense of justice.

The first person I saw as I passed along the back corridor was Mrs Faulkner, standing in the servants' hall perusing some list or other. To some a housekeeper was just a small woman bustling round a house, however impressive that house might be. Instead I saw her as the captain of a great ship – the brew-house, the dairy, the laundry, not to mention the cleaning and the cooking were all ultimately her responsibility, though she never gave the impression of having to do anything herself.

'Good morning, Mr Rowsley – and what a fine one it is,' she called.

Naturally I entered, raising my hat in response to her curtsy.

She raised her voice: 'Maggie!'

A maid, surely no more than fourteen with her pretty round face and plump childish arms, scuttled in, took the hat, and went to hang it up somewhere. Half turning to me, as if to say something, Mrs Faulkner watched her. In the end, she shook her head, saying nothing. I sensed that for once her smile was polite, not welcoming.

On reflection perhaps the cheer in my voice grated. 'I have news to make it finer, Mrs Faulkner. Mrs Kenton was safely brought to bed this morning. Both mother and child – another healthy boy – are doing well.'

A slight frown replaced her smile. 'Dear me, all those children! Ada used to be in service here, you know – and she could have done very well for herself if she hadn't fallen for young Silas Kenton. But of all the young men working on the estate, I'd say he was the best, though I'm not so sure about his brother.'

I nodded. 'Silas seemed happy to take Dr Page's advice about the size of his family.'

'Dr Page was in attendance? No wonder everything went well. He's a good doctor and a good man,' she declared decisively. She lowered her voice as she explained, 'I believe it is his habit not to charge the poorest families for his services. But he would not want that to be widely known.'

I bowed. I risked saying, 'My godfather, also a country doctor, had the same creed. So no one will hear of it from me. Do you think, Mrs Faulkner, that her ladyship would wish to send a few items – perhaps some nourishing jelly – to the Kentons?'

'It is most likely,' she said calmly. 'If she is well enough, she might wish to take her gifts herself, when she takes the air in her new dog-cart. If not, I will undertake to walk down this afternoon and deliver them. I like to see the progress of the improvements his lordship is making,' she added.

Did this mean she would like me to accompany her? Or was she making a simple statement? It was strange to think such a practical woman enigmatic, but in truth I found it hard to describe her, even to myself, though we had been acquainted since Lady Day, when I took up my position here. In person, she was neither tall nor short, neither plump nor slender. Her face was equally unremarkable, except for her eyes, which were always watchful but showed a certain brilliance when she was amused. As for her age, though there were hints of grey in her hair – always, of course, mostly covered with a cap – her skin was as clear, as youthful, as the youngest maid's. She was not much older than me, I would say. Perhaps she was forty.

'If there is anything you would particularly like to see, please let me know and I will be at your service.' I was ready to bow myself out.

Before she could reach for the bell, another small figure materialized in the furthest doorway, bobbing a deep but not elegant curtsy.

'Thank you. I will. Meanwhile, Mr Rowsley, Bessie here has just made – under Mrs Arden's supervision, of course – her first batch of rolls.' It was typical of her to know what was going on in what was really the cook's realm.

'Bessie? I thought something smelt very good.' I smiled down at her. It was hard to tell her age – if born into a family like my employer's, she would be eight or nine, but poor children never grew so fast. Perhaps Bessie was twelve, a very tiny scared twelve.

'I am sure she would be honoured if she could take one to your office to enjoy with your morning coffee.'

'Please, sir. Yes, sir. I'll take it directly. But please, Mrs Faulkner, ma'am, Mrs Arden has just made her ladyship's special coffee, ma'am, and she says there is a good jugful left over. Would you like it?'

Mrs Faulkner's smile was immediate but very formal. 'Yes, please, Bessie. Mr Rowsley? Would you care to partake? So, Bessie, please prepare a tray and take it to the Room.' This was the term by which everyone, Mrs Faulkner included, referred to her sitting room, where all the senior staff gathered for late supper every evening. This was the first time, however, that I had ever been there with no other guests. But she added, 'And invite Mr Bowman to join Mr Rowsley and myself. That will mean . . .?' she prompted gently.

'Three cups and saucers, three plates and three rolls, Mrs Faulkner. And knives and butter and jam and spoons for the jam and a butter knife.' It all came out in a great rush. 'And three napkins, ma'am.'

'Excellent. There may be some cold beef, Mr Rowsley? No? Off you go, then, Bessie. Best ask Mr Bowman first. And don't forget to knock his door very firmly.' She busied herself smoothing the non-existent creases from the tablecloth. 'When I need a new girl I try to take one from the workhouse, but . . .' She shook her head. 'They don't even know the words for common kitchen objects, so they annoy Mrs Arden, and if I let them try their hand at dusting, the mortality rate amongst the china and crockery is alarming. The superintendents are supposed to educate their poor young female charges for a life in service but what they are taught – pff! Nothing! Nothing to the point,' she corrected herself. 'They deserve better, whatever Mr Pounceman says. Much better.' Before I could reply that I often found it hard to listen to Pounceman's sermons without standing up to object to his opinions, she turned decisively and gestured me towards her parlour.

It was, as always, immaculately clean. But I had never known it immaculately tidy. There was always a book or two on the table beside what was clearly her favoured chair. Before I could ask her what she was reading, Mr Bowman appeared, his gait as ponderous and stately as if he were approaching the Queen herself. He bowed rigidly from the hips, an exertion that made his face even redder, his breathing more stertorous. But he sat with a certain grace, despite his bulk and height; he must have been a fine-looking youth, just the sort a household would want for a footman. Like all his fellow footmen at Thorncroft House, he was clean-shaven, leaving extravagant facial hair to outdoor workers. I myself also declined to be fashionably hirsute.

Bessie came in with the tray, almost staggering under the weight. Under Mrs Faulkner's gaze, she transferred everything to the table. Bobbing another flatfooted curtsy in response to the kindly approving smile, she scuttled away.

For a moment perhaps, Mrs Faulkner tensed, glancing swiftly at her guests; should Mr Bowman or I take precedence? To me it mattered not a jot, but in establishments like these, triviality assumed staggering proportions. In terms of age and experience, I should certainly defer to him. On the other hand, she might reason that while he ruled the household, I ran the entire estate.

The old man solved the problem, if indeed problem it was, by asking for coffee but refusing the roll before either was offered.

As he sipped, very genteelly, I told him the good news. 'Perhaps,' I ventured, 'his lordship might wish to send the family some port wine. I understand it to be very nutritious.'

He creaked to his feet. 'I shall see to it forthwith.' He at least was prepared to admit that the Family left all their good deeds for their employees to carry out.

I barely had time to ask Mrs Faulkner to pass on my compliments to both Cook for the coffee and Bessie for her bread when he returned with two dusty bottles sporting cobwebs which Mrs Faulkner flapped away with her napkin.

'The best wine comes in old bottles, does it not, Rowsley?' Somehow the observation sounded indecent, as if he had nudged me in the ribs.

Mrs Faulkner, impassive, looked at both bottles. 'Are they both for the Kentons, Mr Bowman?'

I wondered too. They were the sort that used to grace my father's table when the bishop dined. How many guineas' worth was he giving away?

'I think his lordship could spare them.'

So, in fact, did I.

'On the other hand,' he was saying, 'according to that milksop Pounceman, we should not encourage the lower orders to take strong drink. Did you know he wants his congregation to sign the pledge, as if they were Methodists?' To my amazement he added, 'Poor souls, they have little enough joy in their lives and now he wants to take away what they have. The servants here expect small beer with their meals. As for the workers, what harm does it do for a man to spend the odd evening at the Royal Oak nursing just half a pint of ale? Take one bottle now, Rowsley, and I will put the other aside for when Mrs Kenton has finished the first – for it must be for her, of course, while she is feeding the infant, and not for that hulking husband of hers.' He produced a huge knowing wink. 'Now, which would be more health-giving, ruby or tawny? Mrs Faulkner, which do you prefer?'

'I have no opinion, Mr Bowman.'

'Then you must taste them,' he declared jovially – as if, indeed, he was in his cups. 'All port needs to be decanted, of course, so I will bring some from my pantry that his lordship didn't finish last night.'

Mrs Faulkner's face tightened further, as if she was not enjoying this interruption to her working day.

'In my experience,' I said quickly, 'people who are not used to port prefer the sweeter tawny. Thank you.' I put it on the table. 'I will take it on my next visit.' Then, as if as an afterthought, I turned to Mrs Faulkner. 'Would you be kind enough to tell me what would be an appropriate gift from a bachelor like myself? Perhaps we could discuss it when I show you the developments

by the lake this afternoon. Would three o'clock be convenient?'
I rose to my feet.

She rose too, bobbing a curtsy. 'I will jot down some ideas,
Mr Rowsley.' She looked with some ostentation at the big clock.
'I fear, gentlemen, that her ladyship will be wishing to give me
her orders for the day.'

We bowed ourselves out, going in opposite directions.

I

I must be dead and have been carried up to heaven. The light! The sweet singing! But as my eyes get used to the glitter of the candles against the mirrors, and to the strange echo of all our voices, I know I am not dead. I am in the Great Hall. There beside Nurse is Cook, in her best cap and apron, there is Tom, the footman who often slips an apple into my hand because I remind him of his little sister back in Derby, and there Mr Drake, the butler. Mrs Baird, the housekeeper, looks nearly as grand as Miss Martha, her ladyship's maid. But her ladyship and his lordship – yes, they might be angels, so beautiful do they look in their finery. His lordship stands beside her ladyship's chair, all smiles. Young Master Augustus hands each of us a package, oh, so beautifully wrapped, some with ribbons – those are for the women and girls, of course. Everyone has their gift in order of rank, so I have to wait till the very last. The very, very last.

At last it is my turn. I mustn't snatch, however much I might want to. I must walk the length of the row of maids, past the footmen, past Mrs Baird and past Mr Drake. Curtsy. Three paces forward. Curtsy. Take the parcel with not a hint of a snatch. Three paces backwards. Curtsy. A slow walk back to my place. Then, line by interminable line, we troop back to the servants' hall.

Back to the places we have to sit at table.

We sit.

We are to undo the ribbons carefully. Mine is a lovely blue ribbon, just the colour of my mama's eyes, as I remember them at least. Even though I know I won't be allowed to wear it, I long to put it under my pillow each night, where I can stroke it.

The ribbons – pink, yellow, red, and my lovely blue – all have to be laid on the table. Mrs Baird walks behind us, taking up each in turn. No one says a word. We still have the paper to pull back, after all. There are no cries of joy. No cries at all.

My present is a pair of pinafores, one coarse for when I carry the chamber pots, the other tough cotton for everyday use.

At last a cry rings through the servants' hall, as if a sick animal has been kicked.

The howl comes from me.

TWO

I t was another perhaps foolish whim of mine, having seen the world below stairs, to leave via the circular entrance hall, its height enhanced by the domed ceiling. Inside one had no sense of how inappropriate it seemed from the outside; all was elegance, indeed grandeur. I was halfway across, the footman hovering there ready to throw open the grand front doors, when I realized that my hat remained wherever young Maggie had hung it when I arrived. I could easily have walked back. But the footman would have thought the less of me if I had. Having despatched him on this most trivial of errands, I wandered round, looking at the portraits decking the walls. Had they been more easily visible under their years of accrued grime – I must be able to find an expert capable of cleaning them properly – perhaps they would have been impressive, though personal beauty did not seem to be part of the Croft inheritance.

Raised voices were so out of place here that I felt it was my business to see what was going on. But the echo that characterized the hall baffled my ears – were the shouts coming from the top of the double staircase, or from the dining hall corridor? It was a man's voice I heard most of, then the higher tones of a woman. Frustratingly the echo distorted them even more than the bass notes; try as I might I could not positively identify the participants in what seemed a very unpleasant argument. Surely they could not be his lordship's and his mother's? But here was the footman – Broomfield? – back with my hat. It would not do for me to ask him what was going on.

When I had agreed to show Mrs Faulkner the work on the nearest part of the estate, I had forgotten about my appointment with the rector, whose belief in the perils of drink had clearly not endeared him to Mr Bowman. If I rode to the rectory, and if I cut short discussion of what I had to say, I should not be late. I told Luke to have Esau brought round.

One of the no fewer than six servants I encountered at the rectory took Esau to the stables. Six! And no doubt more unseen below stairs. My parents would have been either amused or enraged at such pretension in a bachelor man of the cloth.

The Reverend Theophilus Pounceman received me in his study, with a handshake fit to break my fingers; clearly he was a believer in muscular Christianity. He gestured me to sit opposite him as he retreated behind his extremely handsome desk. I did so, laying my papers between us. He must be roughly my age, in his mid-thirties. Like me he was a bachelor. Tall, broad-shouldered and handsome, with the most flourishing of lamb-chop whiskers, he surged through life as St George might have done, looking for a dragon to slay – but not perhaps for a maiden's sake; I had a constant sense that no woman would ever be good enough for him. In one or two of his sermons he had been so disparaging about what he called 'the weaker sex' that I had had to point out after the service that more than half his congregation were women, who between them did a great deal of good, however poor they might be.

'You have come about my plans,' he said, observing the rolls of paper.

I bowed, without irony, I trust, at his swift deduction of the obvious. 'Yes. About Stammerton.'

'St Stephen's,' he said in a tone of patient correction.

Stammerton was a sad huddle of farm labourers' dwellings scarce deserving of the term cottages. His late lordship had accepted Pounceman's proposal that the workers should have their own church nearer to where they lived; in Mr Pounceman's mind, it was clearly already dedicated to the first martyr. On face value, a new place of worship was a very generous idea, but I could not see why a building for the worship of the Almighty should have such lowly ambitions. It was to be built in the least desirable location in the village, with steep steps leading from a lych-gate to the rather perfunctory porch. The building itself was a simple rectangle, with a tiny bell-tower a couple of feet high, and a roof that reminded me of nothing more than a barn. At best, the edifice recalled the humblest non-conformist chapels, whose plainness reflected less the spiritual aspirations than the sheer poverty of the community devoted enough to erect it.

It was only as I opened my mouth to condemn the meagreness of the design that Pounceman's opening words took on any significance. *My plans.* Could it truly be he wanted such a dismal little place? Could he really believe it would raise hearts and minds heavenwards?

'I am interested to see what can be done about the whole of Stammerton, including, of course, the church,' I said. 'I see that his late lordship was prepared to be very generous and I am sure that his heir will honour his commitments.' He almost certainly would if I blithely assured him that his father had agreed the expenditure was necessary. 'Those apologies for cottages – leaking roofs, earth floors, shared stinking privies – they must and shall be improved, replaced, for preference. Imagine it, Pounceman: two or three tidy rows of decent houses, all with pumps and privies, and each with a decent-sized garden. Or perhaps small cottage gardens, with allotments within easy walking distance, might be preferable.'

Despite my passion – perhaps because of it – his face was impassive. I was implying a criticism, to be sure, but in his place I would have been more enthusiastic. A moment's reflection would have told him that he was dealing not with the old lord and his lickspittle agent, but with the new lord and his equally new but very eager representative.

'My interest is the villagers' spiritual lives,' he declared grandly.

I bowed. My grandfather had taught me a variety of such movements. With a flex of his spine he could denote any emotion from gratitude to cold anger. I trust that my inclination showed a polite acquiescence but a hint that I did not consider the matter closed. 'Of course.' Grandpapa would have nodded approval if he'd heard the wealth of meaning behind those two syllables.

But Pounceman seemed to have accepted them at face value. 'I assume you are here to tell me when building can begin.'

Grandpapa would have applauded my ambiguous smile. 'I am here to ask if you might want to make any amendments to the design. Architects do not always put on paper what we who commission them actually envision.'

'But you mentioned cottages and goodness knows what else.'

'So I did. Let me show you.' I unrolled another sheet of paper.

'This is how the village is now, with the new church here.' I pointed. 'This is what I sketched out the other day – I hope you will forgive its amateurishness. I thought that in addition to the houses I mentioned we might turn that patch of mangled grass into a village green, with – why not? – a dew-pond for ducks just here. I would hope there is enough space for a game of cricket.' I might not share my father's somewhat extreme view that the fact that English gentlemen played cricket in the same teams as their hired hands prevented an English Revolution to match the French one, but I certainly knew from my own experience that the summer game enhanced the spirit as well as the body of those involved. 'Decidedly a school, with a house for the master or mistress.' My grandfather had changed village life when he had appointed a teacher; Stammerton deserved nothing less.

'Surely that is not necessary.'

'Reading and writing, Pounceman!'

'And what might they read? The scurrilous notion that we are cousins to chimpanzees? Never.'

'There are other things to learn,' I said mildly, feeling that discussion of the eminent Mr Darwin's theory would not be fruitful. The information that my father regularly corresponded with him would certainly not be.

'Of course. And these children could learn them at Sunday school when not required elsewhere.'

'They could, if there were one. But – correct me if I am wrong – there is no Sunday school here in Thorncroft, though there must be sufficient demand.'

'Do you not recall the words of the charming children's poem, sir?' – I did not like his smile as he recited it – '"The rich man in his castle, The poor man at his gate, God made them high and lowly, And ordered their estate."'

'I do not recall reading those words in the Bible,' I said repressively. 'But back to the matter in hand. The village plan. Why not – forgive me, my dear Pounceman – why not place the church here, where it would add its benign presence to the village at all times? A clock on its tower. Some trees which would grow to provide comfortable shade—'

'And where will the poor, benighted men and women worship while all these castles in Spain are built?' he demanded.

'Why, here, of course. Here in Thorncroft. As they have done for generations.' If not, I had tacitly to admit, in great numbers.

'Here? Amidst all the gentlefolk? No, Mr Rowsley, I venture to suggest that you fail to understand the dangers of envy. Think of Chartism. Think of Peterloo, of the Swing Rebellion, of the Tolpuddle Martyrs – we do not want their like here!'

'Indeed we do not. This is why I contend that we need to attend to the bodily as well as the spiritual needs of these people. Pounceman, I have sprung all this upon you. Pray, cast your eyes – cast your mind! – on my poor scribbles and see what the future could be, in as little as five years perhaps.' I got to my feet, picking up my hat. 'I regret I cannot continue our discussion now. I have another appointment.'

Mrs Faulkner appeared wearing not a bonnet to conceal her face but a flattish, wide-brimmed hat, which somehow offset the spread of her crinoline. She did not demur when I offered to carry one of the two baskets she had filled with necessities for the Kenton family. She handed me the heavier one, from which the neck of the bottle of port protruded. Hers contained linen and knitted garments, she said.

I noticed something else. 'Will the baby need tops and whips?' I asked quizzically, but genuinely confused.

'No, to be sure – but it seems to me that Kenton's other children may not view the new arrival with unalloyed pleasure, and to have a new toy may distract them. Everyone will coo over the baby, but few will talk to the children.'

'Do I gather,' I asked with a smile, 'that that will be my role?'

'If you are prepared to take it on, Mr Rowsley. Now,' she added, adjusting her shawl, 'since both baskets are heavy, shall we deliver them before you show me the alterations to the grounds?'

'An excellent plan, Mrs Faulkner. Now, in view of what you said about toys, might my gifts include bats and balls?'

She beamed. 'They might indeed!'

Half an hour later, having distributed the gifts and promised more, we set out again, approaching the lake. It was so pleasant in the sun that I had forgotten the shouting incident I had overheard earlier. Introducing the topic out of the blue might give it more importance than it merited, and might also reduce me to the status of a common gossip. I realized that I must bide my time.

'Where do you put all the waste?' Mrs Faulkner asked, pointing at a cart being loaded with the dripping, stinking sludge from the bottom of the lake.

'It will be added to compost heaps all round the estate. Some people like to apply it direct to the soil – in fields, for example, where the odour will not offend.'

'Unless you live near them, of course.'

'Indeed! However, I was taught that it is advisable to mix it with other rotting matter, such as dead leaves and even the waste from the kitchens, so that is now the practice I observe. The sludge will stay in the heaps for months, in some cases years – at least until everything smells sweet and, if you run it through your hands, you find it light and friable. If you can tell what it once comprised, it is too soon to use it.'

'You will need a lot of compost heaps!'

'We have them. At present many are just piles of dead leaves, which take a long time to rot down, so the sludge will be a boon.'

'And there is so much if it!' She waved away a sudden gust of the foul miasma. 'So soon his lordship will be able to sail – or at least row – down here.'

'He will have company. The lake must have been sadly neglected for years; the men have found no fish to speak of, so I propose to restock it. With carp.'

She raised her hands in mock horror. 'Dear me, I have never found a cook or chef capable of making the wretched fish even barely palatable. Yet they say it used to be a popular dish. Did I not read that monasteries relied on carp ponds?'

I had never expected the study of history to be part of a housekeeper's leisure. Yet I rebuked myself immediately. My dear mama was as widely read as most of my masters at Harrow, and, I suspect, far shrewder in her understanding. 'Perhaps it was part of their determination to make life as harsh and unappealing as possible!'

'A culinary hair-shirt, perhaps?'

'Precisely,' I agreed with a smile. 'So if Mrs Arden is in

agreement, I think I shall encourage the notion that many fish-
ermen seem to have, that it is wrong to eat carp, so they must
immediately be thrown back whence they came.'

Laughing, we walked on, heading gently towards the former
meadow. 'Of all his lordship's improvements,' I said, 'in the
grounds at least, this is the one that gives me most pleasure. My
father was a very keen player, like his father before him. Whenever
he was unhappy or in doubt, he would oil his cricket bat. I suspect
he still keeps it for that purpose even today.'

'And you, Mr Rowsley? Can we look forward to applauding
you as you stride out to the wicket?'

'It will be the only applause I get, while I hold a bat. But put
a ball in my hand and I would hope to acquit myself better.'

Her gaze dropped, as if she was looking into the past. At last
she smiled. 'Once, when I was very young, I had to learn to
bowl. The eldest son of the house where I was then employed
fancied himself a master batsman in the making. One of my
duties – I know not how it came about – was to spend hours
bowling for him.'

'Indeed! Like the great Christiana Willes!'

'You have heard of her!' For a moment her face was beautiful
with joy. Then it closed again, as she resumed her anecdote.
'Eyebrows were raised, of course, by both my employers and
my fellow servants, until an enthusiastic house guest, who also
wanted to practise, asked if I was related to the great Miss Willes,
at which point my credit and indeed my wages went up!' Her
smile waxed and swiftly waned. 'But indeed, Mr Rowsley, I
would be grateful if I might ask, in confidence, for your advice
on a very delicate matter.'

'In my experience, simply listening to the problem is often
better than giving advice,' I said quietly. I stopped and turned to
her.

'I would welcome both. I am anxious about Maggie.'

'The plump little maid?'

'Exactly. I have spoken to Mrs Arden, who is, I think, inclined
to think I am worrying unnecessarily. But she has been weeping
a lot recently – though she claims she's suffering from a summer
cold; if she is, it has been going on for a long time. I have asked
her – because with girls that age, one always fears the worst!

– but she insists, "They always puff up my eyes, Mrs Faulkner, ma'am. And put me off my food something shocking".'

'Yet she appears to be blooming – rosy cheeks, pretty hair. I should imagine half the footmen are in love with her.'

'Exactly,' she said dryly.

'Does she have a particular follower?' I was reluctant to spell out the problem more clearly, lest I embarrass her.

'There's young Harry Kenton, who has been sweet on her for months. But it seems to me that she's cooled towards him, as if someone has told her she could do better. I've not seen her exchange so much as a glance with any of the indoor staff, or self-consciously look away from any of them either, which is more significant than a smile, in my book.'

'Who does that leave? One of young Harry's fellow labourers? Someone she met in church? Surely not: those horrible bonnets her ladyship insists on for all the maids keep them as close as Quakers and mean there's little possibility of a chance encounter there. A tradesman delivering to the door?'

'No: it's only Mrs Arden's kitchen staff who would have a chance to meet and flirt with a butcher's lad, and when they call young Maggie would be busy making beds and dusting the Family's rooms.' She stopped abruptly as one of the workmen marched over.

'Begging your pardon, sir,' he began, 'but it's the sludge.'

'We will discuss this tomorrow, Partridge,' I declared curtly.

'But Gaffer—'

'I can see the matter is urgent.' With a slight curtsy, Mrs Faulkner excused herself and was gone.

As Partridge spoke, his attention to minutiae as pedantic as any schoolmaster's, I speculated. If poor Maggie had been betrayed, could it be one of the young gentlemen that his lordship used to bring along, before his father's illness and death put a stop to that? No: that would be too long ago. And now of course the House was in mourning, with no guests. Should I speak to his lordship? Not without Mrs Faulkner's express permission. In any case, he was what my old nurse would have called a hey-go-mad young man, throwing his money at any scheme that took his fancy. I could not imagine him to be interested in moral problems. As for her ladyship, it was a brave person who tried to make her speak on any topic she had not chosen.

II

I want to cry but I know it is forbidden.

No one has treated me particularly badly, not today at least. It is my own thwarted desire that draws the tears.

Every day I have to come into the nursery while the young master is asleep and clean it so well you could eat your dinner off the floor. That's what Nurse Butler told me. Off the floor and off every chair and table and even off the grate, once I've black-leaded it. Only then can I light the fire. It must burn first time and make no smoke to get in Master Baby's eyes, Nurse says.

I don't mind any of that. Now I've got it clean – the last nursery maid wasn't as particular as Nurse likes, and I can see Nurse's point – it isn't hard to keep it clean. And if Master Baby doesn't wake too early I can look at Miss Susannah's books. I know those black marks mean something. Each day I make a little more time to try to work out what it is. Not long, though: there is the schoolroom to clean, and the latest governess can neither control the three eldest children nor make them tidy up afterwards, no matter how loudly she shouts. And she is so above herself too, Giving Herself Airs. That's what Mrs Baird, the housekeeper, was telling Cook. And Foreign. That's the worst sin. It might be even worse than being an Orphan. I don't know. But she must know about what is inside those books; if only she would help me.

I can hear movement. It is time to take the overnight slop-bucket downstairs and to deal with Master Baby's napkins. And his clothes and sheets. The proper laundry-maid won't touch them, and I can see why. I can smell why.

When I'm a grown woman I'll be able to refuse. I'll be able to get an underling to do it. I shan't pinch her and pull her hair to make her, though.

I wonder what Master Baby will do when he's a grown man. He'll be able to read, won't he? And take his place in the world?

What place is there for me, if I can't read?

THREE

While the vast majority of the staff ate in the servants'
hall, the upper servants always foregathered at eight
thirty for the last meal of the day in Mrs Faulkner's
parlour – the Room, as it was always called, though there were
at least a hundred others under the roof. Tonight there were Mr
Bowman, Mrs Faulkner, Hargreaves – his lordship's valet,
Mademoiselle Hortense – her ladyship's personal maid, and
Cook – Mrs Arden. They were waited on by Mr Bowman's
servant, Tim. Sometimes I preferred the privacy and plain fair
of my own home, a five minutes' stroll from the House. But
since I had had no more than Bessie's excellent roll since breakfast I decided that I needed more than bread and cheese for
supper. I sent Dan, my diminutive outdoor boy, with a note
asking for an extra place to be laid, the repast being as formal,
in its way, as the one upstairs.

When I presented myself it was clear that the ultra-smart
Hortense was wearing a dress that her mistress had probably
given her, much altered, I supposed, to fit the younger woman's
slight figure; Hargreaves' dress-shirt might well have emerged
from his master's wardrobe. Bowman's waistcoat was old-
fashioned enough to have been his late lordship's. Without her
voluminous apron and huge cap, Mrs Arden was almost unrec-
ognisable in an elegant dark blue woollen dress, the skirt almost
as full as Mrs Faulkner's. In a cap much more decorative than
her severe daytime wear, Mrs Faulkner wore heavy maroon
watered silk. I had dressed carefully: there was a fine line between
being too expensively formal in my own tailored clothes, and
disrespectfully casual.

As usual, I found myself at the head of the table, offering up
grace. I followed Papa's tenet: brevity might not be the soul of
wit, but it certainly encouraged reverence amongst would-be
diners.

Today the Family would have dined on consommé, braised

guinea fowl and rib of beef; we followed their menu. Technically we received their left-overs, but Mrs Arden, with an expansive wink, confided that she had got into the way of cooking enough for us to have our portions. 'Otherwise we've had suppers with practically nothing,' she said, once Tim had slipped away to eat what he could in the servants' hall before he dashed back to serve us the entrée. 'And the servants' hall nothing at all except cold meat and a few vegetables. That's not how I like to do things, with all due respect, Mr Rowsley,' she added, as if suddenly realizing I, holding the estate's purse-strings, might have other priorities.

I hoped my face expressed judicious approval. My mind was trying to suppress the image that sprang unsolicited into my mind, as conjured by Dean Swift:

So, naturalists observe, a flea
Has smaller fleas that on him prey;
And these have smaller still to bite em,
And so proceed ad infinitum.

Swift might have been alluding to fellow poets at the time, but for me it conjured the interdependence and rivalries in this establishment.

It was rare for me to initiate a conversation in the gathering, but tonight I clearly had to. The wine that Mr Bowman had conjured from the Family's table, or from another source, was excellent – just the quality for the toast I was about to propose.

'Let us raise a glass to the health of Mr and Mrs Kenton's new baby boy,' I said, leading the way.

There was a tiny frisson – of shock? of disapproval? – but everyone joined in, albeit raggedly.

'Indeed it is not inappropriate to celebrate an outdoor worker's baby,' Bowman said, with the intention, I suspected, of trying to cover what seemed to be seen as a gaffe, 'since his father has the reputation of being a good, reliable man.'

Mrs Arden nodded firmly. 'Did he not win the prize for the best runner beans at last year's fete?'

'And the year before that,' Bowman agreed. 'He has some

notion of digging trenches for them, does he not? I seem to recall he begged some of the wallpaper when it was stripped from the nursery, though I cannot conceive why.'

I kept my peace. This was not the moment for me to lecture people who lived their entire lives like troglodytes within the house on the finer points of plant nutrition. In any case, at this point Tim scuttled in to clear the soup plates and serve the entrée so that he could return to his own supper. Whatever his hunger pangs might have been, however, he was as decorous and dignified as if he had been an altar boy.

'Our numbers will be greatly swelled,' Bowman remarked, as Tim left, 'when her ladyship permits us to receive house guests again.'

'Assuming Lady Adelaide is one of them, do you think his lordship will make her an offer this time?' Mrs Arden asked.

'Why break the habit of a lifetime?' Hargreaves responded. 'I don't know how many times he's proposed, but I can't see her taking him, not ever, if you ask me. Mind you, now he's got his hands on the title, he might seem a bit more eligible.'

Mrs Arden looked doubtful. 'Is she the sort of lady who'd be impressed by such a thing? She comes from a far older family than ours, and they say she's worth fifteen thousand a year.'

'What about that brother of hers? It's well known he's in dun territory and still spending hand over fist. Ten to one her father'll have to settle his debts and that means Lady Adelaide waving goodbye to her dowry.'

'No. It was settled on her by her grandmother – can't be touched, no matter what,' Mademoiselle Hortense declared, her accent veering closer to London than to Paris as it always did when she'd had a glass of wine.

I floated a question. 'What does her ladyship think of the possible match, Mademoiselle?'

'Says she's too flighty and headstrong. Says she's got a reputation for being fast. But if you ask me,' Mlle Hortense said, taking another sip from her glass and dropping her voice to conspiratorial level, 'she'd rather have an altogether different daughter-in-law. Quiet. Shy. Knowing when and when not to make changes,' she added meaningfully. 'Preferably when not to.'

'So the old lady won't have to let go of the reins, eh?' Hargreaves said with a laugh that Bowman clearly thought was unseemly.

He coughed. 'We all know what we think, do we not? But there are some things best not shouted abroad, Hargreaves.'

'Sorry, Mr Bowman, Mrs Faulkner. Sorry, Mr Rowsley, Mrs Arden.' The young man looked chastened indeed.

I pointed to the ceiling. 'So long as all our conversations remain what the Tudors called *sub rosa.*' It was the wrong observation: at least two of our company clearly did not pick up my allusion.

Mrs Faulkner responded, smiling round the table. 'We will need Jackson to paint a rose there next time he whitewashes the ceiling, will we not? Then whatever we conspirators say can remain beneath it. Now, Mr Bowman, more of this excellent broccoli?'

'Indeed. Then I fear I must adjourn upstairs to serve dessert.'

Why had such an old-fashioned custom remained here? It was considered passé, except at the very grandest of dinners. Perhaps it was no worse than our expecting poor Tim to interrupt his meal in the hall as he now did to clear the plates and bring us our own dessert – but at least he was learning his trade, whereas Bowman had no need of any more skills. He rose ponderously, treating us to a creaking bow as he reached the door.

It was noticeable that the atmosphere lightened as he departed.

'What the maids would like to see,' said Mlle Hortense, allowing her elbows on to the table, 'his lordship becoming a settled married man and ceasing to invite other unattached young gentlemen here.'

Mrs Faulkner's eyes flickered. 'I believe we all share that hope. Propriety forbids me to mention any of the Family's friends in public, but pray assure our girls, Mademoiselle and Mrs Arden, that should they ever mention anyone in particular, as soon as I am informed I will find a way of dealing with the situation.'

I nodded firmly. 'My mama used to say that a gentleman is as a gentleman does. If any of our own footmen overstep the mark, I am sure Mr Bowman will deal with them. Or anyone else,' I added. Or was I implying I knew of some badly behaved young gentlemen myself? That shouting this afternoon – but that was certainly not something to reflect on in public.

A bell rang sharply. Mlle Hortense glanced at the board behind my back, and got to her feet with a sigh, looking longingly at the impressive jelly, so far untouched.

'I'll save you some, so just slip down when you can,' Mrs Arden promised with a smile.

At last, I walked slowly back towards my house, the young moon providing just enough light to tempt me to take the short cut through the shrubbery. I was halfway through when I realized I was not alone. A young female spoke, to be cut short by sharp words in masculine tones. There was what sounded like a slap, and a gasp. This was more than a simple tiff. I stepped forward. But I trod on a twig, which cracked loudly.

The ensuing silence was instant and absolute.

I called out, 'Who's there?'

Still silence. I frowned; I had no idea who the girl might be, but the man's voice wasn't that of a yokel. Was I foolish to believe the accent was one from a public school like my own? There were instances where a young man with that background had serious feelings, honourable intentions, towards a servant girl. But there were far more, in my experience, of a man simply toying with the other's emotions, with nothing but his own pleasure in mind. It was not the job of a steward to make enquiries, of course. Were Mr Pounceman a man of sympathetic under-standing, I could approach him. But Mr Pounceman was not my grandfather, who despite his loving and steadfast union with Grandmama, had once as a very young man truly loved a cham-bermaid.

Much as I hated the idea, surely I must confront the couple? No, I would feel soiled by the act.

III

I must. I can. I will.

The slate is in my hands. I pick up the chalk. I copy each line and curve of the letters. Some must touch the lines. Some must drop below them. Some must soar above. But what do they mean?

Our Father, which art in Heaven

FOUR

'Of course I mean today. Is that not what one means when one says "immediately"?' Lord Croft slapped his desk. 'You inform me that there is a dispute on one of my estates in – where did you say? Somerset? – and I tell you to deal with it. Now.' He picked up a letter and pretended to read it.

'My Lord.' I bowed and withdrew, furious – both at his lordship's imperious folly and my own reaction to it. I was a servant, neither more nor less than young Maggie, was I? Yes, of course, that is precisely what I was, which is why I was so galled. I strode to my office, to write brief but courteous notes to all whose appointments with me would have to be postponed, from one with his lordship's lawyer to another with a tenant whose roof had collapsed, narrowly missing his wife and child. Another note told the estate builder to institute immediate repairs: the family must not sleep in a stable another night.

Then I seized my hat, and marched out, meaning to leave, as usual, by the grand front doors, as my own petty assertion of pride. Instead, I turned, as befitted one in servitude, to the backstairs. There were very few of my fellow-servants in evidence. Should I tap on Mrs Faulkner's door and make my excuses for missing this evening's supper? There was no need even to tell her, as his lordship would see it, but I felt . . . yes, an obligation. Even as I raised my hand, I heard voices. Should I interrupt?

Instead, I returned to my office to write another note, which, like the others was brief. Should I ask a footman to deliver it?

I was just about to slip it under her door when it opened. Three or four servant-girls trooped out, curtsying as they went. Mrs Faulkner watched them on their way.

'I have just come to the end of our reading hour,' she said, with a smile. 'Reading may not open physical doors, Mr Rowsley, but think of all those in the mind it can fling wide!'

'Indeed! Alas, Mrs Faulkner, I may not even stay to hear what book they were enjoying: I am bound urgently for Gloucestershire, where I understand civil war is likely to break out on the Snellworth estate.' I bowed, donned my hat, and was gone. It was only as I left the building that I remembered I still did not know what it was that had troubled her the previous day.

I rarely saw Mrs Faulkner looking anything other than in calm control – of her staff, of any situation and most of all of herself. But today, returning from my trip to Gloucestershire, when I tapped at the door of the Room, I found her with an expression of weary exasperation on her face. Her cap was askew and two or three curls had escaped from their stern knot. Her curtsy was perfunctory. She gestured apologetically at the wicker case, shawl and bonnet which lay by her bedchamber door.

'I can see I have come at a bad moment,' I began, sympathy outpacing tact. I tried to redeem myself. 'And I was truly hoping to sit with someone for a reviving cup of tea.' Yes, I was cutting a wheedle, but I was rewarded with another, mock-gracious curtsy.

'I could not think of a better suggestion,' she said, smoothing down her hair before ringing her bell. 'Unless,' she added, almost impishly, 'it was a glass of Mr Bowman's medicinal port. Tell me, how does Mrs Kenton go on?'

'Alas, I was hoping you might be able to tell me. I was sent . . .' I waited until she had given her orders and Bessie had bobbed her way out before continuing. 'I went all the way to Snellworth to cast judgement on some infertile field – a little patch of ground—'

'That hath in it no profit but the name. To pay five ducats, five, I would not farm it,' she concluded, sitting down carefully and easing the small of her back.

'Exactly so. As soon as I saw the papers relating to the issue, I cut what they claimed was a Gordian knot and, having banged a few heads together, headed back.'

'Through all that rain! The roads must have been quagmires.' She shifted in her seat again.

'Indeed. But – far more important – you are in pain, Mrs Faulkner!'

A tap at the door. Bessie had returned, placing the tray and its load, which included scones, cream and jam, just out of Mrs

Faulkner's reach. As soon as the child left, I stood to pour and hand the tea. 'May I find your laudanum drops?'

'Do you imagine me to be an artist or a poet? You will find no laudanum drops anywhere in the part of the house I run, I assure you, Mr Rowsley. I have read – I have seen! – the harm they can do.' Raising an eyebrow, she nodded upwards.

'You mean – her ladyship?'

'You will excuse me if I do not answer your question. The tea will suffice,' she added, holding out her hand for the cup I still had not yet poured. 'Thank you. I have been on a fool's errand too. It seems that Lady Keynsham over in Wellington told her ladyship that she feared that her housekeeper was failing to keep proper accounts, and that someone reliable and respectable—'

'Like yourself!'

'Should inspect them. However reliable and respectable I may be, I am not an expert bookkeeper. Indeed, I spent most of my time gossiping and helping her in her still-room.'

'Which is how you hurt your back?'

She snorted. 'The Keynshams' drive is as full of holes as a Gouda cheese. And John Coachman failed to see a particularly deep one.'

'You were sent in her ladyship's coach?' I could not conceal my surprise.

'I was indeed. And came back in it too. But I find – Mr Rowsley – I do not yet know what I find. An atmosphere. Something is amiss. Do you sense it too?'

Placing a tea-plate in front of her, I made sure the scones and their accompaniments were within easy reach. 'I have had little opportunity to.' As soon as a weary Esau was stabled, and I had changed my travel-stained garments, I had made my way up to the House. Surprising myself, I said aloud, 'My presence here always unnerves the younger staff, and not just the indoor workers. I suspect they see me as an ogre about to throw them into the workhouse. I am always greeted with downcast eyes and the most formal of responses whenever I speak, whatever I say.'

She nodded sadly. 'Any agent will always create anxiety – though I should imagine that to many you are a welcome change.' She took a scone, buttering it and adding jam, but not cream. 'You and I and Mr Bowman, Mrs Arden too – we are neither flesh nor fowl, nor ever will be. That is the way of the world, Mr Rowsley.' There was pain in her sigh that I suspected might not have been caused by her injured back.

'Indeed.' I met her eye, but she turned away. Whatever the cause, she did not wish to discuss it now. For a few minutes we spoke of something but nothing. I put down my cup and saucer. 'I fear I must take my leave. I'm sure his lordship will wish to know that the business he deemed so urgent has been satisfactorily concluded.'

She raised a finger. 'I believe his lordship is not at home. Luke Hargreaves said he had just ten minutes to pack for his lordship and himself – of course, he accompanies his master. They travel to visit some old friends in his lordship's latest toy – a landau that outlandaus all others on the road. You'll be asked to settle the coachmaker's account soon enough!'

I felt a huge surge of anger, that at his whim I had wasted time that could have been far better spent and now he did not even wish to know the outcome. 'Another carriage? When he might travel more swiftly by train? He even has his own private station!' I shook my head. 'And how long does he mean to stay away?'

'Who knows? I believe his friends are to embark on some sort of tour of each other's houses, playing cricket at each one.'

'You, not he, should be there,' I said. I got to my feet. 'No, pray do not stand. And promise me you will not try to lift your case yourself. In fact, with your permission, I will put it into your bedchamber myself.'

As I walked to my office, I paid special attention to those I passed. Mrs Faulkner had been right: there was an extra tension in the air. I wrote a memorandum to his lordship, stating the facts and little more; the dispute was now settled, after all. And who was I to criticize my employer for assuming that I would deal with it without his needing to see if I was successful. Perhaps I should be flattered, that he trusted me.

Yet our last meeting still rankled.

My grandfather had warned me that I would have to learn to be obsequious to fools. In body I had. But not, it transpired, in my mind.

* * *

A great deal of work had accrued while I was absent, so much that by the time I had sorted it into baskets according to its urgency I barely had time to dash back to my house to change for supper in the Room. The company was depleted. Naturally his lordship's valet had accompanied his master; Mr Bowman had taken advantage of his lordship's absence to visit his aging mother in Stafford; Mlle Hortense was permitted to partake of the entrée only, her ladyship having a migraine that required her maid to be in silent attendance with cloths soaked in iced lavender water to apply to the ailing brow. Then she was to finish her ladyship's packing; she had a notion that bathing in the waters of Droitwich Spa might ease her aching joints and she was leaving on the morrow.

Mrs Arden was unwontedly quiet, confining herself to a gracious acknowledgement of our praise of her cooking, till Tim had gathered the last plate and left, closing the door behind him. Now, with a faint smile, she pointed at the ceiling. 'All that we say remains beneath that, doesn't it?'

'Of course.' Mrs Faulkner moved painfully to the door, opening it silently and shutting it again.

'I'll make sure you have a hot brick for that back of yours,' Mrs Arden promised. 'Now, Mr Rowsley, many would say what happened while you were away is beneath the notice of such as you, but Mrs Faulkner and I think you have your finger on the pulse more than most, and I'd further venture that you like to keep it that way.'

Bemused but intrigued, I nodded.

Mrs Faulkner took up the story. 'It seems one of the maids has disappeared.' She snapped her fingers. 'Just like that. Young Maggie Billings,' she added, her voice showing how hard she was trying to control her emotions.

'Short? Plump, with a round face?'

'Yes. Plump. And maybe with good reason,' Mrs Arden said sagely.

'There is no proof,' Mrs Faulkner said quickly. She added more soberly, 'But it is not impossible – sickness, Mr Rowsley, for a few weeks and . . . other signs.'

'If she had only come to us for help!'

'We could have given her advice,' Mrs Faulkner said quickly, and perhaps a little too loudly. 'As it is there is no sign of her, apart from her few pitiful possessions. Her fellow tweenies might have had their lips sewn together. I would have asked Mr Bowman to summon the men, both indoor and outdoor, to ask if they might have seen anything.'

'You would like me to take on that role? Of course I will. But – if she was indeed with child – would any man admit to being the father? Because that is whom we should seek. He, if anyone, would know where the girl has gone. Perhaps if I questioned them individually . . .?' That would be a week's work on top of what I needed to do urgently. 'Have you spoken to anyone yet?'

They shook their heads. 'This only came to my knowledge two hours ago. It will be my first task in the morning. Mr Rowsley, her last sweetheart was Silas Kenton's brother. Yes, of course she was too young for any sort of follower, as I pointed out to her. She seemed to relinquish his attentions with no backward glance.' She gave no hint that we had already spoken about this. Neither would I.

'Suspicious in itself,' Mrs Arden chipped in, with what seemed a triumphant nod. But her tone was more apologetic, as if she feared she had implied something she would regret, as she added, 'A more handsome young man in the offing, wouldn't you say, Mrs Faulkner? A footman?'

'Mr Bowman would no doubt be able to offer information there. But we speculate. The child is gone. Her bed was not slept in last night, and no one recalls seeing her about her duties during the day.'

'Did anyone think to send out a search party? She may have gone for a stroll and hurt herself – in the woods, perhaps.'

Mrs Faulkner cast me a pitying look. 'I fear no servant in this house or any other is encouraged to go walking in the woods during the working day. My reading hour is known only to people like Mrs Arden who want girls to have a chance to improve themselves. And I would be grateful if it stayed that way, Mr Rowsley. If some good man wished to organize something similar for the young men it would be a blessing.'

I thought of my daily schedule. 'In many parishes it is the rector who undertakes such tasks, or at least his curate.' The women's snort of derision told me not to pursue this suggestion.

'But we wander from the point. We must search for the child. I will set the men on to it at first light, whatever else they might be doing. I will also speak to this man Harry Kenton.' I clicked my fingers in irritation. 'Her parents – have they been informed? No? That must be done at once – after all, it may be a simple case of homesickness, and we will find her there. Can you furnish me with their address?'

They exchanged a glance. 'Lord love you, you passed their home on your way in. The Billingses keep the main gate. At least she does. He fathers a brood on her and gets himself paralysed with a stroke. Some might say it's a pity he didn't do a proper job and die of it.' Mrs Arden nodded home the information as if Billings' illness were a deliberate act of idleness.

Mrs Faulkner said quietly, 'It would be kind of you to do it. But—'

'It would be better done by a woman? However, you are unwell, and I should imagine that Mrs Arden has to be up and working before six.' We exchanged rueful smiles. 'I can do it: my father was a parson, you know, and I hope I know how to be gentle.'

IV

If I might only ask for help. But it is not my place to know things. But I must not be stupid either. Not like Effie, who was beaten for not knowing what a bain-marie was. As if they had such things in the workhouse.

Hallowed be Thy Name

FIVE

The main gates were firmly locked and the lodge itself in darkness when I reached Maggie's home. I could have rung the enormous bell on the gate pillars, as if I were an impatient traveller demanding admittance. In fact I hunted for a knocker on the heavy oak front door – a door far sturdier in appearance than the rest of the cottage, which was very small in scale and must have been designed when the Gothic style was all the rage. It must also have been designed to house very short people, perhaps as a visual jest for visitors. I cannot imagine that the people living there thought their cramped conditions a source of laughter.

How many children had Mrs Billings raised in this doll's house? Where had they all slept? But of course, as soon as one was old enough to be put out to service or sent as a labourer to a neighbouring farmer, off they would go. Only tiny children, who would in my own village have been in school, were allowed to be under the maternal feet – and how many of them would be out in the fields scaring birds or picking stones? I felt my jaw tighten. There should and would be a school in Stammerton. And in Thorncroft and in every other village within his lordship's estates. There was talk that universal education would soon be required by law; those in my care must not wait that long.

Eschewing the heavy knocker, I tapped the door with my knuckles, wanting to summon Mrs Billings but not disturb her sick husband's rest. At last she appeared, swathed in a shawl that meant I could barely see her face in the deep dusk that had now enveloped us. She brought no candle.

'I am sorry to disturb you, Mrs Billings, and sorrier to be the bearer of disquieting news, but I have to tell you something. It concerns Maggie.'

Did her eyes widen? Did her head jerk back? She made no other response.

'It grieves me to tell you that she is missing. Neither Mrs Faulkner nor I knew anything about it till we returned from our duties elsewhere, which is why no one told you before. But I promise you that we will do all in our power to find her. Tomorrow every man on the estate will be searching for her, and every indoor servant will be released from their duties to join them. I promise we will do everything we can to find her – God willing – alive.'

What response did I expect? Hysteria at the news, especially as I was telling her so late? A tirade that we were leaving it till the morrow to search? All I got was a stiff bob of a curtsy, her head lowered and her shawl pulled even further over her face. And to my amazement, she stepped back inside and firmly closed the door.

I was up at first light, despatching Dan, my stable lad, to the House with messages for the grooms there to despatch to all the tenant farmers and labourers. Maggie had been lost, on her own, for at least thirty-six hours now. The odds were not in her favour, but as Dr Page, riding alongside me in the sweep through the woods, remarked, country people were tough.

'They have to be,' I flashed, too quickly for politeness.

His eyebrows rose, but not, I thought, in offence, more to express agreement.

No more words were said. We rode on, occasionally standing high in the saddle the better to scan the undergrowth, even now being lifted then beaten flat by the farmhands, many of whom had been toiling for four hours now.

As for me, I had long since emptied my water bottle, but I refused to touch the spare one in my saddle bag. If the child were still alive, water would be the first of her needs.

Suddenly I heard a female voice, and was ready to raise my own in delight. The call was not one of despair, but of encouragement. A group of women had gathered at the far end of the ride and were waving to us. Did we dare hope?

All too soon I realized we were being called for another reason altogether. But I could not fault the reason. Mrs Arden and some of the kitchen and scullery maids had set up station around two trestle tables. An urn bubbled on a spirit stove and a large barrel stood invitingly on a stand. Between them, on a cloth so snowy that it would not have disgraced her ladyship's own table, were bread and beef, cheese and ham.

Mrs Arden waved aside my thanks – indeed, my congratulations. 'There's small beer, Mr Rowsley, like we serve at harvest. Or there's tea if you prefer. Some of her ladyship's special coffee, too,' she added in an undervoice. 'Mrs Faulkner said you were partial to it. She should have been a general, Mr Rowsley, the way she's organized this. We've been up since dawn, both of us with our sleeves rolled up as if we were skivvies again. The footmen were dragooned into helping set up tables all round the estate so no one will go hungry or thirsty.'

'It's my belief, Mrs Arden,' I said quietly, watching the men tucking into their repast, 'that most of them never see such quantity – and indeed quality – of food in the whole of their working lives. The farmers, yes, and the House servants, but no one else.'

'Save at Harvest Home and Christmas,' she agreed. 'And it has to be said that his late lordship never stinted.'

'I trust the tradition will be maintained,' I said. It would, even if I had to fund it out of my own pocket.

She gave me a sharp sideways glance, as if reading my thoughts. Then she said, 'When you've all finished here, tell me where you'll be looking next, and I'll make sure that's where I'll set up.'

I was afraid I might have to urge the men on, a latter-day Roman centurion urging his foot soldiers into battle, but I was mistaken. Each man toiled as if for his own child, some ready to make their lunchtime rations into rough sandwiches so that they might eat on the march. At three, however, one of the gamekeepers broke from the line, suggesting, with a jerk of the head, that I should join him.

'What is it, Purvis? Have you seen something you don't want the others to see?'

'No, gaffer, 'tis that I've seen nothing all day that makes me think anyone would have strayed this far from the House. And I'm a-thinking there may be a reason. I'm not saying she did, mind, but if a young maiden like her was in any sort of trouble, sir, if you get my meaning, mightn't she be walking somewhere else?' He looked meaningfully over my shoulder at a mound of lake mud. 'She'd not be the first, nor, alas, the last, to seek that way out.'

'You think we should drag the lake, Purvis? It'll break the men's hearts if they see us doing it.'

He rocked his head. 'Is it better to do it at the end of the day, when we're all fair worn out, or to set a small party on to it now? Better while it's light, and before that thunderhead brings trouble to us all.' He looked anxiously to the horizon, where I'd seen nothing but what I thought was fair weather cloud.

I nodded. 'Thank you, Purvis. You're quite right. Can you carry on as before? I'll gather together a team – but first I'll warn Mrs Billings what we plan to do.'

He knuckled his forehead, giving a smile I suspected was rare, and all the more valuable for that.

'No.' Mrs Billings' response to my information was that simple flat negative. At last, in the face of my silence, she added, 'There's no need, sir.' She shifted awkwardly, as if in physical pain as well as embarrassment. But she kept her head averted, so the brim of her ugly bonnet almost shrouded her face.

I inclined my head, the better to hear: the poor creature had virtually no teeth and an ugly sore at one corner of her mouth must have made it hard to move her lips. How old might she be? She still had a babe on her hip, or I would have taken her for seventy. 'How so, Mrs Billings?' I asked gently.

'Her's gone. Her and the babe within her. Skipped off – her and her fancy man, as far as I know. Walked out of those very gates, proud as a peacock. I promised on the Bible to tell no one, though. No one at all. But I didn't know it would cause all this trouble.' She dabbed at the sore with the corner of her sacking apron.

Half of me believed her – perhaps the whole of me, had she not referred to the Bible. How did a family as poor and almost certainly as unlettered as this come to possess one, let alone retain one, when any item of value – and some of none at all – would be sold or used to barter for necessities. But I confined myself to saying sternly, 'You have indeed put a lot of people to a great deal of trouble, Mrs Billings, and I am very disappointed in you. For now I must go and call off the search, but I may wish to speak to you later – about the identity of that fancy man, who I assume got her with child?'

'Silly girl, to be so taken in! But tell his name she would not, and so I cannot either,' she said, all in a rush. 'Sir,' she concluded, rather belatedly, with a stiff curtsy.

She was hiding something I was sure. But what could I do? Shake the information out of her?

'Are you sure you have nothing else to tell me?' I asked, trying to sound as if I was speaking more in sorrow than in anger.

Her reply was a silent withdrawal into the lodge and a quiet but firm closing of the door.

I rode briskly to dispel my anger and irritation, and I was able to deliver the news with a wry smile. It was received with obvious relief; most of the workers must have known her or her family, and though no one could approve of the pregnancy and the apparent elopement, there was an undercurrent of hope that all could yet end well – better than the alternative for which they had been bracing themselves, to be sure. As for the men, they had been royally fed, and the women had been able to emerge from their sunless, housebound existence into the blessed open air. All had had a chance to mix and gossip – even flirt.

'If only we had a decent man of the cloth to serve the parish,' Mrs Arden said, allowing Tim to pour her another glass of wine. 'And you didn't hear that, young man – understand? Is everyone else's glass filled? Good lad: off you go.' She waited till he had closed the door. 'You mark my words, next Sunday he'll be up there in his pulpit, preaching fire and brimstone and cursing womankind for being temptresses. Jezebels! Do you see young Maggie as a Jezebel, Mrs Faulkner?'

Mrs Faulkner's face was tight. 'Indeed, I see her as a poor child with scarcely two thoughts in her head capable of forming an idea who has been led astray by someone who should have known better – whoever, whatever he is! A child, Mr Rowsley – you've seen her. And though she's pretty – and prettier since she's been with child – I can't imagine a man being charmed by her for long. It's to be hoped she's already wed, or you know what happens to girls who are not. And their children, poor innocent babes!'

'The workhouse! Work? Slavery more like. And the children torn from their mothers' arms, and given an education worth this much.' Mrs Arden snapped her fingers. 'Forgive me, Mr Rowsley, my feelings got the better of me.'

I pointed to the ceiling, and smiled. 'The rose that only we can see guarantees my word that I will say nothing of this conversation. And indeed, it is only what my parents and my godparents say, and I would say myself.'

Mlle Hortense, who had sat in what seemed an apprehensive silence throughout the exchange, suddenly smiled, and mimed applause. But before she could speak the words on her lips, her bell rang, and, with a last sip of wine, she excused herself and returned to her mistress.

The three of us sipped in companionable silence, until it was time for me to walk home through the balmy evening. I had half a mind to turn back and invite both ladies to take a turn with me around the formal garden, but the moon went in, and suddenly the estate looked less inviting.

V

lthough none of us can read, we all open our Prayer Books and sit with dutifully lowered heads as if we can follow every word. The paper is very thin. The print is very small, not like that in the books in the nursery. I mouth the words, because I know them by heart, of course; we all do, though deaf Jenny always gets some of them wrong.

The sermon is about one of Christ's miracles. I would love to ask the vicar if he thinks there are still things like miraculous draughts of fish, or blind people being given sight by a mixture of spit and dirt. I might have asked kind Dr Martin. Why is he called a doctor when he is not a medical man? But Mr Sproggett is not the sort of man a girl would wish to speak to on such a matter. So in a quiet moment, I ask God if I might have a miracle, like getting that blue ribbon back again to keep forever.

Perhaps I haven't prayed hard enough. It doesn't appear before my eyes.

And then – and then! Yes, a strange thing does happen. I see the words I have been so carefully copying in front of me, on this very page! I trace them with my finger, and Mr Sproggett and all around me are saying them: Our Father, which art in Heaven, Hallowed be Thy Name.

I follow each and every word for the rest of the prayer.

This is better than a blue ribbon. This is the key to everything.

SIX

S till in the cricket whites favoured by about half the men, I sipped ale with the other members of Thorncroft village team, including both the Kenton brothers, on benches outside the village inn. The Royal Oak might well have dated to the time of King Charles: the building walls were so far from the vertical that it seemed impossible that it should not have collapsed years ago. It would have entranced an artist with a taste for the romantic, as would much of the village, which straggled along the road, on to which some front doors opened directly. Set back were the grander ones, such as Dr Page's. Although it still lacked a school, there was a post office and a couple of tiny shops. The village green sat at the heart of it all.

At first, talk was all about the match: how badly some of the players had fared, so that we got very few runs, and how it looked as if we had no hope of saving the game.

'Until you came on to bowl, gaffer,' said Alf Hargreaves, his lordship's pig man, supping from his tankard, 'and showed us all how to do it, in a manner of speaking.'

'But it was your fine catches that brought about their downfall,' I countered, truthfully, swatting a gnat. 'Yours and young Elias'.'

'Ah, I reckon he catches them with those whiskers of his,' Alf snorted, smoothing his more modest moustache. 'If ever Shropshire gets round to having a proper county team, I reckon he should be in it – though they'll choose gentlemen over any working lad, no doubt.' He spat, copiously, then waved a brawny arm. 'Bring Granfer Hawkins over – not him, so much as his pipe. Foul it may be, gaffer, but the thing is, the damned midges and gnats – begging your pardon, gaffer – can't abide it. Now, gaffer, Granfer there is uncle to John Coachman.' He drank again. 'My lad Luke's gone up in the world, compared with me – his lordship's valet, see. Imagine, me, the pa of a valet! I never leave here, where I was born and raised, except when we're playing another village, but he's jauntering round all over the county, aye, and further afield too. Sometimes without a moment's notice, too – not like the old lord, who liked to plan things to the nearest milestone, or so it seemed. He gets an invitation and – pff! – off they all go. And just when you think he's going to be all quiet and reasonable, blow me if there isn't blood for supper if Luke forgets a favourite necktie or set of studs!' He looked from left to right and dropped his voice. 'There's things young Luke has to turn a blind eye too, mind, like—' He clapped a hand over his mouth, as if it suddenly dawned on him that he was not being tactful. 'Begging your pardon, gaffer.'

'Luke always strikes me as a very efficient and well-presented young man,' I said smoothly. 'And now, if I'm not to be bitten to death, or veritably kippered by Mr Hawkins' pipe, I must be on my way. But I've left enough with Marty Baines for you all to have another half.' Marty Baines, the landlord, was an amazingly sober man, rumoured to be more Chapel than Church, who could be relied on not to let anyone get fighting drunk. He'd shown me the pump at the back, useful for making men quietly presentable to their wives. He wanted no violence laid at his door.

Alf tugged his forelock. 'You'll be playing for us regular, will you, gaffer, from now on?'

I smiled as I thought of the unalloyed pleasure I'd had this afternoon. 'If you'll have me, I'll be there as often as my work with his lordship permits.'

To my surprise, he got up and fell into step with me, just until we were out of earshot. 'This is a bad business for the Billingses, gaffer. Who'd have thought a quiet young maiden would be so foolish?'

'Foolish she may be, but then she's little more than a child,' I said, not quite mildly. 'And there's a young man in the case too. Have you any idea who he might be?'

As if puzzled by my attitude, he shook his head. 'There's always gossip. Word is, gaffer, it's someone from the House, not an outside man. But I'll have to wait till young Luke comes back before I know anymore, won't I?'

'You underestimate yourself, Alf. You'll pick things up that I never will.'

'But not as well as Marty. He's the eyes and ears round here. But not the mouth, if you take my meaning.'

'I do indeed. But maybe even a discreet man might talk to you. And you know where to find me, don't you?' I slipped him a florin.

He looked as if he was about to protest, but pocketed it none-theless.

My walk back took me past the little row of cottages, all belonging to the estate and none as well-maintained as I liked, though most of the gardens showed the pride and effort that went into them. Some women were catching the evening sun as they weeded the flowerbeds; others were simply chatting across garden fences – all in all, an idyllic sight such as my imaginary artist might want to paint. But how many of the women were as prematurely aged as Mrs Billings? I knew Mrs Faulkner was always ready to help in an emergency, doing the work that many other dowagers in Lady Croft's position would have thought an essential part of their duties – indeed, in many cases, the only part of their duties. My mother would have been horrified by what she would have considered idle inertia. I recalled her setting up a sewing class and teaching women about growing herbs and vegetables, hitherto in our village an exclusively male occupation. Mysteriously she always discovered a glut of fruit and an apparently endless supply of sugar so that every household had a supply of blackberry jam and preserved plums, damsons and greengages. She would have approved whole-heartedly of Mrs Faulkner's still-room, and been delighted to know that the contents were not kept for the Family's use alone.

I had hoped that Mrs Faulkner would be able to spend the day at leisure, giving her injury a chance to recover; many a woman would have taken to her bed. But here she was, strolling through the park, wearing another of those pretty little hats to shade her eyes against the westering sun, which cast a rosy glow across her features. It was easy to fall into step with her. I enquired after her health.

Her voice was bracing. 'I find a good walk will cure most ills, Mr Rowsley, backs included. Now, I'm afraid that with all your play and probably your ale with your teammates you have missed supper. But Mrs Arden has a soft spot for you and I believe you will find a shepherd's pie awaiting your attention if you call round to her kitchen.'

'Thank you. I'm sure my feet will find their way there in a few minutes. But I've just seen young Harry Kenton in his brother's garden. It's time I spoke to him about Maggie. I know they were no longer walking out together but he might know who replaced him in her affections.'

Briefly she touched my arm. 'Unlike his brother, Harry has a temper, I hear – especially when he has been to the Royal Oak.'

'Yes, I saw him there, but I did not want to speak to him in front of anyone else, particularly as he had just taken a magnificent catch which brought me my third wicket. And this might be a good time to talk, since we still share the golden glow of sporting success. I'm sorry, Mrs Faulkner, that you could not be there. We managed a famous victory – and they've invited me to be part of the team for the rest of the summer.' I must have sounded like a silly schoolboy.

'Perhaps one good thing to come of his lordship's improvements will be that I have a chance, very casually, very accidentally, to watch while I supervise the team teas.' Her words were mild enough, but I could feel the anger behind them. She turned her face away.

I thought of my mother's words: *It seems to me that as the years go by we are determined to cast a veritable corset round women's activities, just as we put them round our bodies. All this fainting and fading – cut our stays and give us less to eat and we'd be ourselves again.*

'I truly hope so. How, why, did we forget that once girls were encouraged to climb trees and play? At least Jane Austen would have us believe that they did.'

She faced me again, her smile of delight transforming her face. 'Ah! You have read *Northanger Abbey*! But remember that Catherine had to give up being a tomboy to become a heroine!'

'If I ever had a daughter I would like her to be both. But now I have to do my duty and confront Harry, do I not? Mrs Faulkner, I would welcome your views on what the young man has to say. May I hope to join you in a cup of tea when I have eaten what I expect is a magnificent shepherd's pie?'

'You would be welcome.'

* * *

Mrs Kenton greeted me as if I were an angel from heaven. Silas likewise, rosy with ale and exercise, shook my hand with fervour, and ready to talk through the match. When at last he understood that I was there for a less pleasurable conversation, he melted into the shadows but did not quit the garden. Harry, who had been silent and watchful throughout Silas's chatter, did not refer to the match, and, arms folded, waited for me to begin.

'I think we have the same aim, Kenton,' I began. 'We both want to see Maggie's seducer brought to book. When you and she parted company, did she indicate who might have replaced you in her affections?'

'It was that . . . It was that Mrs Faulkner who stopped me walking out with her, that's who.' He was about to spit, but clearly thought better of it. He looked at me almost appraisingly. 'Sorry, gaffer.'

'It is not to me that you should apologize, but to Mrs Faulkner, who was in fact so concerned for the girl's welfare that it was she who set in train the search for her. There must be no more disrespectful behaviour towards Mrs Faulkner, Kenton, understand that. And understand what the consequences would be if you do ever behave in any way and at any time without absolute politeness.'

He nodded, but did not otherwise acknowledge what I had said. Indeed, his next words might have seemed like a justification of his resentment. 'I loved Maggie. She was as loyal and true to me as I was – still am – to her. And I treated her like one of them china cups, delicate-like, so she was still a true maid, believe me.'

'I do, man – of course I do. But it seems she did . . . like . . . someone else. Why else should she leave the safety of the House and—'

'Maybe because the House wasn't safe!' he shouted, turning on his heel and striding off into the dusk.

Mrs Kenton materialized. 'Mr Rowsley, sir – he's not in his right mind just now. He's a good, gentle man, mostly.'

'I'm sure he is,' I assured her, not quite truthfully, and not failing to notice the word at the end of her sentence. 'And I truly hope he continues to behave himself.' Then I smiled. 'Now, Mrs Kenton – how's the latest addition to your family? Flourishing, I hope?'

'He's doing very well, sir. Sir, we were hoping, Silas and me, that you might sponsor him at his christening. And that you might let him be called Matthew, sir.'

'I would be honoured, Mrs Kenton, both by the choice of name and by the chance to be a godparent – so long as one of my duties is to help his father teach him how to handle bat and ball.' I would also make sure I opened a Post Office savings account for him, the contents of which he could not reach till he was of age.

She curtsied again. 'Like those you had sent for the others, sir? That was so kind, so generous.' When I waved away her thanks, she continued, 'Look – you can see where they've been playing . . .'

I delayed my supper by no longer than it took to sluice myself down under the pump in my yard. Evening clothes would clearly be out of place, but, just as Mrs Faulkner had looked neat as a pin, so I chose a good summer suit – a wise decision because Mrs Arden had had the table laid in the Room, where she was sitting opposite our hostess, with a glass of port to hand. For me was a tankard of ale, a clear nod to my afternoon of sport. Sensing, however, that another rodomontade about my prowess would cause either pain or amusement, I told them that I was to become a godparent.

There was no doubting the look that passed between them.

Mrs Arden openly chuckled. 'Well, Mr Rowsley, I know you are a good Christian man with a true Biblical name . . .'

I blushed. 'Do you spy a trace of veniality? I tried to suppress the notion, I do admit.'

'And it is kind of you that you did,' Mrs Arden concluded quickly. 'They are a good, hard-working couple.'

'And Harry?' I asked dryly.

'He once threatened to kill me,' Mrs Faulkner said with apparent calm.

'He . . .! Do you want me to dismiss him?' I was far from calm. 'I rebuked him firmly tonight when all he did was speak of you with anger, but such a threat is truly unpardonable.'

'It was a while ago. It's clear he still hasn't forgiven me for what he perceives as my part in his broken romance, but he is polite enough when our paths cross.'

'So I should hope! But you didn't answer my question, so I will put it another way – would you feel safer if he were not on the estate?' She wandered around it freely – protecting her would be well-nigh impossible.

'If you had asked me that six months ago I might have said yes. But recently I have felt able to resume my unaccompanied walks without feeling any fear.'

Mrs Arden put down her glass with unwonted firmness and looked her straight in the eye. 'Remember, my dear, that some say that revenge is a dish best eaten cold.'

VI

*S*hall I start with one of the children's books? I would get into trouble if I touched without asking first. What about that sampler on the wall? It is in strange lumpy letters, but there are a few words, in the middle, at least.

Thou, Lord, seest me

I know Thou. *Yes, and* Lord. Seest *takes longer. Then* me.
For a while I am afraid. But then I remember that God forgives, which Nurse rarely does. I shall have to find a way of working out the rest of the letters, which just seem a jumble of C's and X's. An I. No, I can make no sense of it. But I mustn't bite my nails, or Nurse will paint them with something she says will make me ill.

SEVEN

'**A** whore and a harlot, a Jezebel ripe to be whipped at the cart's tail!'

Theophilus Pounceman's lips were wet with passion. His spittle probably reached the front row of pews. His venom certainly reached right to the back, where the House servants were huddled. I heard sobs and sniffles. I felt a rising tide of anger, a desire to knock the conceited and unforgiving sneer from the face of the man in the pulpit. If only I could shepherd the servants away, as I would from an angry bull in a field. But to do so in the middle of the sermon would cause an uproar, possibly one which could see me dismissed from my post and losing what I truly believed was my opportunity to good, however little it might seem. My fellow servants – and I – had to wait till the interminable service ground to an end, each minute the longer for the fury growing in me.

But now Pounceman wore a sanctimonious smile, as he shook the hands of the richer members of his congregation, no doubt trying to conceal his vexation that his lordship and her ladyship were not there to applaud what he had said. Mrs Arden and Mrs Faulkner did not, of course, merit a personal word, and I deduced from the expression on their faces that neither would have welcomed it. But I was of course a man with power, if not a title, and with an oily smile he proffered his hand.

I stared him down. 'We will speak of this at the vicarage in exactly ten minutes,' I said quietly, but he looked so shocked I might indeed have swung – as I wanted – at his chin. I wished the encounter had not had an audience. I thought I heard a couple of outraged gasps at my temerity.

'You are a man of the cloth and I a layman, with, you will no doubt observe, no legal authority over you. But let me make this clear, Pounceman, I will not have my staff spoken about like that. If you have a complaint about one of them, you take it to Mrs Arden, Mrs Faulkner, Mr Bowman or even myself. You will claim you wished to put the fear of God into the other girls – but let me make it plain, it takes a man to get a girl with child, and, whatever his rank, he should bear at least equal blame, since he is certainly not going to be the one enduring the tribulations of pregnancy and the hazards of childbirth.' I leant over him as he sat at his desk. In his place I might have stood to match my interlocutor, inch for inch, but he stayed in his chair. I could not work out whether he was daring me to strike him or so arrogant that he simply assumed I was making a terrible mistake. And had he – I could not be sure – reacted when I mentioned rank?

'Your passion is misguided, sir.' He lent back, as if he was addressing a schoolboy. 'This woman is a vile sinner—'

'Are we not all sinners? Did not Our Lord Himself come to earth to save us all? Women as well as men? And did he not tell those determined to stone to death the woman taken in adultery that only a person without sin might cast the first stone?' With an effort I restrained myself from pointing an accusing finger at him, as if he were a felon in the dock.

He narrowed his eyes. 'You are well versed in the New Testament, sir.'

He made it sound like an accusation. But, controlling my temper, I gave a guileless smile. 'My father is an archdeacon, sir.' I wish it could have been an exit line.

'There are all too many appointments of lax individuals in the hierarchy. Kissing goes by favour, they say,' he added waspishly.

If he was referring to my father's titled family he would get no rise from me. I waited in silence, often, I found, the best weapon.

Predictably, he found it necessary to speak first – and bluster. 'As you yourself admit, sir, you have no place here. So—'

'My dear Pounceman, I think you will find I have every right to be here – his lordship, your patron, has bestowed a very generous benefice upon you, has he not? And your moves and manners will always be of interest to him,' I added with a slight smile. Blackmail? Possibly. 'Now, let me think – you will take Evensong this afternoon, will you not?'

'Of course!'

'Good. Now, we need no more sermons like that to disturb the tenor of our dealings,' I said gently. 'So I imagine this afternoon's will feature a good woman.'

'But—!'

'I'm sure with your superior knowledge you will find an unsung heroine, in the Old or the New Testament. A good woman. That's what your sermon will be about. And now I will bid you good day.'

The encounter left me feeling angry with myself for being reduced by his snide allusion to scoring cheap points. But I was even angrier with him, particularly as I did not feel I should tell anyone about the encounter. Yet Mrs Arden and Mrs Faulkner, who had even predicted the term he used to describe a child I was beginning to see as a victim, deserved to know I supported them. The answer surely lay with Esau, who would be my unquestioning mentor as I took him for a long ride.

As his name implied, he was hairy, with a prolific mane and an extraordinarily long tail; he was clearly unhappy when it was cropped or plaited. Apart from that, he had comparatively little personality for a horse, preferring simply to make his way along whichever way I directed him. This time it was along the lanes, dusty in the sun, heading out of the main gate and turning to the south. I kept him at little more than a walking pace, trying to think of nothing in particular but knowing, in my heart, how ashamed I was of my petty exchange with Pounceman. Somehow I would have felt cleaner if I had broken his jaw for him. And yet – why did he receive me in his study, seated at his desk? I too had a study and a desk, but would always receive guests in my sitting room, where we could sit in civilized comfort, assisted perhaps by a glass of sherry or Madeira. We could still have exchanged stern words, of course – even got angry. So why did I so object to that desk?

I followed the road on its south-eastern route. The Royal Oak was firmly closed, in accordance with Marty's beliefs, no doubt, but I must make sure I spoke to him as soon as I could. At last I was out of his lordship's territory, but I was still able to greet people I had met at market and indeed at yesterday's match. After an hour, however, I was both thirsty and hungry, and would have turned back but for the sight of a weather-beaten old woman sitting on a bench outside an alehouse, which was so small and dilapidated as hardly to warrant the name. I dismounted, doffing my hat as I led Esau into the shade. I bade her share a jug of ale with me, and find me a hunk of bread and cheese. Both were excellent.

It seemed she often sat there, watching the world go by, sometimes serving gentry, she said, adding, 'Such as you, master.'

'I suppose,' I said slowly, appalled that I had been so unenterprising in my search for young Maggie, 'you didn't see a pretty young woman and her sweetheart go this way last week?'

'Sees a lot of them.' She sucked on her clay pipe. 'But not necessarily last week.'

I was about to slip her a shilling in the hope it would restore her memory when she spoke again.

'Be you sure the maid was with her sweetheart?' she asked. 'For I did see a pretty young wench wend her way past here midweek. Plump as a partridge and pretty as a picture. Gave me the sweetest smile.' She sucked again. 'Asking for the Wolverhampton road she was. But I'll tell 'ee this for nothing, she weren't a maid, not to my way of thinking. Maybe it's only an old woman like me would notice how her stays were straining. And smile she might, but she'd been a-weeping, you mark my words.'

I described Maggie as best I could, sick to the stomach as the old woman nodded at each adjective. Hoping she was agreeing merely to please me, I threw in a few more words – a rich gown, perhaps. I earned no more than a scathing snort. 'In service, I'll be bound. Stupid wenches – why don't they use their heads and their pennyroyal? Bless her, I could have helped if she hadn't been so far gone.'

'And she was on foot?' I asked stupidly, too horrified at the implications of what she was saying to ask anything more to the point.

'She weren't on no fine horse, were she, master?' She looked at me shrewdly, laying a gnarled hand gently on my wrist. 'Sometimes a girl's a bit late, master, now and again. Ain't no harm in making her regular again. But kill a babe, never, so God's my witness,' she added with a piety I almost found convincing. 'I love delivering a babe,' she added. 'I do the layings out round here too. Your corpse needs a tender wash and I'm the gentlest round here – you ask folk about Mother Blount.'

'I will, Mrs Blount.' I found my anger at what I had construed to be infanticide had subsided. 'That was good ale and better cheese.' I got to my feet.

'Hey!' She grabbed my cuff. ''Tisn't you who's her fancy man, is it?'

'No. I wish I knew who it is, Mother Blount, because I would make him pay, believe me.'

She looked me in the eye. 'Aye, master, I believe you. Now, don't 'ee forget. The Wolverhampton road.'

As if doing her bidding rather than following my own inclination I set out southwards till I reached the next alehouse. This was decidedly superior to the first, boasting a servant to take Esau and a cleanly dressed landlord nodding politely in greeting.

He responded equally politely to my questions, but echoed Mother Blount's words – he'd seen no fine young couple, just a girl inclined to be stout and a bit weepy about the face. Seeing the mixed emotions on my face, he summoned his pot-boy and the cook: no, they had seen no one else, not this past week or more.

Thanking them for their help with some coins I had to trust the landlord to distribute, I mounted Esau again, turning him back home. It was too late to seek more possible sightings of poor Maggie today. In fact, if I didn't urge Esau into a bit more pace than he liked, I would miss Mr Pounceman's sermon, one in which after all I had a particular interest. Fewer servants would be in attendance: some would be engaged in preparing the evening meal and as to the others Mrs Faulkner was generous in allowing free time. She had declared that unless the Family were in the congregation, she regarded the second service as optional. I wished I could. But I had set myself a task and must follow it through. Now which woman would he choose? Would he pick a woman, like Miriam, who had started well but ended badly? I hoped he had more sense. Perhaps the Canaanite woman, who had answered Jesus back and achieved the miracle she needed? Naomi? But that might be seen as a young woman tempting a man, albeit a story with a happy ending – no, I did not expect that. The Queen of Sheba and her hairy legs? I must wait and see.

VII

Nurse doesn't know what the letters mean either! I make sure she catches me cleaning the frame.

'That sampler? That be one his lordship's cousin worked. You can see her blood on it – never very handy with her needle, Miss Honoria! But those letters in a funny order – no, I never could make sense of them either, so don't worry your head about them.' She actually smiled at me. 'You're a good girl and working well. Some would say you're wasted tucked away up here and you'd do better for yourself working where folk that matter can see you.'

'Please, Nurse, I like it here!' I cover my mouth with my hands. That's answering back! 'Sorry, Nurse.'

She laughs. Nurse laughs! 'Bless my soul, Hatty, you're a funny one. Tell you what, I'll ask Mamselle what those letters mean.' She nods a smile, but raises a finger. 'Just make sure you don't get above yourself, miss.'

EIGHT

Mrs Arden was the sole representative of the household when I entered the church, not taking my usual place but slipping in beside her. I wished, as I knelt in a private preparatory prayer, that I might nudge her – or even wink – to show her I had planned something, but clearly neither was appropriate in God's house. If only I had had time to prepare her – but here was Pounceman, sweeping in with his usual flourish and we all rose to our feet respectfully. Without doubt he registered the drastically reduced House contingent and my presence – though I kept my expression bland and, I hoped, unreadable.

I was pleased to note that his usual rich resonant tenor was squeakier than usual as he led the sung part of the service. I also thought I saw him busy with his pencil during the two Bible readings, neither of which referred to women – so he would have had to work hard to accede to my request.

The sermon was about hard work.

Mary and Martha.

He almost persuaded his congregation that Christ was wrong to suggest that listening to Him was better than toiling in the kitchen, but he resisted the temptation, grudgingly. He managed to include Milton's observations about standing and waiting. Mysteriously he construed this as waiting on your master at his table.

'What was that sermon all about?' Mrs Arden demanded, as we walked back towards the House together. 'I couldn't make head or tail of it. And what's that poem got to do with the price of coal? Begging your pardon, Mr Rowsley, it's what we say where I come from. It means—'

'That it's irrelevant? And so it was,' I agreed with a smile. 'But I sympathize a little with Mr Pounceman. It had to be produced at short notice. He and I had a brief discussion after this morning's service,' I added.

'Ah! We saw you heading out to the rectory.' She stopped, looking up at me, her expression stern but possibly approving.

'I've been elsewhere, too,' I said. 'Asking questions about Maggie. And receiving some disconcerting answers.'

She seemed to read my mind. 'Perhaps you should say no more till we gather for supper. I hope Mrs Faulkner is well enough to join us; her back was too bad for her to walk down for Evensong, I'm afraid.'

'I quite understand.' My voice was grave, but my eyes responded to the ready twinkle in hers. 'And I am sorry that so many of the staff are similarly afflicted.'

We set off again in a companionable silence. With no warning she suddenly asked, 'Tell me, Mr Rowsley, why is there no Mrs Rowsley? A fine young man like you should have a pretty wife and a quiverful of children.'

'My wife would not necessarily have to be pretty,' I said with an embarrassed laugh.

'Well, goodness knows there are plenty of plain women to choose from! But, Mr Rowsley, I fear I have upset you.'

'Not at all. I should imagine, Mrs Arden, that you are only saying out loud what is whispered in the corridors and in the cottages. Since you have been open and frank, I will be open and frank with you. I grew up surrounded by the most admirable women, who never regarded themselves as the weaker sex – any more than I believe you or Mrs Faulkner would. No? I thought not. But while they have not changed, society has. It seems women are to be cherished, cosseted, sometimes to within an inch of their lives.'

'May I correct you, sir! *Ladies* are to be cosseted and cherished. They are to swoon and blush. We loosen our stays and get on with our tasks.'

'That would be the philosophy of my grandmamma and my mother. They regard themselves as relics of a bygone age – not a better one, not a worse one, just a different one. They raised me to be friends with women, to like them, to argue with them, to challenge them. But it seems that the days of easy camaraderie between the sexes are over. Men like me are to tell their womenfolk what to do and when to do it, what to wear, how even to dress their hair – in, I have to say, styles that may be modest and submissive but which very rarely flatter.'

'Indeed – how many of us can carry off a centre parting? Just because the dear Queen thinks it makes her face look thinner. Dearie me, what am I saying?'

Laughing, I took my penknife and cut off a rose, holding it high over our heads. 'Sub rosa!'

She took the bud and tucked it fetchingly into her bonnet.

Mrs Faulkner greeted us in the kitchen, where the rest of the female staff were waiting talking quietly among themselves. She was moving stiffly, but she assured me that the discomfort was subsiding.

'I can tell you something that'll help your back more than embrocation,' Mrs Arden declared cheerfully, taking off her bonnet and hanging it on the back of a chair. 'A sermon, that's what!' She broke off to speak to the senior kitchen maid, nodding in approval at the answer she received. 'Good girl.'

Mrs Faulkner said, almost repressively, 'Perhaps we should speak of it in the Room.'

I grinned. 'I am quite happy for Mrs Arden to tell all her staff, if she so pleases. And for you to tell yours, who I am quite sure will tell the footmen and other manservants. It will be all round the village anyway by this time tomorrow.'

'Indeed?'

I could detect very little enthusiasm. Had I somehow challenged her authority? Serious again in a second, I said, 'There is something I do need to tell you both, in private. Perhaps we should start with that.' I bowed; she was to lead the way.

As usual, a pile of books lay on the table. Her tastes might have baffled and enraged our employers in equal measure: *The Mill on the Floss* sat cheek by jowl with a text I'd not yet read myself, *Utilitarianism*. I must ask her if I might borrow it when she had finished it. More respectably, there was a Bible, held open by a pair of spectacles I had never seen her use before. She moved to stand in front of her treasures, notably not inviting us to be seated.

Without thinking, I asked, 'Mrs Faulkner – have I offended

you in some way? Or are you in more pain than you care to admit?'

Her smile was stiff. 'I believe my visit to church this morning exacerbated the problem.'

'I cannot imagine otherwise. However, I think I can assure you that Mr Pounceman—'

Mrs Arden snorted. 'Pounce*woman*, more like, though actually I doubt if he'd touch a woman with a bargepole! Sorry, Mr Rowsley. I interrupted.'

I grinned forgiveness. 'Our esteemed rector will not preach a sermon like this morning's again. I believe he may be . . . chastened . . . by the reaction to it. I am not sure that this evening's effort would rate highly in ecclesiastical circles, but at least he did not insult either Martha or Mary.'

'Jesus might not like being shown to have made the wrong judgement, though,' Mrs Arden murmured, pouring three glasses of sherry, an informality I would not have risked. 'Go on, Mr Rowsley, tell us how you achieved the turn-about.' She sat down, uninvited.

Now it came to it I felt like a schoolboy told to stand and recite. I fear I even blushed. 'I was forced to remind Mr Pounceman that it takes two for a woman to be with child, and that to harangue only the one likely to suffer the most is barely Christian.' I broke off as someone tapped at the door.

'That'll be young Tess,' said Mrs Arden, who opened it herself, returning with a plate the contents of which smelt as manna might have done. 'Cheese straws. A new recipe, the one you recommended, Mrs Faulkner. Will you both try one? I believe they will suit the sherry very well.'

Until I too had tasted one, I had no idea how hungry I was. 'They – literally – melt in the mouth! But, if you will forgive me, lest I eat the whole plate, I will give you the other news.'

Mrs Faulkner raised an eyebrow. 'But did not Mr Pounceman object to your Turkish treatment?'

'Of course he did. But he . . . he let me persuade him. Although he is by no means an employee of his lordship, he is beholden to him for a very lucrative benefice. I cannot imagine he would want anything to disturb his relationship with him.'

Mrs Faulkner shook her head. 'You took a risk, Mr Rowsley.

A great risk. I say that as one who has known his lordship no short time. But I am grateful that you took it, as I am sure we all are. You are right: everyone on the estate will be aware of what you did by noon tomorrow. But you spoke of other news,' she continued, as if wishing to shake off a dangerous topic of conversation.

'Indeed. News which, I fear, can bring no joy, just anxiety. After my . . . discussion . . . with Mr Pounceman, I needed to clear my head and went for a ride – to the south, as it happens. Eventually I had a conversation, the gist of which was that a witness saw a girl like Maggie, but not with a handsome beau. She was alone and with a tear-stained face. The witness also swore that she was with child. I rode further: another witness said much the same, though without mentioning her condition.'

The women nodded as one, as they digested the implications. Mrs Arden looked at Mrs Faulkner: she was to speak first. 'I did suspect. Of course I did. I questioned her, as gently as I might. But she was firm, emphatic, even in her denials. Yet this witness recognized her condition immediately?'

'Mother Blount.'

'Ah! Of course. In the old days she'd have been burned as a witch, but she does a lot of good. Tops and tails the villagers, you might say – there at their birth, there to lay them out. Well, I feel embarrassed, of course, that she should be so much more observant than I, but bow to her experience.' Her smile was wry. 'Do I recall, Mr Rowsley, that it was Mrs Billings who told you that Maggie was with . . . a young man?' She seemed to be choosing her words with extra care.

'She implied it. I must have been mistaken – perhaps I heard what I wanted to hear, that the child had at least a protector with her. The thought of a child of fifteen, on her own, knowing she is carrying a babe, and . . . I am truly lost for words.' I covered my face with my hands. Yet pity was not enough. 'I need your advice, please. You will both have known girls like this equally betrayed. What should I do? Go in search of her?'

With a dry cough Mrs Arden refilled my glass.

Mrs Faulkner waited while I drank down far more than was seemly. Only then did she say quietly, 'Firstly I think her mother must be questioned again. You may feel that this is a task for a woman. If you do, I will undertake it. Her answers may save you what might be at best a wild goose chase. At worst you may be compromising yourself and your reputation, which could well lose you your position here. If you were dismissed, you would be leaving the House without an effective master. Between us Mrs Arden and I can manage the household, even the men, but we cannot manage the estate, and it is on the estate that everything and everyone depends – yourself included, I should imagine. *Festina lente*: that would be my counsel.'

Mrs Arden shot her a surprised look.

I hope I managed not to do the same: not since I left home had I heard a woman offering me a Latin adage. And somehow I had to translate it without humiliating Mrs Arden.

But Mrs Faulkner was doing it already, with grace. 'Tell him, Mrs Arden, there is no point in dashing off like some romantic knight errant when he could – with a little pause for thought – make much more progress!'

Her friend laughed. 'Might this pause include a bite of supper? It is ready for the table, I should imagine. I hear the men coming down to the hall now, ready to hear you say grace. As for ours, Tess will bring it in, but I fancy – with your agreement, Mr Rowsley – that we should serve ourselves, as we often do when there are just a few of us.'

Our supper might have been more of a war cabinet, largely as a result of a question Mrs Faulkner posed, apropos my urge to dash off to find Maggie.

'Suppose you do find the child, Mr Rowsley – what then?'

'I restore her to her family, of course,' I said. I might have begun confidently but I stuttered to a halt.

'You have seen her family's home? Exactly. How can she return there?' Mrs Faulkner asked.

'And she can scarcely return here,' Mrs Arden said. 'With the best will in the world, Mrs Faulkner cannot have her working in her usual capacity, any more than I would have a girl in a similar situation in the kitchen. We do not expect our fellow-servants to be nuns or monks, but to be seen to reward . . . No, it will not do.'

'So, having found her, we must persuade her to name her betrayer and compel him to marry her? One has often heard of this happening, but so many times it has brought much distress to both parties,' I observed, thinking of cases my father had tried to deal with.

'Some would say that they deserve to be punished. Both.'

'Speaking to Maggie would help mean the circumstances of her pregnancy could be determined, and blame apportioned,' Mrs Faulkner pointed out. She raised an index finger. 'But who would do the questioning? And who make the judgement? Who enforce any verdict? You? Or Mr Pounceman?'

I had no answer. 'Has there been no talk amongst her fellow-servants? The girls she shares a room with, for instance?'

'Now we know more of the situation, and we can point out the child needs help, not a lonely walk where harm could befall her, I think the staff will feel more able to confide in us,' Mrs Arden said. 'Between us we can speak to all the females, but who will question the men? It is Mr Bowman's job, and he will not return till Tuesday.' She looked hopefully at me.

I spread my hands. 'Mr Bowman might resent my interference. And probably the young men, who fear me anyway, would not co-operate. If, however,' I added, capitulating, 'any specific names come up in your questioning, then of course I will speak to the man concerned.' I looked from one woman to the other. 'And then what? What if the man turns out to be married?' I shook my head. 'Oh, for the wisdom of Solomon!'

Mrs Faulkner's laugh was dry. 'As Mrs Glasse might have said, "First catch your hare".'

VIII

I *must not get above myself – but I must and will learn to read. I make sure I give every book an extra-careful dust; in other words, I turn the pages, scanning them for words I recognize or can at least put together. But the letters on the sampler defeat me. Perhaps Nurse has forgotten to ask Mamselle what they mean. I dare not ask. Not if that means I am getting above myself. When Nurse calls me* Miss *– worse still* Missie *– I know that though she is smiling, she is giving me a serious warning.*

What if Mamselle herself does not know what they mean?

NINE

Monday's weather was bad, heavy low cloud bringing rain driven by a southwesterly gale. Having ridden a reluctant Esau briskly round the estate to give my orders for the day, which entailed as much indoor work as could reasonably be found, I was glad to return to the House. Esau was to be rubbed dry and kept in the comfort of his stable; I withdrew to my office and the pile of paperwork I had reserved for just such a day as this, even if it meant sending for extra lamps. I longed to be able to introduce gas-lights, like those in the homes of so many of my acquaintance, but would have to choose my moment – and probably wait till all the pleasure-giving changes had been paid for.

However, as the rain hurled itself at the window, I knew that other expenditure might be even more urgently needed. This was just the time to inspect the fabric for leaks. I sent a note to George, the estate carpenter, bidding him to join me in my tour of the House – he would know better than I what might need immediate action and what could be postponed.

While I waited, I wrote more notes, this time to neighbouring farmers, offering tarpaulins and labourers to deal with any urgent storm damage. Two hapless outdoor lads had the unpleasant task of delivering them. I worked my way through a pot of coffee and two thick files of correspondence before George presented himself, clearly soaked to the skin.

''Tis a regular cloudburst, gaffer,' he said, as if apologising for the puddles he was leaving on my carpet.

'So I can see. Look at you, man – you're dithering as if you're in an ague.' I eyed his height and girth. In his fifties, he was shorter than me, his shoulders broad in proportion. His hands looked strong enough to throttle someone with one of them tied behind his back. 'If you don't mind being decked out as a footman, we'll get those clothes of yours dried in the kitchen, yes, and your boots. And I'm sure Mrs Arden can find some hot coffee for you too.'

He was inclined to demur, but I was entitled to insist, which I did, sending him off with Eliott, one of the more sensible footmen, whom I called back: 'There is to be no open mockery, nor behind-the-hand sniggering. Am I clear?'

Within a quarter of an hour George was back. Someone had found him not livery, but a Sunday suit, predictably too long in the trousers, so he had to hitch them up with string tied below the knee. Far from being relieved, George looked remarkably hang-dog.

'The only thing to do, man, is laugh at yourself before others do. Turn it into a joke at my expense – "Gaffer's turned me into a scarecrow!" That sort of thing. My shoulders are broad enough,' I said, more hopeful than convinced. 'Now, where do we start? You must know this place like the back of your hand, but I've been worried about the roof since the day I arrived.'

'And you're right to worry, gaffer. To my way of thinking, we should look at the attics first, begging your pardon, gaffer.'

'Lead the way. But let me make this clear, George, you are the gaffer here. You are the expert and I will listen to your advice – and act on it, if it's in my power.'

Nodding, perhaps doubtfully, he led the way straight to the back stairs, stumbling as he left the brightness of the front of the House for the ill-lit stone stairs, dark green paint on the walls making the matter worse. How on earth did people carry items without tripping in the near Stygian gloom?

The first note I made was to have them painted cream and have them covered with drugget. Not ideal but better.

'Lord bless you!' George puffed as we reached the first attic. 'All these stairs. Now, gaffer, this is the oldest part of the House – right?'

'It may well be – I'm completely lost!'

'Look at the size of the bricks: smaller than ours. Hey, look at that lot.' He gestured at a double row of paintings stacked against the far wall. 'Isn't that a picture of Good Queen Bess?'

'Probably. Painted during her reign by the look of it. And look at all those other pictures too! Surely that's a Holbein – and that's a Kneller.' His lordship wasn't so much as sitting on a fortune but lying beneath it. 'And the furniture – how on earth did they get such heavy stuff up here? This table – it must weigh a ton!'

We wandered round like children in a bizarre fairy-tale. In the end we were recalled to the task in hand by a persistent drip in one corner. 'Blocked gutters or a missing tile,' George said, 'and dead urgent, or we shall be getting dry rot – if we haven't got it already.'

We: he clearly identified himself with the Family in a way I couldn't now, even if I ever would.

Leak after leak went on my list. A rumble from his stomach reminded me that it was well past the hour of the servants' morning break.

'Shall we take a breather now?' I asked with a laugh.

To my delight he laughed too. 'Bless you, gaffer, I might as well work on till dinner – it only wants an hour.'

'And by then your clothes might be dry,' I added with a grin, as we headed for the stairs and the nursery wing.

By the time we had reached the guest wing, my stomach was joining his in protest. By mutual consent we suspended our task, heading to the servants' hall for a veritable trencherman's feast of roast lamb. There was no doubting the suppressed giggles and sniggers as George sat down; when I took a seat near him, the silence that fell upon the gathering was tense and awkward. It was only as Mrs Arden and Mrs Faulkner rose, catching my eye, that I recalled that the others could not speak until the senior servants had adjourned to the Room for their dessert.

I touched George amicably on the shoulder as I left. 'We'll resume at one fifteen, shall we, where we left off?'

He stood, touching his forelock. 'One fifteen it is, gaffer.'

'I should think your own clothes will be dry by then, George,' Mrs Arden said, over her shoulder, as she curtsied to me to precede her.

There was a plate of fruit for our dessert, and a bowl of early strawberries from one of the succession houses, which also, incidentally, cried out for George's attention. Clearly there was far too much for one man to do, even if we added two or three skilled men to his apprentice, but I was aware, as his lordship was not, of the limitations of my budget.

'Mr Rowsley?' Mrs Faulkner was gesturing at the fruit.

'I do beg your pardon. It has been a dispiriting morning, ladies.

I cannot conceive why much of the work was not done years ago. I hate seeing neglect in a great house like this.' Might I persuade his lordship to sell some of the attic's contents? But that was a matter I ought not to discuss with even trusted companions like this. In any case, they probably had more pressing matters to discuss. 'Strawberries, if you please. Pray, tell me: is there anything to report more to the point than dry rot in window frames?'

The women exchanged glances. Passing a jug of cream, Mrs Arden spoke first: 'To my mind there is no doubt that Maggie's situation was suspected by a number of girls – I believe you felt the same, Mrs Faulkner? – but even now they are reluctant to break what I presume is a vow of silence, especially after that sermon yesterday morning.'

Mrs Faulkner pondered. 'Do you think there is more than what I might call a sisterly bond? I wondered if one or two were actively afraid to speak out – they were looking over their shoulders as they whispered their replies, as if they were afraid they might be overheard, with dire consequences. Shall I ring for coffee? I suspect we are all a little behindhand with our work today.'

'Afraid? Not just esprit de corps?' I asked. Mrs Arden's blank face told me I had made a gaffe. 'The junior servants sticking together against people like you two ladies with the power instantly to dismiss them?'

'No. Absolute fear,' Mrs Faulkner said decisively. 'You could almost smell it.'

'Does this mean that the man involved was – important? Someone – I can hardly believe I am saying this – someone like Mr Bowman?'

There was a scratch at the door. The latest tweenie arrived with the coffee tray. Bobbing almost frantically, she backed out.

Getting up awkwardly enough to suggest that her back was indeed still troubling her, Mrs Faulkner checked that the door was fully closed. 'Mr Bowman may never be entirely sober but he would never trouble a child of that age. He's more likely to kill the man who did. He sees himself as a father to them all, young men and young women alike, you understand: remote, perhaps bullying, but a father nonetheless.'

I dared not voice my thoughts, that one of his lordship's guests might be responsible. I dared not voice another thought even to myself.

'By the way,' Mrs Faulkner continued, still on her feet, 'I have to confess I did not make my way to the gatehouse this morning.'

'No sensible soul would!' her friend exclaimed. 'There's no good to be gained turning up like a drowned rat. She'd just wonder what you were there for!'

'Exactly. And I wanted to imply the visit was casual, and build up to what I fear will be an interrogation.' She passed the cups of coffee – some of her ladyship's special blend – before she sat down. 'Did you get any information from George?' she asked, so casually I knew my answer would disappoint her.

'I am biding my time. All our conversation this morning was about the poor state of the roof and much of the woodwork. I thought he would be readier to talk when he was comfortable in his own clothes, and, of course, after his dinner-time beer.'

'That's another matter Mr Pounceman wants to stick his nose in – the beer allowance,' Mrs Arden snorted. 'He says water is good enough. Which I suppose it is, if it's good water. Ours is so hard – you've no idea the effort it takes to get good lather. Ask the laundry maids. You wonder if he'll dare tell his lordship that water is better than his burgundy.'

'Not when he's coming to supper with the county set, that's for sure,' her friend laughed.

I hesitated. The idea of making beer part of anyone's wages worried me. There were people who might want to follow Pounceman's precepts, but the pressure of their fellow servants, sitting round the communal table, must be very hard to withstand. 'I would like to be a fly on the wall if he did!' I said truthfully. 'Now, I fear I will keep George waiting, and in truth there is much to be done. We will be ready for our cup of tea this afternoon, without doubt.'

The list of essential repairs got longer by the minute. We were now in the family wing, much extended to give loftier rooms for honoured guests and his lordship. In line with custom, her ladyship had given up her room, and now occupied the dowager's suite further down the main corridor. Though the décor was the best in the whole house, her former quarters would be redecorated ready for the day when his lordship brought home a new wife.

George gave a dry laugh. 'When I was a lad it was my job to oil all the locks and hinges in the bedchamber corridors so people could go about their business each night without anyone knowing. Creaky floorboards too – I became an expert on them. So's my apprentice. Not that he needs to be. It's all changed now, hasn't it, gaffer? The Family and their friends are supposed to behave themselves the same of the rest of us. People are so damned pious – begging your pardon, sir!'

I laughed. 'You sound regretful.'

He sucked his teeth. 'There's good and bad to be said for it. Back when I was a lad, a wench in young Maggie's state wouldn't have had to run away. She'd have been looked after, proper. Yes, she'd have been sent away to another estate, but she'd have been cared for there, and the babe brought up decent. If it was a lad and a Family by-blow, then it would be educated and found a position. Apprenticed, if there was any doubt.'

'And what if the baby was a girl?'

'Same thing, really – a respectable position would be found. Then the mother – well, she might marry a local worker, or just be given a ring and become Mrs Something or Other and found a post in another great house. None of this "Never darken my door" business!'

'"Darken my door business"?' I repeated sharply.

'Don't get me wrong, gaffer. I'm just drawing a conclusion. A girl isn't going to flit off like that if she was going to be properly looked after, is she?'

'So, assuming you're right, and I'm not arguing, who would show the young woman the door?'

He paused. 'Many places, it'd be the housekeeper or the cook, wouldn't it? Or even the steward. But I can't see any of you three doing that. Can you?' He looked me straight in the eye, suddenly if only briefly treating me as an equal. 'Now, I have to say I don't like the look of that frame, do you?' he continued with an awkward cough.

I had to admit I didn't, and made a note. So who would have dismissed young Maggie? Or did she indeed believe, when she left, that she was going to meet her lover?

His lordship's room was occupied by three or four maids, ostensibly beating curtains and wiping paint but actually giggling behind their hands. The laughter stopped immediately, and eyes were lowered as they curtsied. Off the main chamber was a dressing room, big enough to accommodate a full-size bed, but currently empty but for the usual cupboards and wardrobes, all in the latest style, and several free-standing mirrors. One of the cupboards was not properly closed. Had the contents of that been the cause of their hilarity? With George beside me I could hardly investigate.

'That door in the corner connects to his late lordship's dressing room,' George said.

'Can you imagine if one of them was turned into a modern bathroom?' I murmured. 'It would save all that tedious business of hip baths and washstands and chamber pots.'

He stood stock still. 'But what would the maids do with their time?'

We had checked three or four more rooms further down the corridor before I raised the question of Maggie again. 'There must be rumours around the House and the estate about who got Maggie with child, George. I'd rather they reached me, you know, before they got to young Harry Kenton's ears. I'd say he'd be quick with his hands, if he was crossed.'

George sucked his teeth, digging a thumbnail into a suspect sill before he spoke. 'More dry rot there, gaffer.' He looked around the room. 'You may not like to hear this.'

'Is it I they accuse?' I tried to sound more disbelieving than furious.

'Not exactly, gaffer. But they do say you must know. Or someone in the House must know. Mr Bowman, or Mrs Faulkner. Specially her, because – you know – of the . . . evidence . . .' He turned bright red. 'When my wife was a wench in service, it was part of the housekeeper's job to check, you know, every month, that she was having . . . So the housekeeper would be the first to know if . . .' He coughed. 'If there was no blood, like.'

For the life of me I could not imagine Mrs Faulkner indulging in the ritual monthly humiliation. I returned to what he had said earlier. 'And they think whoever it is – and I can assure you it is not me – should have done more to protect her?'

He looked at me shrewdly once again. 'You would have, wouldn't you, gaffer? But tell me, why has Mr Bowman flit off? He'd hear the footmen whispering and sniggering if it was one of them.'

With her ladyship and his lordship both suddenly called away, there was no reason for Bowman to be in residence. But I did not care to follow out loud where that thought was leading me; after what Mrs Faulkner had said, it was certainly not to imagining the butler as a seducer. 'Mr Bowman returns tomorrow. I give you my word I will speak to him then. Meanwhile, what about this room?' I tried the handle. And again. I looked disbelievingly at George.

Although most of the rooms had locks, very few had keys in the doors – after all, the House was always full of people ready to detect an interloper. We had simply walked into those we had checked so far, the locks and hinges beautifully oiled. This door refused to budge. Frowning, he fished in his pocket and produced a bunch of keys, some simply skeletons. With some confidence he tried one of them. Then another and another.

'Looks like we'll have to get in through the next-door room. It's kept for particular friends of the Family,' he said, leading the way. That door opened easily, but the connecting door was as tightly fastened as the one to the corridor. 'Do you want me to force it?' he asked. 'It'll show, of course.'

'Any more subtle way of opening it?'

'I can unscrew the lock. But even that might be noticed.' He looked at me anxiously: if it were discovered, and he truly offended his lordship, would I be able to help him?

I responded to his unspoken question with a slow shake of my head. 'It would be hard to justify unless we had evidence of anything needing urgent repair. Let's think about it, George. Now to the next. There should just be time.'

There would have been, but for an urgent summons. Farmer Twiss's milking parlour was losing its roof. George looked at me. 'I'd best lend a hand if you'll excuse me, gaffer.'

'Excuse you? I'm leading the way!'

IX

I can hear them arguing, Nurse and Mamselle.

'I am employed,' Mamselle is saying, her voice rising and rising in anger, 'to teach the Family's children, not some workhouse guttersnipe.'

Nurse is stern. 'No one said anything about teaching, Mamselle. She just asked about those letters and I said I'd ask you, as a favour, like.'

'Well, I tell you no – no favours!'

So Mamselle doesn't know what the letters mean, either.

TEN

I t was a weary band of men, trooping back to the estate after we had not only covered the roof with tarpaulins, but shored up the end wall, which had been in danger of collapse. We were all soaked to the skin, and I was acutely aware that very few men would have the luxury of a hot bath and a change of clothes. It seemed I was to have both, and a good meal too. Mrs Faulkner had sent a note down to my house, telling me that she had the copper heating water for me, and a bedroom prepared for me to bath and change, if I cared to bring my evening clothes in a portmanteau.

Like George earlier in the day, I left wet prints all through the passageways. A junior footman led the way up the back stairs, but I was gratified to be ushered into a guest bedchamber, complete with a roaring fire and a steaming hip bath. The footman, surely no more than sixteen, was solemn and silent as a valet, carefully unpacking and laying out my suit and removing the soaking garments I discarded. I was happy to turn down his offer to assist me as I dressed for dinner, but nonetheless he waited for me in the corridor to escort me back downstairs, where I received, to my embarrassment, a hero's welcome and a glass of champagne.

'Mr Rowsley,' Mrs Faulkner said slowly, laying down her knife and fork at the end of a perfect meal, 'Mrs Arden and I have been thinking. It might seem . . . strange . . . that the Family and Mr Bowman all shoot off at the same time. And do not forget my quite spurious errand for her ladyship,' she added quietly.

'And my trip to solve a trivial problem, of course.'

She nodded. 'Just because servants are told never to question their masters doesn't mean they cannot speculate amongst themselves. As we are doing now. Mr Rowsley, what are your thoughts?'

I clicked my fingers in irritation. 'How could I forget? A few days ago, before the general exodus, I heard voices raised in what sounded like anger. But the noise was distorted by the rotunda – I couldn't tell where the sound was coming from or who was speaking. And one night, passing the shrubbery on my way home, I heard another exchange – this time it was clearly between a young man and a young woman. When I heard what might have been a slap, I called out. But whoever was there melted into the darkness.' I spread my hands apologetically. 'I'm sorry. This doesn't add anything to your . . . your speculation. But I agree with you that there have been a number of coincidences. I don't know the Family well enough to say whether their behaviour is typical of them – though I can assure you that one or two of the employers I have served have been breathtakingly high-handed, changing their minds with complete indifference to others' commitments.'

Mrs Arden laughed. 'Oh, indeed. I recall the day one lord told us to take our annual holidays the very next day – and then, just as we were ready to leave, changed his mind. Just like that. And you must recall Lady Miller, Mrs Faulkner . . .'

Much as I would have liked to accompany Mrs Faulkner to the gatehouse, I knew it would make her delicate task worse. In any case, I had enough work to do, from riding round the estate to authorize essential work caused by yesterday's weather to suggesting to George that he should pull together a band of skilled men to help him in the repairs to the House. Ideally I'd have told him to use estate workers, but we were so overstretched by the storm and by his lordship's improvements – which could not indeed be stopped at this stage or even more money would be wasted – that we simply did not have enough hands at our disposal. Disconcerted by the sudden mental image of giant thumbs and fingers attached to tiny bodies, I corrected myself: we did not have enough skilled carpenters to call on.

'Wellington or Shrewsbury, I thought. Maybe Ironbridge, though I don't know there'd be many chippies there,' he said. 'Factories, mostly, that way.'

'Where you have factories, you have workers' houses. And where you have new houses you have all sorts of artisans.'

'And not one of them good enough to work on the House, surely, gaffer. Jerry-sneak workmen, all of them!'

'Fair enough. You know better than I. But I'd like you to talk to folk wherever you go.'

He opened his mouth to argue, but shut it again firmly. Then he looked at me sideways. 'And am I to be asking questions of them? About a certain young person?'

'I see no harm in combining two errands, do you, George? Mother Blount may have seen another girl in distress, not Maggie at all. Let's face it, innkeepers and publicans are likely to tell you the truth than me if I went poking my nose in – especially if you said, maybe, that a friend's daughter had gone astray.'

Nodding slowly, he shot out a strong, scarred hand. 'You're a good man.' He rather spoiled the compliment by adding, 'Whatever they say.'

The behaviour of the maids in his lordship's dressing room had intrigued me. So, when I had a moment, I made my way up again. Occasionally – and not just for show – I made use of my pad and pencil, adding items to the list we had made yesterday.

A cursory opening and shutting of drawers and cupboards revealed nothing other than clothing. Until I found the cupboard which had been left open but was now closed – even locked. My key ring soon provided the answer – and soon I discovered the reason for the sniggers. The shelves were lined with books that were clearly pornographic. It was fortunate that most of the girls were farmers' daughters, who would know about animals' natural functions, even if they did not associate them being mixed with human inclinations. I locked the cupboard again. What were the implications of my find, other than that his lordship had pleasures I associated with some of my less likeable colleagues at school and then university? It was information I did not care to share – and certainly not with Mrs Faulkner and Mrs Arden. Possibly not even with Mr Bowman, who was returning later today. I had a sudden frisson of far from pleasurable anticipation: it was clearly my duty to accost him beforehand and ask if he had heard any rumours about Maggie's condition. There might be other questions: if he had, had he acted on them?

To some extent, of course, the discussion would depend on how sober I found him.

By chance late in the afternoon I was in the courtyard when the pony cart arrived, and was able to help him down from it. A stable-boy appeared as if by magic, conjuring, with a piercing whistle, a footman, who gathered Bowman's luggage and made off with it with satisfactory briskness. Bowman might have been surprised by my request to speak to him privately in his room before supper, but he agreed readily – not like a man nursing a conscience guilty of a sin of commission or even omission. He suggested we took sherry as we talked; his advice had been that we should wear smoking jackets as a point midway between formality and the relaxed code we had no doubt adopted in his absence, he added with a twinkle. I suspected the decision would filter as if by osmosis to the women. More important than what they wore, however, was whether they would trust their colleague enough to discuss in front of him any revelations Mrs Billings might have made. I was not entirely sanguine.

Though Bowman was often too full of bonhomie for my taste, this evening he was serious as one might wish when I broached the topic of Maggie's disappearance, his normal professionally equable demeanour crumbling further as I unfolded each extra detail.

'The poor child!' He hauled himself to his feet, as if to reach for the sherry decanter, instead pacing from one end of his room to the other. At last he sat, collapsing into his chair. 'For God's sake, there are enough women in the House – or even the village – to help her. Pennyroyal, isn't that supposed to work – only when it's not really a baby yet,' he added hurriedly, as Mother Blount had done. 'But who could have betrayed the poor maiden, Mr Rowsley?'

'I was hoping you might speak to the footmen. I would have done it myself but you know them so much better than I do, and would know when they were telling the truth and when dissimulating.'

'I trust I will!' He swallowed – possibly his pride, as he said, 'Would you want to be with me? You have the authority I lack.'

'Not in this house,' I said firmly. 'As far as I am concerned, your word is law here, yours and Mrs Faulkner's.' I was gratified to see his shoulders set more squarely. 'Do you have any suspects already? I know that young men will always indulge in banter, sometimes horseplay, but do any show signs of taking things beyond the acceptable? Or,' I added, despite myself dropping my voice and leaning forward confidentially, 'were there any rumours amongst the footmen of bad behaviour from his lordship's guests or their servants?' To my chagrin I had to repeat what I had said more loudly as he cupped his hand to his ear: I had forgotten he was hard-of-hearing.

'Do we know – I'm sorry to be indelicate – how far into her . . . her condition . . . she was?'

I shrugged. 'I'm in no position to so much as hazard a guess. I never noticed, because, to be honest, she was just a quiet, self-effacing maid.'

'Maggie? Quiet? Self-effacing? I always thought her a lively enough young lass. But others must have noticed the change.' His look was shrewd. 'Surely Mrs Faulkner—?'

'It is not a subject I felt comfortable pursuing with a lady,' I admitted, 'as I am sure you will understand.'

'Quite so, quite so . . .' This time he did reach for the sherry, filling both glasses to the brim. Nonetheless, the sip he took was small, discreet. He changed the subject violently: 'Have we had word when his lordship plans to return? And her ladyship, of course?'

'Not yet. The staff have been working very hard in their absence, as you can imagine.'

He nodded absently. 'Yes, Mrs Faulkner has a long-established routine for when the Family are away for short periods. Mrs Arden too.' He sipped again. 'You know, Mr Rowsley, I am no longer a young man. I had thought to settle down as the master of a genteel guest house. The usual procedure in such a case is to marry the housekeeper one has worked with for many years – but I am not sure that Mrs Faulkner would . . . Mrs Arden, now – do you think *she* might welcome my addresses?'

I managed to say with what I hoped was a becoming gravity, 'I think there is only one person who could answer that.'

'Ah! Of course! Mrs Faulkner!' he declared confusingly.

'I beg your pardon? I gathered that . . . I understood you to say . . .' Perhaps I spoke more sharply than was tactful.

'Yes, Mrs Faulkner. She would know her colleague's inclinations.'

I raised my glass. 'Let us drink to a suitable outcome to your enquiries. All of them,' I added firmly.

'So the gate was guarded not by Mrs Billings but by a scrap of an urchin who greeted me with the news that his ma was a-working at the ditching,' Mrs Faulkner said, with a mixture of pity and exasperation and a not altogether kind mimicry of the child's delivery.

'He was still there this afternoon,' Mr Bowman agreed. 'But Mrs Billings, working at ditching? Why on earth should that be?'

'To relieve the flooding after yesterday's downpour,' I said quietly. 'I told Garbutt, who is in charge of the lake dredging, you'll recall, to employ as many as were needed at double their hourly rates. I never imagined he'd take on a woman.'

'The women from round here pride themselves on their endurance,' Mr Bowman declared. 'And down in what it pleased Her Majesty to call the Black Country women make great chains, and iron nails! Heavens! Their arms are like Hercules'! A man would fear get on the wrong side of one! As for the women on the narrow boats – my goodness, what with their fearsome muscles and their shockingly coarse language they truly make one believe there was once a race of female warriors!'

Mrs Arden slipped a swift glance in my direction: clearly she recalled our conversation about what women could manage if needs be. I responded with the briefest of smiles. Would Mr Bowman really make her, with her capacity for impish humour, a happy woman? In her place I would worry about his pomposity, his deafness and his drinking. But marriage gave women security they lacked in the single state. How many women did I know – yes, and men too – who continued to work almost till their death because there was no other way to survive?

I would welcome Mrs Faulkner's views. She was very quiet this evening, however, almost subdued; perhaps her back still troubled her. Yet I sensed an anger about her too. If only I might contrive a word in private. That, however, would almost certainly prove impossible, given her understandable respect for propriety.

I smiled at her briefly before observing, 'But poor Mrs Billings is no Amazon. I wonder if the exertion will have harmed her.'

'She would not admit it if it did. And the extra money will help her household. But, if you think it a good idea, I will speak to her tomorrow.'

'Thank you. I would be very grateful.'

Bowman gave a troubled laugh. 'Take care, Mr Rowsley. A word to the wise. If you take too much interest in Maggie's family, there'll be those who draw the wrong conclusion.'

Much as I would have liked to choke an apology from him, a deep breath gave me time to reflect. The warning might have been tactless but was sincere, and in truth only echoed what Mrs Faulkner and Mrs Arden had hinted. 'I think it is the responsibility of all of us to care what happened to the child, and I am grateful to Mrs Faulkner for doing so much. Now, may I say grace?'

'You're a cad, sir, and a bounder!' My interlocutor had stopped me as the following morning I rode towards Twiss's farm to see that the repairs still held. He jabbed his riding crop into my chest.

I left it where it was. 'Indeed, Mr Newcombe.' I looked as calmly as I could into the furious face. Tertius Newcombe was one of the churchwardens no doubt seeking to uphold the morals of the congregation. A portly man in his fifties he owned a prosperous farm the other side of the village. 'And why should you say that?'

'You know damn' well why I say it. And will say it again.'

'I might think better if you removed your whip, sir.' I wanted to say a great deal else, but I knew my temper of old and did not wish to become reacquainted with it. 'Thank you. I collect you are referring to the disappearance of young Maggie Billings?'

'Who else? They say you want to find her to silence her.'

'I certainly want to find her, but buying her silence is the last thing on my mind. As her employer, we – the household – are after all to some extent *in loco parentis*, I believe – and the idea of a child walking off unaccompanied into the night appals me.'

'A child!' He was clearly nonplussed.

'According to Mrs Faulkner, at most fifteen – and already a vital means of her family's support. Let me make this clear: I don't like the notion of a child being betrayed by a man in the house for which I bear responsibility. It doesn't accord with my notions of decent behaviour. I doubt if the man in question will confess, so I believe it is the Family's responsibility to ensure that Maggie, wherever she is now, is given enough money to have a roof over her head and to provide for the child.'

His eyes narrowed. 'That's rewarding loose morals.'

'Some would indeed think that, and why not? But if a second child is involved, an innocent baby, then I cannot see how we can judge it, morality or not.'

Newcombe raised an eyebrow. 'There are plenty of orphanages – there's also the workhouse.'

'Either of those would make not just Maggie but also her innocent baby suffer.'

His eyes narrowed. 'And his lordship approves of what you're doing?'

'His lordship is away from home. I don't think this matter can wait till he returns. A girl of fourteen or fifteen on her own? Who knows what danger she is in?'

'She's in greater danger of eternal damnation!'

'Yes, I heard Mr Pounceman's sermon. I hope her seducer did too. I can see, Mr Newcombe, that we are not likely to agree in this matter. So let us change the subject to one we can talk of in amity. Your son – Gerald? – seems to me to be a most promising batsman. I hope you will let him continue to play in the village team . . .'

'Indeed – is there any doubt?'

I coughed gently. 'His lordship's plans for a ground on the estate?'

He shook his head firmly. 'A team's a thing that binds a village together, Rowsley. Which reminds me – good work on Twiss's farm. Neighbourly.'

'The least we could do. We had the men and the tarpaulins.'

'Hmm. Very well.' He stared. 'You'd best make your peace with the rector, though. We must all stick together. Good day, Rowsley.' His nod was at least polite.

So was mine, as we shook hands. But my heart was still racing with the effort to keep calm.

At least I was ready to smile warmly when I encountered the next neighbour, Oliver Page, the doctor. We rode together for a while, talking of nothing much. But I had, of course, to ask if he had heard any rumours about Maggie.

He sucked his teeth. 'It's not impossible she might be six months into her pregnancy.'

'Six months!'

'Tight lacing. Voluminous skirt. Huge ugly apron. I've known women practically ready to pod before I knew what was up. Now, what's this I've heard about Stammerton?'

'So it's all round the village already,' I said ruefully. 'But you'll be aware that not everyone approves.'

'Not everyone has the sense they were born with. It's music to my ears at least,' he declared with gratifying enthusiasm. 'Those apologies for dwellings will fall down soon enough, and it would be far more sensible to replace them, rather than attempt futile repairs. Yes, it makes good economic sense as well as – dare I say – moral sense. But never to underestimate the enemy,' he said, bringing his horse to a standstill. He leant towards me like a schoolmaster, wagging his finger. 'I am sure you know that your benevolent concern for young Maggie Billings is scandalising the half of the village that doesn't cautiously admire what you are doing.'

'I've just been roundly rebuked, as it happens.'

He nodded gravely. 'It's not just the gentry who disapprove because they fear you are encouraging dissolute behaviour amongst their servants, it's some of the poor too, who perceive she may be rewarded for behaviour they avoid.'

'Avoid! Are you telling me that at least half the couples that Mr Pounceman joins in wedlock don't already have a child on the way?'

He snorted with laughter. 'Well, many a countryman wouldn't buy a bitch to breed from if it hadn't already littered. I fear many of our young men have the same approach to a potential bride. And, for heaven's sake, these are young people who might as well get what pleasure they can, bless them. Except that so many of their babes are born into such desperate poverty: after all my years in practice it still grieves me beyond measure when a child succumbs to an illness that a healthier, better fed child would survive. Still, in your new Stammerton, they may thrive. I hope and pray they will. But a word to the wise, my friend: to build Stammerton, you need to keep your job.' He kicked his mount into action.

*   *   *

I chanced to encounter Mrs Faulkner that afternoon after she had called at the lodge. She was carrying a basket, now empty: I deduced she had contrived to make her errand one of mercy as well as subtle interrogation.

She admitted, as we strolled together, that her back still gave her pain, but said, with a shrewd glance, 'But not as much as Mr Bowman's observation gave you, I fancy.'

I stopped in my tracks. 'I give you my word—'

'Mr Rowsley, now we are alone I may speak more freely. If my calculations are correct, you could not be the father. But in a sense Mr Bowman was right to warn you, if not in public like that. We all have to be like Caesar's wife, entirely above suspicion. As to Maggie, I believe Mrs Billings was not being straight with me. She still talks of her daughter meeting her fancy-man, in highly derogatory terms. But – you know how a child who has been primed to tell a particular story is rarely convincing? – I felt that with Mrs Billings. If she is indeed telling the truth, she is not telling the whole truth. And I am at a loss to discover what that may be.'

We walked on slowly. 'I can't think of anyone else who might question her more profitably,' I mused. 'Unless perhaps Mrs Kenton? Maggie is her own sister, after all – and I, as the putative godfather of her son, might ask her to do that as a favour?'

'And how might her brother-in-law react to that?' Her voice was cool and considered – but Harry had threatened her, had he not?

'I'm sorry. It was a foolish idea. But I have one or two others. Alf Hargreaves—'

'The pig man?'

'The same. He is keeping his ears open for me. And I hope to persuade the landlord of the Royal Oak, Mr Baines, to divulge some of the secrets Alf is sure he has overheard.'

'So long as hope comes with an open purse, he might. No, I misjudge him. In his line of work he has to keep secrets as well as a priest does. As for Alf . . .'

'You don't like him?'

'I know of nothing against him. He's very proud of Luke, his lordship's valet, of course. He's done very well to get so far so quickly.'

'It's no mean achievement for the son of an unlettered father.'

'Oh, Luke's a quick learner – yes,' she added, with one of her rare smiles, 'he was one of my reading hour pupils. In fact, he was one of my first pupils. I could see – just see – he had ability, Mr Rowsley. Oh, he was a joy to teach!'

'I should imagine you are a very good teacher.'

'I am better now,' she said, without a hint of pride. 'Practice has not made me perfect, but it has helped me see other ways of imparting what I learnt myself.'

'Who taught you?' I asked, eagerly. I was getting closer to her inner life than I'd ever been permitted, unless it was the revelations about her sporting talent.

She blushed. 'I mostly taught myself. Like Luke I was a child servant in a great house and I realized . . . that I needed to read, to know my numbers. And now I love passing on my knowledge.'

'In other circumstances you would be a schoolteacher, perhaps?' I had a sudden image of her running my model school in Stammerton.

'In ideal circumstance, yes. But you must know, Mr Rowsley, I am well rewarded for my work here, especially as you insisted – I cannot imagine it was his lordship's idea – that all our wages should be raised. And a teacher is not well remunerated.'

'Mr Bowman,' I said, 'plans to run a genteel boarding house when he retires. That would not be your idea of pleasure?'

'With him! The very idea!' With a sudden embarrassed laugh, she covered her face. 'Oh, dear: I beg your pardon. That was not polite of me.'

This time I cut a whole spray of roses, which I held over her head with a smile before passing it to her. 'No one will know of it from me. But I should warn you he wishes to speak to you of his plans – for another lady,' I said hurriedly.

'Not dear Beatrice Arden! Dear me. Should I warn her?'

'You might prefer to warn him. As I said, he wishes to consult you, as her best friend.'

Her grimace was word enough. 'I shall have to work out something tactful, will I not? Mr Rowsley, this has been a most delightful interlude in our day, but I fear it has not moved our knowledge of poor Maggie forward by one iota.'

'We spoke about what might.'

We exchanged a smile, the sort that like her calculations about Maggie's pregnancy would not have been given in front of others.

I made myself look at my watch. 'I believe I have time to go and talk to Baines.'

As I turned, I reflected. Beatrice Arden. The formality of our lives meant we never used each other's Christian names, and it was almost shocking to hear Mrs Faulkner break the unwritten rule. Beatrice: I couldn't imagine she knew anything of Dante. I couldn't imagine Mrs Faulkner not having read his entire works, albeit in translation. And as for her – what might her name be? As I walked, swatting away encroaching bees, I tried and discarded various names. Suddenly discovering the true one became a matter of urgency.

X

Mamselle finds fault with everything I do, although Nurse, who has always been far stricter in the past, calls me a clever little duck.

'And I say what I said before: you should be down in the main part of the house, where people can see how hard-working you are. No, no arguments. If you don't move at my suggestion, chances are you'll be thrown out altogether – and you wouldn't want to go back to the workhouse, would you? Mrs Baird will know my feelings, and, you mark my words, you'll be on your way up in the world before you can say "Thank you, Nurse!" and make your curtsy. Come on, give old Nurse a hug: we shan't be seeing so much of each other soon, but I want you to promise me something. If you're ever in trouble, whatever the reason, you come to old Nurse. Promise.'

'I promise, Nurse. Thank you.' And I cry all over her crisp white apron-bib.

ELEVEN

Estate business stopped me going down to the Royal Oak as I'd intended, but to my surprise early the following morning Mr Baines called on me before I left home and set off for the House. I had been hard at work in my study since seven dealing with paperwork, and was just about to go down to the kitchen in search of coffee when William, my servant of all indoor work, announced that I had a visitor. Marty Baines was one of the last people I'd have expected to come to me, being important enough in the village to expect me to go to him. Short and delicately built, he was as dapper as the owner of a gentlemen's outfitters. He greeted me with a polite but by no means toadying bow. I responded in kind.

'I was just about to take a cup of coffee, Mr Baines. William! Could you bring it to us in the morning room? The sun is very pleasant there at this time of day,' I added.

Baines looked around him as I led the way, with so much interest I suspected he'd never been in the place before. Instead of sitting down, he went to the window, as if checking that the estate gardeners were acquitting themselves well. He nodded his approval before taking the armchair I indicated.

'I hear you're interesting yourself in young Maggie Billings,' he said, but then paused while William came in with a tray.

'Thank you, William. I'll pour. I don't suppose we've got any of Mrs Arden's biscuits left? Yes, a plate would be excellent.'

The boy bowed himself out.

Baines laughed. 'He's clearly got an eye on a career up at the House when Mr Bowman retires.'

'He'll have to grow a few more inches,' I said ruefully. 'Her ladyship prefers tall footmen. It's a shame. He's a bright boy, and deserves to do well.' I waited while William served us with as much grace as if he were indeed Bowman. 'Thank you. Now, Mr Baines, what can I do for you?'

'It's not so much you helping me as me helping you, Mr

Rowsley. But before I tell you what I know, I want your word you mean well by her. Maggie. I think you understand me.'

I met his eyes. 'If I loved a maid enough to get her with child, I give you my word I would have married her before I put her in that situation.' He nodded. I was to continue. 'Mr Baines, neither of us is in our dotage. But I cannot imagine either of us . . . she is almost young enough to be my daughter.'

'As if that stopped some men – indeed, I read of some who find youth a positive, indeed the only attraction, in a female. Imagine, it is still legal to have sexual congress with a girl as young as twelve! I marvel, Mr Rowsley, I marvel. My wife and I had a daughter of that age. They were both struck down by a cholera outbreak in Manchester.' He paused to drink his coffee. When he put the cup down, he was calmer, though it rattled in its saucer. 'That's why I moved here. I couldn't bear to stay in a place where so many I loved and respected died like animals.' For a long time he looked not at me but into what I suspected was the past. 'I ramble, Mr Rowsley. All I came to say was that I heard from a fellow Baptist, a minister who runs an Ebenezer chapel in a poor part of Wolverhampton. Mr Ianto Davies, a man with Welsh passion in his veins and his sermons.' He gave a dry smile. 'He found a girl sleeping in the chapel porch. He and his wife took her home, and cared for her as best they might. She slept a long time. When she was well enough to talk, she told them she was looking for an aunt, a respectable widow, to seek sanctuary. They escorted her there – it was a disappointing street, they say, but the widow's house was clean enough, and she consented to give the girl a roof over her head. The child refused point-blank to say anything about her family, and implored her aunt not to reveal where she came from. But Ianto did catch a name. Maggie.'

'This is news indeed!' I said. 'But I sense your friends do not believe that all is well.'

'Mr Rowsley, I plan to go to Wolverhampton myself tomorrow: would you care to accompany me? The train journey doesn't take long. Such a boon, these railways, though his late lordship fought tooth and nail against them . . .'

*   *   *

I must make sure everyone had their instructions not just for today but also for tomorrow. First I headed to the Home Farm. Everyone was going about their business with a sense of purpose. Even the animals seemed to be on their best behaviour. Alf, however, let the side down with a truly disreputable hat. He was scratching the ears of a magnificent Welsh boar, sire to an apparently endless stream of piglets produced by our Shropshire sows, but broke off to tip the offending headgear. The boar objected. The scratching resumed. We discussed everyday husbandry leaning side by side on the gate.

'Have you heard from young Luke?' I asked at last.

'I was hoping you might tell me when he'd be back,' he countered. 'I'm not much of a one for reading, gaffer, so it's rare I gets a letter from him – maybe if his lordship chooses to stay away for months, not just weeks, at a time. And someone will read it to me,' he told the pig, shame lowering his voice.

'You must be very proud of him,' I said before he could apologize for being unlettered.

'Aye, he's a good enough lad. Had to box his ears a bit when he was a youngster – I dare say Mr Bowman had to. But not now. Service suits him – wouldn't have suited me, would it, Arthur?'

The boar apparently agreed.

'I'd have thought you'd be the one telling me what the lad's doing,' Alf observed reasonably.

'His lordship's too busy to write just now, I should imagine.'

'Oh, ah.'

The two simple syllables conveyed a wealth of meaning, very little of it appreciative of any pressures that might constrain his lordship.

Unable to argue I turned the subject to the enjoyable prospect of the next cricket match before setting off to harangue and cajole the rest of the workers in pretty well equal measure. There was no sign today of Mrs Billings.

'Indeed, Luke did have a temper when he was a lad,' Bowman agreed later that afternoon, when I spoke to him in his pantry. 'But – we speak in absolute confidence, do we not, Rowsley? – seeing his lordship in his rages did a great deal to reduce the frequency of Luke's tantrums. It was as if his lordship held a mirror up to them, and the lad did not like what he saw. Between ourselves, he is wasted here. He would grace a gentleman in a . . . in a distinguished public role.'

'You never had that ambition yourself?'

The old man shrugged. 'I had hopes of his late lordship, I will confess, until he settled down here and closed his town house. Then I knew it was not to be. A man becomes set in his ways, does he not? You, for instance, will ensure all is in good heart on his lordship's land and then seek to run one of the grand estates – I can imagine you at Chatsworth or Blenheim, if not for your next post then the one after that.' He paused. 'I have to confess I have not yet discussed my hopes for Mrs Arden with Mrs Faulkner yet. I wondered – I have to admit – if someone else might have engaged her heart.'

My answer was almost truthful. 'I have heard no rumour of that. In any case, should you not be approaching the lady yourself? However good a friend to her Mrs Faulkner may be, she might not have access to the deepest secrets of her heart.' But had I seen joy in Mrs Arden's eyes when I gave her that rose? I truly hoped it was only the happiness of having a friend.

It was time to turn the subject. 'Does his lordship never give any indication of his movements?'

Bowman looked amazed. 'Why should he? The House must always be in perfect readiness for its master. Likewise for her ladyship. It is a matter of pride to us indoor staff that whatever the whim of our employer we are always prepared to indulge it.'

I acknowledged the implicit rebuke with a bow. 'Of course. You are quite right.'

'Do you care,' he began, obviously accepting my apology, 'for a glass of sherry?'

At five in the afternoon? 'Forgive me if I decline. I have work to organize for tomorrow. But will you excuse me if I don't explain now? It's news I should give to everyone together.'

I chanced to return to Mrs Faulkner as I returned to my office, to which she gestured: might we speak in private?

She declined to sit, asking, 'Do you think the problem of Mr Bowman and Mrs Arden may have gone away? At least he has not spoken to me. I wonder why he has changed his mind? Perhaps he's spoken to her already and we are to have a betrothal!'

I shook my head. 'I fear he fancies her affections are already engaged.'

Absolutely still, she looked at me. 'Are they? And are they requited?' The message was clear.

I said carefully, holding her gaze, 'I value Mrs Arden as a dear friend and as a colleague. But that is all. And I truly hope that that reflects her feelings – if any – towards me.'

In the ensuing silence a lot more was said.

A tap at the door announced the arrival of a tenant farmer.

XI

*T*he library! I am to dust the library! His lordship's special domain, where no one is permitted to disturb him. I am to light the fire, and even as it catches, I am to start dusting, from the top of each high shelf to the bottom. Some of the books are behind grilles: I must not touch these unless the grilles are unlocked. If there are books on his desk, I must not touch them, but must whisk the feather duster around them. I must be finished by nine o'clock sharp. If his lordship appears early, I must curtsy and back out, even if I have not finished. Even if he speaks to me, even if he talks very kindly, I must curtsy and back out.

And, adds Mrs Baird, with such a straight face I think that inside she is laughing at me, I am not even to think of borrowing any of the books. Not a single one. Ever. And then I do not think she is laughing any more.

TWELVE

With the blessing and good wishes of my colleagues, but no further private conversation with Mrs Faulkner, I set out betimes the following morning, collecting Mr Baines in my trap, which I left at the estate's station, the horse in the tender care of the station-master's middle daughter, a child with a gappy smile and intelligent eyes.

'Thorncroft Station! Imagine,' Baines said drily, 'his lordship having his own station just for him and his guests. Oh, and his employees, I suppose.'

'It is not an unusual arrangement. But it is not one that pleases me – though that must be between ourselves, Baines.' I hoped he was not the sort of man to capitalize on my indiscretion.

'Mum's the word,' he said obligingly. 'You're in an awkward position, aren't you? An employee, but gaffer to the other employees. It could be a very lonely existence . . . You're always welcome in my parlour, Rowsley, when you want a pint in private.'

'Thank you. I'll remember that. It's all too easy to forget that there's a world that's not connected with the House and the estate. Some days, although the London papers arrive regularly, and Mr Bowman certainly irons them, I believe no one even looks at them. I do my best to read them before they are discarded unread, but to my shame I don't always manage it.'

We stopped at the next station, a public one, of course; a motley group got on, but none of them penetrated the first-class carriage we occupied. Nonetheless, conversation became desultory as we watched Shropshire passing before our eyes.

'Dear God,' I said, as the train left the sunny countryside and headed into Wolverhampton, 'we go straight from heaven into hell! How can people endure such filth? Look, that line of washing will be blacker when it comes in than when it was hung out.'

'But people still have pride,' he said sharply. 'Each day you will find women on their knees in the street, scrubbing at their doorsteps. They will black-lead their fireplaces. They will clean their windows.'

As the train slowed to judder over points I could see he was right. But the women were as thin as Mrs Billings. Some were pregnant. A young child might have drawn their round bodies and stick arms.

'What sort of life will Maggie have here?' I breathed.

'Who knows? She may even flourish.' The train was slowing. 'Ah! There is my friend, waiting to meet us.'

Ianto Davies was short and stout, his face so cherubically round I could not imagine him so much as raising his voice, let alone producing a fiery sermon. But behind his pebble glasses his eyes were shrewd.

'Mr Rowsley, to my mind two strange men, three, including me, presenting themselves on this woman's doorstep – Mrs Batham, by the way – would be a mistake. May I go myself to prepare her for such a visitation: we don't want her to imagine the Magi have put in a reappearance, do we?'

'No. But one of them might bear another's gift,' I pointed out. I produced a purse. 'You know better than I how much to give – too little it's an insult, too much and perhaps that's a worse insult.'

He took the purse and looked inside. 'I think you've erred on the side of generosity. What I might suggest, my friend, is this. If you are sure, absolutely sure, you want her to have all this, then may I offer to dole it out on – say – a weekly basis. That way I ensure that my wife or I can keep a regular eye on her well-being.'

Mr Baines nodded. 'It also ensures it won't all be spent on the demon drink as soon as it gets into her hands. Not, I hasten to add, that I've ever heard drunkenness imputed to the young woman.'

We waited while Mr Davies trotted off. I turned to my companion with an ironic smile. 'It's strange to hear such words come from the mouth of an innkeeper!'

'Perhaps. But there's a world of difference between having a companionable half of mild with your fellow men, and downing so much mother's ruin you end up senseless in a gutter. If villagers didn't come to the Royal Oak, they'd go somewhere else where the landlord might let them drink all their wages and let them go home empty-handed to their families. You must have seen enough of that in your time.'

'I have indeed.' My laugh turned to racking coughs.

'Ah, you're not used to the smoke. But I have to tell you that this is nothing compared with the real industrial areas. The good folk here would be enraged if you said Wolverhampton was part of – yes, let's use Her Majesty's name for it – the Black Country. But go to Oldbury, to Smethwick, to West Bromwich: that's where you'll see heavy industry and smell the coal dust, taste it, drink it, spend all your hours in it.' He stopped, nodding up the road. 'Here's Ianto, and he's not looking very happy.'

Nor was he. The mouth that nature intended to turn up turned downwards, his face a comic mask of tragedy. 'Maggie's there, but Mrs Batham, her dragon of an aunt, says she won't show herself. Too ashamed, she says. So I gave her just half a sovereign, and the information that Maggie must come to the manse this time next week for some more.'

'Thank you. I hope she turns up.'

'I just hope she gets the money, to be honest with you,' the minister said. 'Just because I'm a man of God, Mr Rowsley, doesn't mean I don't know what the Devil can get up to. Half a guinea is a lot to a woman in a two-up two-down back-to-back. A lot. We must pray she doesn't get led into temptation, mustn't we? Mrs Batham, I suppose I mean. And Maggie. Now, gentlemen, Ethel, my wife, has prepared a few refreshments, and will be terribly upset if you don't partake of them . . .'

Ianto Davies' grace was one of the longest I'd ever heard, and his wife's pastry some of the heaviest I'd ever tried to eat. I swear if one of us had dropped our slice of pork pie on the plate it would have shattered it. But it tasted good, as did the pickles, home-made and bought, she proudly declared, from the chapel sale-of-work. She was passionate about teaching poverty-stricken women skills that saved a few pennies; she encouraged them to donate one jar of every batch to the church, simply, she said, so they could feel pride in their work.

'And I cadge ends of cloth from haberdashers in the town so they can dress their babies – sometimes themselves! – with a little dignity,' she added.

'I wish you could meet my mother,' I said truthfully. 'She carries on my grandmother's tradition of helping the poor help themselves.'

'Better by far than the workhouse!' she declared, stopping to pour tea so strong I could have stood a spoon upright in the brew. She continued in the same crusading vein, her fervour and determination a joy – if a trifle exhausting – to hear.

'She'd make a fine MP, wouldn't she?' Mr Davies said proudly, jerking a curly thumb in his wife's direction.

She did not see it as a joke. She spat out the words, 'And I can't even vote!'

Her husband patted her hand. 'No. It's not enough you tell me where to put my cross! But when I hear Ethel speak like that, I do wonder, gentlemen, I do wonder . . .'

Mr Baines was shaking his head disapprovingly, but I had already jumped in. 'Exactly what so many of my friends are saying. One day, one day – though we may not live to see it – people like you, Mrs Davies, and my mother may get their chance on something other than the domestic stage.' People like Mrs Faulkner too – I wondered what her views would be on the subject. On the other hand, there was Mr Pounceman . . . 'Though I know people whom I admire and respect disagree with me.' There was no point in annoying Baines unnecessarily.

It seemed that the business in Wolverhampton Mr Baines had spoken of was a fiction. Certainly he headed nowhere but back to Queen Street Station, one, confusingly, of two stations in what was still but a middle-sized town. Had his business been to see me living up to my word? Or to introduce me to Mr and Mrs Davies, who would both keep an eye on Maggie? – I could not imagine Mr Davies being allowed to operate on his own in such circumstances. Perhaps he simply wanted a day's holiday in someone's company.

Having established that we both felt Maggie would be safe under the Davies' supervision, and lamented the promise given to Ianto that we would say nothing to the family till he considered it right, we needed to find something else to talk about. As we headed into the cloudless blue skies of the countryside once more, it was easy to find one we could both enjoy. Cricket, and the following day's match.

The mood of the Room was subtly lightened by my good news. It was as if with the responsibility at least for the time being in someone else's hands, everyone could start to live their own lives again. But something clearly caused Bowman a little unease; at one point he left the room quite suddenly, before returning to his place without a word. Then as if nothing had happened, he joined in the general conversation until the convivial evening ended. I was sure that Mrs Faulkner must be at least as conscious as I was of yesterday's interrupted conversation, but she was as calm and quietly witty as usual. For both our sakes I hoped my demeanour matched hers, though I was desperate to catch at least a few moments' private conversation with her as I left. It was not to be. As we rose, Bowman surged towards me. Taking my arm, he edged me out into the still warm evening air, where he produced a cigar.

'This is not a question I would like to put before the ladies,' he began, once it was alight. 'But the money for Maggie's welfare must have come from somewhere, and I do not think, Rowsley, that you would take it from his lordship's petty cash. Am I right? Am I, man? Yes or no.'

'This is strictly between us, then, Bowman. I am a bachelor with very little claim on my resources—'

With a laugh somewhat spoiled by a coughing fit, he clapped me on the shoulder. 'I thought so. You're as straight as a die, aren't you! Which is why I wished to give you this.' He pressed an envelope into my hand. 'No, don't open it now, and by no means seek to return it. I am in the same fortunate position as you, young man, and have the pleasure of receiving some very generous tips when we have guests. I have known Maggie ever since she joined us, and am fond of the . . . the young woman, I suppose we must now call her. Would you fancy one of his lordship's best cigars, Matthew?'

Moved more than I could explain, I put out my hand and shook his heartily. 'I will make sure Maggie receives every penny of this. As for the cigar, Samuel, I thank you, but would rather you kept it for the day we hear she is safely delivered of her baby.'

He nodded, almost absently returning to his pocket. We talked a little about the next day's weather and about the cricket match – an away one against Eaton Parva – and then bade each other a cordial goodnight. At least I hoped I sounded cordial: our meaningless chatter meant it was now far too late to speak to Mrs Faulkner.

Having spent Friday on what was arguably my own business, not his lordship's, I resolved to spend Saturday morning ensuring that every last piece of office and outdoor work was up-to-date.

My stint indoors completed by nine, I set off on Esau to check that all my instructions had been carried out to the letter. It wasn't until I was satisfied that even the most carping of employers – and I did not lack experience with such men – could find nothing to complain about that I could look forward to the cricket match.

My colleagues and I were to travel to Eaton Parva on farm wagons, both of which were provided with barrels of beer. For the first time since I'd played for the village, I was anxious about my company. For the sake of the team I did not want them drunk beforehand; for the sake of my working relationship with my teammates, most of them estate workers, I did not want them drunk afterwards. Equally I did not want to stop them enjoying themselves. There was an easy answer: it was better to appear stand-offish than a spoilsport, so, claiming I had forgotten something, and would catch them up, I ran back to my house, summoned a disconcerted Dan, who was clearly just about to go off and enjoy his usual Saturday afternoon free time, to saddle Esau. I flipped him an extra coin by way of thanks – enough to make him blush and tug his forelock as he muttered his thanks.

The schoolboy lingering in my body would have loved to join my team in a roistering celebration of a famous victory over an old rival, but after standing the first official round of cider and ale at the Eaton Parva inn I slipped quietly away. In truth, I was looking forward to responding to Mrs Faulkner's wistful but mocking enquiry as to how I had acquitted myself with the news I had taken five wickets and actually scored fifteen runs.

XII

All these books. So many books. Apart from the windows overlooking the garden, each side of the room is covered with shelves, running from a low wainscot to the ceiling. Some shelves are covered with a metal grille. Others are not. There are books with titles I can read, with what I think is the name of the person who wrote them under the title. Others have writing on them that doesn't make any sense to me. What a world must live between all those covers! A thousand worlds! How clever, how wise must be someone who can read and understand them all.

I am to use a feather duster to clean them – yes, even those on the top shelves, which I must climb up to on a ladder that runs from side to side of the room.

But I must not touch them, and I must never ever try to read them.

THIRTEEN

'Her ladyship is back, gaffer!'

The stable lad's shout as he dashed across the cobbles in front of me was almost unnecessary, given the bustle in the yard. Despite the estate having its own station for the train travel that Mr Baines and I could testify was swift and agreeable, her ladyship still preferred a horse-drawn carriage, followed, in this case, by another carriage, which was even now being unloaded by a team of footmen, while the horses were being led one by one into their stables.

Perhaps I expected similar haste and anxiety in the kitchen and servants' hall. In fact, knowing the preparedness and efficiency of my colleagues, I should have been ready for what I found: purposefulness, yes, but no apparent haste and certainly no anxious scurrying.

But one footman approached me with a bow. 'Mr Bowman's compliments, sir, but servants' supper has been put back half an hour. If you care to wait in his room, you will find a decanter and biscuits waiting for you.'

Though it was a dispiriting enough place, furnished with cast-offs, and few enough of them, I did care, but I asked him to bring me a tankard of small beer.

My reward was a grin. 'It's all round the staff, sir, your triumph at the cricket.'

'Not such a triumph. Eaton Parva seem to be a team of old men and young boys – not a strong young man in sight.'

His smile was somehow ambiguous, but he said politely, 'I'll bring the beer forthwith, sir.'

It was good to settle down with a newspaper, but even better to reflect on my good fortune in keeping beforehand with all the estate and household work. Should her ladyship wish to speak to me, I would be able to report on George's success in marshalling a team of carpenters ready to work as soon as I could give the order, which I felt I could not do till I had discussed both the expenditure and the possible inconvenience with a member of the Family. I would not mention the Maggie Billings affair until she raised it. Nor the Stammerton business – and certainly nothing of my contretemps with Pounceman, though I suspect he would be swift to put his side of it. Forewarned was forearmed. I abandoned the prospect of beer till, in my office, I had checked one more time the plans, the costings and arguments for and against developing a model village. On impulse, I did what I never did: I stowed all the documents concerning that and indeed even other important matter in the safe, locking it and pocketing the key. A Chubb. For some reason I was pleased by the fact that the beautiful precision engineering was the work of people from Wolverhampton. When at last I sank back in the less comfortable of Mr Bowman's two armchairs, I actually raised my glass of beer in toast to them.

The reappearance of Mlle Hortense at the supper table changed the atmosphere quite radically. Bowman had hinted heavily, when he finally returned to his room before supper, that it would not be appropriate to mention Maggie.

'But surely all the other maids will tell her everything they know.'

'Which is what Mrs Faulkner and Mrs Arden have chosen to tell them – just as I have informed the male staff that she has been found safe. We agreed, the ladies and I, that that was all they needed to know. I hope you agree.'

Personally I saw no need for such discretion. Nonetheless, though I was inclined to feel resentful that they had made the decision without consulting me, I did not argue – they knew their charges better than I did, after all.

Her sojourn away from the House did not seem to have suited Hortense: she pouted with discontent, and freely admitted she was looking for another post. 'Another day of the company of catty old invalids I will not, cannot, stand! I had thought we would stay at a nice house belonging to a friend of the Family, but no, we were trapped in a hotel, with us maids herded together in ugly dormitories – poor food and not a scrap of comfort or privacy. And her ladyship ringing for me at all hours, the way the treatment made her feel – her joints, her stomach, her head

– I don't know where and what she didn't complain about. And she kept on saying she didn't know why she'd gone in the first place. But when I said she could just come back home, she said she would stick it out, no matter what. Touched in the head, if you ask me.'

'Even if you did ask us, you shouldn't refer to her ladyship in those terms,' Bowman said sternly, adding, as he pointed at the line of bells on the furthest wall, 'You may *wish* to leave, Mademoiselle, but if you don't answer that bell forthwith, you may *have* to – and without a reference, I shouldn't wonder.'

The response was a magnificent flounce from the room. I thought Bowman might burst.

Mrs Faulkner said, some amusement in her voice, 'I fancy she may already have found a new post.' She turned to me. 'Sometimes servants do that: they are ready to move but believe that if they get dismissed they may get an extra month's wages in lieu of notice.'

'Good luck to them, say I,' Mrs Arden put in. 'All the fuss some of these young women put up with for less than twenty pounds a year.'

Mr Bowman stared. 'Indeed, she gets all her ladyship's cast-offs!'

'And what can she do with them, all that rich silk and satin? Wear them? It takes hours of work and a lot of skill to make them fit, and even if they ever looked exactly right, what occasion does she have to wear finery? The Christmas party and the Harvest Home? I would not do her job for twice what she earns, let me tell you. Not unless I worked in a great city,' she added reflectively, 'with places to go in my time off, assuming I ever had any.'

Mr Bowman glowed with fury – with possible apoplexy, I thought. Mrs Faulkner was steadfastly refusing to meet anyone's eye. Mrs Arden didn't even look defiant, just relaxed, almost amused, like any of my mother's friends making a reasonable point. What was her real motive, apart from the obvious one, with which I for one could not argue? Was it, perhaps, a desire to shock Bowman so much he would no longer wish to propose to her, possibly embarrassing both of them?

It was time for me to step into a growing pool of silence. 'Now his mother has returned, what are the prospects of his lordship doing likewise?' I asked the table at large.

'Her ladyship has indicated that he may return in the future, possibly with some companions.' Mrs Faulkner's voice was entirely devoid of emotion.

'*Possibly*? How can you all plan for that?'

'It is a matter of pride that we are always prepared,' Bowman reminded me repressively.

'But for a party of young men? Without even female companionship to . . . to leaven the lump?'

Mrs Faulkner laughed out loud. Encouraged, perhaps, so did Mrs Arden.

But Bowman, already irritated by Hortense, no doubt, stared at me. 'I would have expected better of you, Mr Rowsley. It is bad enough to endure young Hortense's levity, but you of all people should not be stooping to that sort of expression about your employer.'

'I believe,' Mrs Faulkner said delicately, 'that Mr Rowsley was speaking not of his lordship but of his lordship's friends, many of whom have in the past given us much cause for concern. All of us,' she added firmly. As Bowman continued to huff and puff, she added, 'Dare I remind you of the time some young blood scaled the flagpole and broke it, endangering both himself and those below him urging him on? Of the assaults – yes, I use the word advisedly, though some sort to hush it up with the term "horseplay" – the assaults on a number of young women about the house? And even on one of your young footmen? Yes, young Simon, who was so distressed he left as soon as he could. On his own his lordship is biddable, and I have no doubt that Mr Rowsley will encourage him to respect his inheritance and indeed leave a fine legacy for future generations. But with some of his friends—'

'He's like a badly trained dog,' Mrs Arden put in, with an air of finality. 'Mrs Faulkner, gentlemen: will you excuse me if I withdraw now? Although, as you rightly say, Mr Bowman, we are always prepared for the Family's return, I would like to make sure that nothing I send up tomorrow will displease her ladyship if she is not feeling well.' She rose, curtsying with a hint of irony as she left the room.

Mrs Faulkner got up too, belatedly clutching her back. 'I am in some pain, gentlemen. I fear it is laudanum for me tonight.'

She looked me straight in the eye. I was to understand that she was lying. And also that I was to get rid of poor old Bowman for her.

I did. Much as I hated cigar smoke, I suggested we blow a cloud together, resolving to keep any conversation both short and neutral.

In the event, it was neither. Far from denying that his lordship had a poor choice of friends, he told me some of the horseplay they had got up to, some amusing, some, such as when drunk on communion wine urinating in the church font, markedly less so. 'Anyone would think it was like the days my father spoke of, when gentlemen were expected to do wild things in their cups . . . when people bet huge sums on which raindrop would run down a window first, or which young blood might ride a horse up the main stairs. I recall myself as a young footman dodging a boot as I carried hot water to one lord's bed-chamber to find his bed occupied by another lord's wife. We laughed, in those days. Some of his lordship's friends still do. But now we cannot find anything funny in such antics. It is natural to be irritated by them, to judge the perpetrators badly. Have you ever thought we are becoming puritans again? Losing our sense of humour in our desire to be pious?'

It was a discussion worth having, but I wished to keep to the subject in hand. 'If so, clearly the young man who assaulted one of our colleagues hadn't caught the mood of the times.'

'Ah, that was a bad business. Between ourselves, Rowsley – I'd hate the good ladies with whom we supped even to suspect this – it was far worse than an assault.' Looking round, he continued in a whisper, 'The lad was raped. Like an animal. In front of other young gentlemen who cheered and stamped as the deed took place. In this house! One of my young men, whom I think of as sons!'

I put my hand on his shoulder. 'That is truly shocking. Criminal. I would like your word, Bowman, that if any of those evil brutes ever return here as guests you will let me know. I have no idea what I can do about them, but I am sure that you and I are stronger together than separately.' I paused. 'I have to ask, my friend: have you ever known his lordship . . . you said he had tantrums . . .?'

His face betrayed an internal battle; loyalty to the family won. 'You must excuse me, Rowsley. He is my employer. And yours,' he added, over his shoulder, as he walked back to the House.

Must I return to my own home? The prospect was not exciting. After the high spirits of our cricket victory, I now felt ill-at-ease, angry and disturbed and suddenly furious that once again I had had no opportunity to speak to Mrs Faulkner alone. Could I go back? It would outrage decorum if I did. So I turned and strode the shortest route, through the shrubbery, kicking anything in my path. I disturbed something. I felt it rather than saw it. My fingers closed around it. A button. I almost threw it away. Instead, I stowed it in my pocket and finally headed for home.

XIII

I am to dust, not even look at any of the books. But one lies open on a sort of pillow in the middle of the huge desk. It is as big as the Bible in church.

I run my feather duster lightly over the edge of the cover, but take care not to touch the pages. The printing is like printing I have never seen before – all thick lines and sharp angles. Some of the letters are surrounded by amazing patterns in colours that glow despite the dimness of the light. That looks like a dog – or is it a snake?

I am about to reach for the magnifying glass left so temptingly beside the pillow. But those are footsteps, and I must run, fast as I can, for the concealed door, making sure I close it silently.

FOURTEEN

'Goodness me, young lady! Where did you get a bruise like that?' Dr Page had pushed back Mlle Hortense's pretty little hat and was peering at her face with obvious concern. 'Does that hurt? This?'

I am sure Hortense would have preferred him to conduct his examination in the seclusion of his consulting room, but he had stopped outside the lych-gate and was dealing with the problem in full view of the congregation streaming out of church. Was I surprised that she insisted all she had done was walk into a door? Everyone who saw the black eye and swollen face must have known that doors were more passive than whatever had inflicted the damage.

'I put some of Mrs Arden's best steak on it, doctor. I am – oh!' A wince cut off her protestation.

'I think you need something more than steak. Pray, Rowsley, will you give the young lady your arm down to my surgery? The eye in particular must be treated, and urgently, too!' He bustled off at great pace down the village street.

Hortense and I followed more decorously. Her fellow servants could not have followed if they had wished – they were due back at the House with Mrs Arden, who had led the morning's procession. I dare say that most of them, fearful of another attack on their gender, would rather have been elsewhere than church this morning. Mrs Faulkner's back was apparently still troubling her – though I suspected she might have enjoyed a miraculous recovery, had she known that the sermon, on the subject of the woman who touched Jesus in order to be healed of her constant haemorrhages, would be given by a man almost moved to tears by her plight and then by her faith. Not Mr Pounceman, of course – a middle-aged locum whose name I never caught. Unlike the rector, he was short and spare, his whiskers sliding apologetically across the deep worry crevasses criss-crossing his cheeks. He had prayed briefly for the health of his brother in Christ, without mentioning any particular ailment.

Once Hortense and I were clear of any other parishioners, I said quietly, 'Tell me the truth about that injury, Hortense. I promise you it won't be you who gets into trouble, just the person who did this to you.' I smiled to interrupt her protest. 'It wasn't a door that did that, not unless a human being deliberately pushed it extraordinarily hard. You know that it could have been even worse. I have never known Dr Page so concerned.'

'I cannot. I dare not. As soon as my face is respectable again, I'm off. I've got a cousin in Warwick. She's found me a situation with a young lady in the town, one who likes to travel.'

'Listen – the day you leave, you will tell me the name of your assailant. I know that you will not get the redress you deserve, but at least it may prevent anyone else getting a similar injury. You understand me?'

Even a slight nod caused her pain. 'I suppose so,' she whispered.

'You promise me?'

Another whisper. 'I suppose so.'

Dr Page may have been trying to elicit the information I had failed to gain: I could hear the rumbles of his voice, sometimes insistent. I hoped he would have more success than I did, but I did not expect him to. In time they emerged from his consulting room, her face now bandaged.

'Remember, you may have tea, soup and bread and milk: no solids. I'm sure my old friend Mr Bowman will provide some brandy if the pain gets bad – but no more than a sip, young lady, because of those laudanum drops.' He patted a tiny brown-paper wrapped package. 'And however tempted you are to continue, you stop taking the drops after three days – you hear that, Rowsley? And you are not to let Mademoiselle Hortense to go anywhere near doors, inanimate or otherwise. She must spend a few days sitting quite still.' He winked at me – yes, he shared my suspicions. 'In fact, I will return you both to the House in my trap so you do not have to exert yourself. Wait here.'

Once he had escorted Hortense safely inside the servants' quarters of the House, where I am sure he gave forceful instructions, he returned to me, as I stood fussing his pony in the warm sunshine. 'That's a bad business, Rowsley. I fear for the future of some of her teeth. She may be deaf in that ear for some time too – in fact, for the rest of her life. Her skull – well, let us hope it's thick. Whoever did that should be prosecuted.'

'Even if that were to involve appearing at the Bar of the House of Lords?'

'Good God, man! Is that whom you suspect? I'd no idea he was back.'

'As far as I know his lordship isn't. But his mother is.'

'But she's frail – well, I suppose she could heft a scent bottle or something similar. So what do we do?'

I told him about the promise I'd extracted. He nodded, gravely. 'Let's hope she keeps it.'

He seemed in no hurry to leave, so I said, 'Tell me, Page, why was our rector absent today? Is he genuinely ill?'

'I fear he's really very poorly, though he will recover in time. Pounceman suffers from a childish complaint. You will understand that I may not tell you more.'

I looked sideways. 'Shall I ask Mrs Faulkner to summon all the women to the servants' hall so they can add their voices to mine?'

My reward was a crack of possibly sacrilegious laughter and a friendly clap on the shoulder. 'I must be off. I want to know immediately if that girl takes a turn for the worse. Immediately, mind. Whatever time of night or day.'

To leave the bright courtyard for the dimness of the servants' entrance and hall was like plunging into the depths of the sea. There was the usual bustle, but Mrs Arden and Mrs Faulkner were not part of it. I asked for Mr Bowman, to be escorted to his pantry, where, head bowed, he was staring blindly at an open safe and all the silver he was responsible for.

He acknowledged my arrival with a nod, no more. Then, as if we had been in the middle of a conversation, he said, 'I would not have had that happen for the world. Not for the world. I wish I had not spoken to her like that at supper. What if it's the last thing she heard me say?'

'Dr Page said he hoped her deafness would be temporary,' I said – though he had implied the opposite of course. 'My dear Bowman, have you hurt your hand?'

He looked at it as if seeing it for the first time. He snorted.

'It looks as if I've turned bare-knuckle fighter, doesn't it? But my opponent had the better of me.' With his left hand he pointed to the safe, which still bore a trickle of blood. In the face of my silence, he suddenly swung round. 'Dear God, you can't think I hurt Hortense like that? I told you, they are like my children! My own children!'

'Children you might wish to punish? No, Bowman, your face tells me otherwise. Let us ask Mrs Arden for some steak for that hand.'

'She's busy – she's with Mrs Faulkner sorting out accommodation for poor Hortense. Both ladies are insisting on giving up their own rooms – a competition of kindness.' I could imagine it. 'There is also the problem of who should take over Hortense's duties.'

'You won't like this question, but I have to ask: do you know who did hit Hortense?'

He looked grave. 'She simply will not tell me. It would have taken a strong young man to inflict that amount of damage, wouldn't it? There's one explanation – what if she has a follower who did it? Someone here or someone she met in Droitwich? That might explain her reluctance to accuse anyone.'

I nodded – and the suggestion was corroborated by Mrs Arden when I ran into her. 'Maybe Mr Bowman's right: I heard horses last night, after dark – two or three. They woke me, but I'm so used to rolling over and going back to sleep I took no notice.'

'His lordship does what he wants, when he wants, for as long as he wants, and I want no more impertinent questions from you. You are here to run the estate.' Her ladyship's hand clenched round the ivory-headed walking stick propped beside her chair. She picked it up and jabbed it at me. 'Run it.'

'There are some matters his lordship might prefer to authorize before I go ahead,' I demurred. I was standing before her, in the sunny morning room, with what would one day be a charming view over the lake. 'Unless, perhaps you, your ladyship . . .?' Seeing her colour rise alarmingly, I broke off and started again, with a deep bow. 'If you wish it, I will make the decisions based on urgency and need, as I always do.'

'So why have you bothered me, a poor, sick, old woman? I am barely back in my own home before you start your impertinent badgering. Get out.' She reached ominously for her stick again, lifting it to jab me in the chest. 'And remember: if you ever dare to question his lordship's movements again, you will be dismissed.'

I bowed, safe in the knowledge that only his lordship had the power to do that, paying me a great deal if he did it without due cause. My contract had been drawn up by my worldly cousin Mark, and not deeply scrutinized by my master's lawyer before his lordship had scrawled his aristocratic signature at the foot, closing our bargain with a dab of wax and his ancestral seal.

Nonetheless, this was not the best way to start a Monday morning.

Before supper, taking with me flowers selected by one of the gardeners, I went with Mr Bowman to visit our invalid. In the event she had been taken to the old nursery, where her friends could easily visit her, slipping up the miserable back stairs whenever they had a moment free from their duties. They had come throughout the day, Bowman told me, with home-made barley water and lemonade, and even ice cream.

Hortense managed a feeble smile when she saw the flowers, already arranged in a vase by Mrs Faulkner's skilful hands. But it was clear she was in a great deal of pain, and I wondered if she had received other blows about the body she'd not mentioned to Page – though I could not imagine that he had not checked for himself.

'Don't hurt yourself more by trying to speak,' I told her gently. 'But remember what I told you yesterday: you are not in any trouble. If you would like one of your family to come and see you, for I fear it will be some days before you are fit to travel, pray tell me, and I will pay all their expenses. Your mother? A sister? Just say the word.' I took her hand and squeezed it very lightly. 'Now, I fear the sun will be in your eyes within moments: permit me to draw the curtain just a little. There.'

Bowman bent and kissed what little the bandages did not cover of her forehead. 'Good night, my child. Sleep well.'

He wiped away a tear as we left the room.

Despite my confidence that her ladyship could not put her threat into action, I spent the next few days travelling around the estate, even some of its further-flung outposts, which I reached by train. Whenever I returned, the news of Hortense was fairly good – her recovery was slow, but Dr Page, who had taken it upon himself to visit regularly, was optimistic. By the time I returned from my last foray, down to Devon, of all places, to a cluster of farms near Honiton, the first fields of hay were ready for cutting, and the weather was set fair. The next few days were extremely busy. All able-bodied men were involved – which included me. Just as the women at the House had prepared refreshment when we were hunting for Maggie, now they worked long hours feeding everyone who turned out. My main task might have been supervising and co-ordinating the teams involved, but I didn't want to lose the men's respect by being thought a slacker, so was usually the first out, and always the last in. My life revolved – in a very satisfactory way, as it happens – between sleep, work and food. Sick maids and sick parsons were as irrelevant as an insect bite; I cannot recall giving either a thought except when on the third or fourth evening a boy slipped a note in my hand after the usual hard-fought Saturday cricket match, which had necessarily been reduced to twenty overs per side. Mr Bowman's compliments and a hot bath awaited me before supper. Would I take a summer suit, to reflect the weather?

Although I would have loved to regale Mrs Faulkner with my tales of bowling derring-do, half of me would have preferred a bite of cheese in my own parlour and an early night. To decline the invitation, however, would be churlish. So I staggered home, stowed the appropriate garments in a grip, and wended my slow and footsore way to the House. I was ushered to the bedchamber I had used before: sure enough, there was plenty of hot water awaiting me, enough to bath an army. I had the choice of ale or lemonade. I suppose I spared a moment's pity for the men who only had carbolic and the garden pump at their disposal, but in truth I lolled back like an emperor.

It didn't take me long to work out that the conversation over our cold collation was strained. At last I looked from one sober face to another. 'Pray, what is wrong?'

'Hortense,' Mrs Faulkner said. 'No,' she added swiftly. 'Her recovery has been remarkable. But she has left us. Just like that!' She snapped her fingers. 'She left a note, however, and a forwarding address. And she asked me to apologize to you on her behalf for breaking a promise.'

It was clear my companions expected me to explain. I was tired enough to snarl that it was no business of theirs – and yet it was. So I summoned a grim smile from somewhere. 'She promised to tell me the name of her assailant before she left – for a position with a young lady keen on travelling? One living in Warwick, near her cousin?' Conscious I had passed some sort of test, I smothered a yawn. In truth, I was afraid I should fall asleep at the table.

'She says that as soon as she's presentable, she and her new employer will be heading to Nice.'

'Excellent.' My only fear, too base to voice, was that Mlle Hortense might not speak the language. But I detected a flicker of amusement in Mrs Faulkner's eye: I responded.

As the table was cleared after coffee, I approached her. 'I wonder if I might see Hortense's note?'

She looked puzzled, perhaps even offended, but I sought and held her eye. 'Of course. I will look it out for you. Shall I send it down to your house?'

'Some things,' I said carefully, but blushing despite myself, 'should not be deferred longer than necessary.'

Would the others never cease their chatter and leave us?

XIV

I am atop the wheeled step-ladder his lordship needs to reach the top shelf of books. If I stretch, I can reach them all with the feather duster. I do all I can, then go down, move the steps, and then go up again. But I do not like being so high. The steps wobble as I shift my weight. I must not look down.

The task takes far longer than Mrs Baird said it should. I dare not hurry, lest I poke the books with the long cane and tear the ancient binding. But I am developing a rhythm, and there are only two bays to finish.

The last! But the floor is uneven, and the wheels seem to be slipping.

The door opens.

His lordship!

I should not be here.

But far from shouting at me he smiles. I hear the rich fabric of his dressing-down whisper as he walks towards me.

'Poor little woman,' he says. 'Up so very high. Here. Let me jump you down.' He holds his arms up. The steps lurch. I am falling.

I cannot leave his arms. I must run but I am powerless. Suddenly I am pinned against the bookcase, and he is pulling aside his nightshirt.

There is pain inside me. It goes on. And on. And on. Worse with each thrust. And the next.

The library is empty. I feel blood running. I see it on my shift.

I must run to Mrs Baird. To Nurse. To anyone.

But my legs will not work and I crawl every inch of the way to the back stairs. The pain takes me away.

FIFTEEN

The expression on her face troubled me – no, terrified me. Her eyes were saying all I wanted them to say, but it was clear that her mouth was framing words I could not bear to hear. Taking her hands, I lifted them to my cheeks and held them while I reached forward to kiss her. For a long moment she was passive; it was like kissing the cold lips of my niece's china doll. But at last, my heart leapt as she responded. We clung to each other.

When I opened my eyes after the wonder of it all, she was weeping. 'Matthew, I cannot. I must not.'

I kissed her again, very lightly. 'Whatever it is you cannot, must not do, one thing I beg: you will tell me your name. It's only fair,' I said, trying to make her smile. 'You know and can use my name. I do not even know yours.' Officially, at least. Dare I add that I must, if I was going to ask for her hand in marriage? No, not until she had told me the source of her sorrow. Her pain. From time to time her whole body convulsed against mine.

Her voice told me the effort she was making to control her emotions, as it came out with a brittle laugh. 'Harriet. Like the Harriet of whom you have probably read, "the natural daughter of somebody".'

'*Emma*'s Harriet Smith?'

'My title is purely honorary; I took the surname from someone who was kind.' She shuddered again. 'I promised you Hortense's note.'

'Harriet, I do not give the snap of my fingers about your honorary title, though I would like to shake the hand of anyone who has treated you well. I do not care about Hortense, so long as she is safe and happy. All I want is to make sure you are safe and happy. Now and always. And I know,' I added, trying to keep my voice as controlled as hers, 'that something has occurred to make you terribly unhappy. Something I have done?'

'No. Not you. Ever.'

I did not think that that was true. I winced as I thought of her face the night I gave Mrs Arden that rose. I waited.

'Nothing that has occurred this evening has caused me distress,' she said. 'Nothing. But in truth, Matthew, you must do as I must. Bury yourself in your work, perhaps find a new situation.'

I shook my head. 'There is too much for me to do here, and I find I can only do it if you are by my side. My dear, my Harriet, I want to extract a promise. Hortense wasn't good at keeping hers. But you will keep your word, because it is in your nature. I want you to promise to come and visit my parents. With or without me, as it happens. That is the only thing I want you solemnly to undertake to do.'

'Why?'

'Because my mother can listen and my father can talk. Both better than I can. You can talk to my mother about the cause of your grief, and listen to my father telling you that nothing in the past ever truly matters.'

She shook her head sadly. 'I will do as you ask. One day, if you still hold me to my word. But one day I know it is you who will – Matthew, please leave me now. Please.'

'I can't. Not with you as unhappy as this. Come and walk with me in the garden. Oh, get your pretty hat if you must, though I would prefer to see your hair.'

'And if anyone sees us?'

What I would like to have said was, 'I shall tell them I am entitled to stroll in the moonlight with my affianced wife.' Instead, I said with something of a grimace, 'I am quite sure there is plenty of gossip about us already – and if there is, would anyone dare go and speak to her ladyship and complain? And complain of what? Neither of us is young; neither of us is married. And, Harriet, if she did dismiss me out of hand, she would regret it, because I do not think the estate could bear the cost of the compensation it would have to pay as well as the salary of a new agent.'

She looked at me askance. 'I had no idea you were such a hard man.'

'My cousin is a hard-headed lawyer. And subtle, so that everyone thinks him the most amiable man on earth. Harriet, we can walk out together, open and honest, or sneak out guiltily like a tweenie meeting the boot boy. Which is it to be?'

'The former. But I will wear my prettiest hat.'

XV

Mrs Baird finds me stealing rags. 'But you had your monthly only a week ago.' She gazes at me, eyes kinder than I imagined. 'Into my room with you. Here, stand on these.' More rags, because the blood is still running.

Before I know it Nurse is with me. 'Poor, poor chicken. Lie down. Let me see. No, no need to scream. I won't touch you.'

Over my head, she and Mrs Baird speak quietly, but with such anger. I say, 'I'm sorry – I didn't mean. I wasn't reading.'

'The library. And someone found you there?'

I nod.

'Who?'

I shake my head. 'Mustn't tell. Our secret.'

'Only one man says that. But Dr Webster should see this.'

'Can you imagine him keeping quiet?' Nurse demands. 'Granny Hughes, that's who we need. She knows more about childbirth than any man I know, and she'll know what to do with that nasty tear.' She stroked my hair. 'Now, my chicken, we're going to make you a bit more comfortable, but before we do we'll give you a drink of his lordship's – hey, what's all that about?'

Mrs Baird's voice is tight and hard above my screams. 'Can't bear to hear his name, and who can blame her? We always knew he'd do it again someday. It's my fault: I should never have let her in there. But I told her she must never let anyone find her there.' She is crying. 'If only I had some laudanum drops!'

'Well, we haven't, so go and find the cooking brandy. And some sugar and milk. The sooner she's asleep the better, poor lamb.'

SIXTEEN

I was dressing for church next morning, when I heard William pounding up the stairs. He barely knocked before bursting in.

'Please, sir, it's the House! They've got the police there and you're to go up. I've had Dan saddle Esau just to save a minute!'

'Well done. My jacket, please. Thank you.' As I matched him step for step down the stairs, I asked, 'Do you know what's going on?'

'Got cuffed round the lughole when I asked, gaffer. I mean sir.'

It was too lovely a day to have to spur Esau into action. I would rather have dawdled along on foot, like the birds raising my voice in song, if, of course, I could have sung, with my face stretched as it was in a huge silly grin. I would have betrayed myself immediately, of course, and Harriet. As it was we exchanged the briefest of glances, as I hurried to the library where a harassed footman told me the officers were waiting.

'Where is Mr Bowman?' I asked as we strode along. I ran through any number of scenarios, including my arrest or his, but none quite made sense.

'Mr Bowman is unwell this morning.' The footman paused and looked around cautiously. 'Shall I see what strong black coffee will do for him, sir?'

I grinned. 'Excellent notion. Now, Thatcher, I have another idea. I will receive the policemen not in a family room like the library, where we might be disturbed, but in my office.'

'Shall I bring coffee and tea there, sir?'

'Another good idea. It would be good if it was waiting there when our visitors are shown in. After that, we must not be disturbed unless I ring.'

'Very well, sir.' His voice sank into that sepulchral tone of acquiescence that Bowman sometimes favoured.

* * *

Ushered with great formality into my office, dominated by the great desk that I had inherited and would never have chosen, the officers were inclined to stand, though at last they responded to my gentle but firm insistence. Experience had long taught me it was harder to quarrel if everyone was seated, equipped, moreover, with a china cup and saucer.

Elias Pritchard, our very talented bewhiskered wicket-keeper, happened also to be our village constable. This morning he looked supremely uncomfortable. I suspected that it was not just the fact he was in the imposing company of a tall thin man my age who introduced himself as Sergeant Burrows of the Shrewsbury Constabulary. It was probably more to do with the fact that we were a good combination on the field of play and he didn't like mixing his professional role with his sporting one – a dichotomy I knew all too well myself, after all. Sergeant Burrows was even more hirsute than my teammate, his bright ginger beard descending to mid-chest. They both tugged their uniforms to straighten them, as if intimidated by such a distinguished residence: even this downstairs room was bigger than the average cottage.

'We were hoping to speak to his lordship, sir,' Burrows declared, firmly replacing his cup and saucer on the extreme edge of the desk. After staring uncertainly at it for a moment, he pushed it in a further inch or two.

'I'm sorry to have to confirm what I am sure you have already been told: his lordship is not at home.'

'That's what young Thatcher said, but that just means he doesn't want to receive visitors, doesn't it?'

'Often it is a polite lie,' I agreed. 'But in this case it's the literal truth. Lord Croft is away visiting friends. I believe he is engaged on a cricketing holiday, going from one great house like this to another to play teams of other aristocratic young men.'

'You *believe*?' Burrows narrowed his eyes: he was clearly more alert than I'd originally given him credit for.

'Officer, I am a mere employee, not his friend. Perhaps her ladyship will have more information but it would be a brave man who tried to speak to her before midday,' I added with a rueful smile. 'You might need to make an appointment too; people – even public servants like yourselves – never drop in casually to speak to her.'

'Would her ladyship's maid be informed? She might have seen a letter lying around, or some such.'

'Mlle Hortense,' Elias put in. 'But she's no longer employed here. News gets around fast, doesn't it, Mr Rowsley, in a village like this.'

'She found a new post with a young lady living some way from here,' I agreed. 'She left a note to that effect for Mrs Faulkner, together with a forwarding address. I'm sure Mrs Faulkner will give it to you. But believe me, I really do not know when his lordship proposes to return. I did ask her ladyship myself, but she assured me it was none of my business.' They exchanged a glance, as I expected they would. 'What is my business is why you're interested, gentlemen, in his lordship's activities.'

Burrows raised a finger to stop Elias interrupting. 'Can you tell me if his lordship drives a landau? Made by Elford and Sons, Shrewsbury?'

What was going on? 'He certainly drives a landau, and he certainly patronizes Elford. I have a lot of bills to prove it.' I turned and patted a document box on the shelf beside me.

'This was a very new vehicle,' Burrows said. 'The coach-maker's name was still as clear as day. We have already asked the coach-maker who had bought it. He said that he was paid nearly two hundred pounds in cash by a young man who claimed to be his lordship.'

Cash! That was surprising. Mrs Faulkner had observed tartly that she expected I'd get the bill very soon. 'If the payment was in cash, I can't say one way or another that it was his lordship who was Elford's customer. I would have expected Elford himself to recognize a valued client, however. Now, before I answer any more questions, I'd like to know the reason for your interest in his lordship's affairs.'

'The vehicle in question was found smashed in pieces and mostly hidden deep in some woodland near Church Stretton.'

'Mostly?'

'It'd make good wood for someone's fire, wouldn't it, sir?' Burrows said dryly. 'As for what was left, it looked as if someone did not want it found. And there was no sign of a driver.'

'There would have been two occupants,' I said, my mouth suddenly dry. 'His lordship and his valet.'

'That'd be Luke Hargreaves,' Elias put in.

'Was there any sign of any violence?'

'No sign. But more to the point, no sign, as I said, of any occupants. Not to mention the horses pulling it – four, I presume?' Burrows asked sharply. 'Seems an extravagant way for a young gentleman to travel. A gentleman and his servant,' he said, sensing that Elias might be about to correct him.

'I quite agree,' I said truthfully. 'I can quite see why you are asking about him. Even for a rich man a landau is not the sort of thing you'd leave lying about in pieces. What about their luggage? There would be various portmanteaux, and all his lordship's cricketing gear.'

Both men spread their hands. Nothing. 'Has his lordship ever done anything like this before? Disappeared?' Burrows asked bluntly.

'I have been here only a few months, and during that time he has been occupied with developing the grounds here.'

'I told you, sir – frittering away his inheritance,' Elias said, to be swiftly hushed.

I looked at the clock. At ten, it was far too early to ask for an audience with her ladyship. 'Gentlemen, I think I have told you all I know. Her ladyship will know much more than I. Why do I not take you to the servants' hall for some more refreshment, and I'll ask someone to rouse her.' Whom I knew not – presumably her ladyship and Mrs Faulkner had chosen an acting ladies' maid.

'Someone braver than I am,' Elias muttered. He looked me straight in the eye. He did not need to say aloud that it needed someone braver than me, too.

I flickered a smile at him. 'But perhaps Mr Bowman might have all the information you need.' I rang. Thatcher appeared as if he had been only a foot from the door. 'Would you accompany these gentlemen to the servants' hall? I'm sure they would appreciate some of Mrs Arden's cooking. Thank you.' I turned back. 'This could be everything or nothing, couldn't it? Maybe the young man has decided to kick over the traces—'

Burrows added pointedly, 'Or maybe someone has decided to kick him over them.'

*   *   *

I took it on myself to check on Bowman, who was at least up, decked in a splendid dressing-gown almost certainly from his late master's wardrobe. Despite the coffee, he looked very unwell, and had not yet attempted to shave.

'Samuel, this is not like you,' I said breezily. 'Come on, my friend, spruce yourself up. Pah, your shaving water is nearly cold. I'll get young Thatcher to bring some more and some more coffee. And you must eat, too. The police are here, with all sort of questions, and I rely on you to help me answer them. Do you understand?'

The eyes he turned on me were bloodshot, and the bags under them deep, but he straightened perceptibly.

'I really cannot manage without you,' I added truthfully, as I left the room, closing the door firmly behind me. It was one thing for him to have been in his cups – I'm sure the entire household knew about his tippling – but another for him to be seen at his dishevelled worst.

Mrs Arden and Mrs Faulkner were apparently preparing to go to church, a duty that had completely slipped my mind. But the former quickly slipped off her bonnet. 'Silly old fool – been at the juice again, has he? I know just the thing.' She reached for an apron.

'Could you ask someone else to prepare it? Thatcher will take it to him. He seems a discreet enough young man. Meanwhile, we three need to talk in private. Mr Bowman too, when he is well enough. My office, I would suggest,' I added, nodding in the direction of the two policemen, currently deep into plates of ham and eggs.

As one, Harriet and I waited in silence while Mrs Arden gave her instructions. I am sure we both craved a few moments' private conversation – even the time it would have taken to walk through the corridors would have been better than nothing – but we had agreed last night to preserve our usual working demeanour as long as we could. When the corridor became too narrow for three to walk abreast, especially when two were wearing crinolines, I fell behind.

I was pleased – but not surprised – to see that the coffee things had been removed.

'We don't have much time. Those men won't be content with eating for much longer.'

Mrs Arden laughed. 'They've got fresh rolls to tackle yet. And some of my best preserves – wasted on them, but not jam to hurry.'

I smiled an acknowledgement, but pressed on nonetheless. 'Firstly, who has taken on Hortense's duties? Because the men won't leave till they've spoken to her ladyship, and someone has to wake her up. She is unlikely to be pleased, as I know from experience.'

The women exchanged a glance. Harriet said, 'It's not a job for young Florrie, is it? Though if she simply took up her lady-ship's chocolate and hot water as if she expected she would want to go to church . . .'

'Then as soon as she is up and dressed, I will undertake to speak to her,' I said, pausing as the door opened. 'Unless – ah, good morning, Mr Bowman! We need your wisdom here.' He bowed from the waist, his corset creaking audibly. He was scarcely recognisable as the wreck I had seen but a few minutes earlier. Whatever was in Mrs Arden's recipe had done wonders for him, as had shaving. As he closed the door, I continued, 'Mrs Faulkner, I will summon Thatcher and send a message for Florrie.' I rang. Again the young man appeared with discon-certing speed, and went off on his errand. 'I do hope he hasn't taken to eavesdropping. Anyway the police can be told truthfully, if they ask, that her ladyship is getting dressed. Now, Mr Bowman, please tell us what you know about his lordship's whereabouts. We know you are as discreet as the grave, and people will say things in front of you they wouldn't tell to their parish priest.'

He sat with something approaching his usual dignity. 'This is in the nature of a rehearsal for what I shall have to tell the policemen?'

'I think it probably is. If there is anything germane, they will need to know.'

He took a deep breath. The effect was rather spoiled by a violent belch. 'I beg your pardon. I fear I know very little of what has become his life. Certainly he has got in with a bad crowd. Young men who behave like schoolboys half their age. I have told you, Mr Rowsley, about the violence of their behaviour. Last weekend, I recall. We were smoking together outside.'

I nodded. 'We were indeed. You were too loyal to the family to go into much detail. You may have to be less . . . delicate . . . when the police speak to you.' Even as I spoke, I remembered another moment, and clicked my fingers in irritation. It was easier to jot down a note to remind myself than explain. *Button*, it said. 'Meanwhile, have any of us any idea why he should have paid for the landau in cash? Not to mention the horses to pull it, all of which are now missing, along with all the luggage.'

'I think he may gamble heavily, out of fashion though such excess may be. I suspect, Mr Rowsley, that your tight control over the estate funds irks him – though his mother insists it is necessary, as we all know it is. So he may have won a big sum. And to spend it all on one piece of wild extravagance is perhaps a rude gesture at all who counsel prudence.'

'Do you suppose,' Harriet began, 'that whoever he won the money from sought revenge? And destroyed his trophy?'

'If so,' Mrs Arden continued seamlessly, 'might they also have destroyed him, Luke and four good horses? And made off with a lot of luggage?'

'Or perhaps his lordship had an accident en route to another venue and simply decided to abandon the vehicle, irresponsible though that might be. If only we knew his itinerary!' Bowman concluded with a wail.

'But her ladyship insisted it was his business and no one else's,' I said with an air of finality. 'And that must be what we all tell the police. Now, Mrs Arden, you mentioned hearing horsemen the night before Hortense was injured. Have you heard any rumours about the identity of the visitors?' I turned to the others. 'Have either of you?'

They looked at me blankly. 'It's the first I've heard of anything like that,' Mr Bowman declared.

I nodded as if they had both spoken. 'Something Mr Bowman said has reminded me of something I found the evening in question. A button. It may signify something or nothing. It's safe in my house. But I would like to show it to you before I hand it over to the policemen.' I picked up my hat. 'Shall we meet again in the Room in fifteen minutes?'

XVI

They talk over my head. Through a strange fog I can still hear what they are saying, although I do not understand their words.

'What if he's got the poor mite in the family way?'

'They say you can't if it's your first time. And she's just a child.'

'But what if?'

'Wait and see?'

'Too late by then.'

'Family would take care . . .'

A snort.

'Got to make sure.'

'Pennyroyal tea . . .'

SEVENTEEN

'I would need Luke to confirm it, but in my opinion this is from his lordship's summer-weight evening suit,' Bowman said heavily. 'And you say, Rowsley, that you heard an altercation between a young man and a young woman?'

I nodded. 'Yes, but on another evening entirely. I thought it was just a lover's tiff, and decided not to intervene.'

'A tiff it might have been. But between his lordship and a young woman?' Mrs Arden put in. 'Between him and Maggie? Such a relationship is not unknown.'

Harriet went so white I feared she was about to faint. But she kept herself sitting upright somehow or other. Lest others remark on her pallor, I said, 'I think we must speak to Mrs Billings again. I know Maggie forbade us to reveal her whereabouts, but if the child she's carrying is his lordship's it puts an entirely different complexion on the matter. Poor child. Poor, poor child,' I sighed.

A tap on the door silenced us all. Florrie, fresh from her ladyship's chamber, was as white as Harriet. She curtsied, but stumbled. Bowman supported her to a chair. 'Such a rage she's in! I let slip about the policemen, and I thought she'd kill me.' She raised her head high and managed a smile. 'She might have done, except with a couple of bobbies handy down here she might have been caught a damn sight quicker than she liked.'

'No swearing, Florrie,' Harriet said absently. 'Mr Bowman, I fancy that a drop of your medicinal brandy might be in order. Florrie's had a nasty shock—'

'Thank you, Mr Bowman, but no, if it's all the same to you. I've signed the pledge. My whole family have. There's a new Methodist chapel down Dudley way, so we started going. And I know Mr Pounceman doesn't approve of the demon drink, so I often feel like having a noggin to spite him, but a promise is a promise, isn't it?'

Unless it was made by an irresponsible man so he could have his way with a girl who allowed herself to believe him.

'It is, Florrie,' I said. 'Now, how did you leave her ladyship?'

She laughed. 'Quickly! To dodge a hairbrush. Nice silver one, too – I bet it got a nasty dent when it hit the door.'

'I hope so. Now, answer me truthfully, Florrie – I know this might mean breaking a promise, but sometimes, except when it's made to God, you have to. Hortense left here with a really bad injury, didn't she? Do you think that might have been caused by a flying hairbrush?'

She considered. 'Summat much heavier, I reckon.'

'Some*thing*,' Harriet said gently.

'Sorry, ma'am. It's just that I'm all het up and I forget what you've learned us. *Taught* us.'

'Good girl. Now,' Harriet continued, her colour returning, 'if Hortense wasn't hit by a brush, what do you think did hurt her? And who? I'm sure she swore you to secrecy but Mr Rowsley is right: we really need to know. Sometimes if someone hurts someone they might want to try again.'

'Ah, and do a better job – do her in, second time round,' Florrie agreed, with a sage nod. 'Don't reckon as how it's – *don't reckon that it was* her ladyship. Thing is, this might get Hortense into trouble.'

'She's left now, so we can't punish her. And only I know where she has gone to live.'

There was a loud knock at the door, swiftly followed by the entrance of Thatcher. He bowed. 'Beg pardon for breaking in on your talk. But the policemen are insistent they speak to her ladyship, whether she is ready or not. They want someone to show them up to her room right now.'

Mrs Faulkner got swiftly to her feet. 'I'll take them.'

And I couldn't even scream at her to be careful.

'Very well, Florrie,' I said as Thatcher closed the door behind her, 'Hortense was hit very hard by something, we all agree on that. By what and by whom?'

'It was a man, and that's all you're getting out of me,' she said, 'until I hear otherwise from Hortense. But I don't want those bobbies to go sniffing round asking for her in case the bastard gets wind of it and finds her first. And that's flat.' She got up, dropped a curtsy that was as challenging as a gauntlet, and marched out.

Forgetting myself, I mimed a round of applause. In for a penny, in for a pound: 'If that girl can lose some of her accent and remember the grammar that Mrs Faulkner is trying to teach her, she'll go far.'

Bowman looked at me curiously. 'I really believe you approve of her attitude.'

Mrs Arden's face was unreadable. 'Do you want Mrs Faulkner or me to accompany you to the lodge, Mr Rowsley? Or Mr Bowman?'

I looked from one to the other. 'It'll be obvious if you leave your posts. No one expects me to be here on a Sunday, so I'll go alone. But I think I should take some food – not quite a bribe, but a little encouragement. Something small and discreet, that will fit in my pockets. Can you help me with that, Mrs Arden? Thank you.'

I do not know how Mrs Billings dragged herself to the gate each time she was summoned. She was nothing but skin and bone: perhaps Dr Page would have known if it was because she did not eat enough or whether some terrible illness had struck her. She leant against the door jamb as if she needed its support – as I feared she would when I had finished speaking to her. I felt my way into the conversation by asking a genuine question.

'Mrs Billings, a week or so a couple of gentlemen, maybe three, arrived at the House very late at night. You must have opened the gate for them. Do you recall who they might have been?'

Her expression was totally blank, but she made an effort. 'Would they have been in a coach, like his lordship's, say, or were they riding?'

'On horseback.'

She nodded. 'Ah, they'd have no call to rouse me then: leastways, if they knew their way around the estate. There's a couple of little gaps in the wall, far side of the woods. Tight fit for a horse, mind.' She did her best to smile. 'My grandfer used to call them the Eyes of the Needle.' She seemed happy that I was laughing. 'As for a coach, gaffer, hasn't been one since her ladyship's.'

'Thank you. I'll get one of the estate lads to point the gaps out to me.' Now came the part I was not looking forward to: 'Mrs Billings, I am sure you told me the truth last time we spoke about Maggie, but I am also sure you did not tell me the whole truth. I don't know why. I know there is some trouble. Yes?'

Her eyes filled with terror.

'I also know she does not want to be a bother to you. Actually, I know where she is, but she refuses to let me tell you.'

Her lips moved but I detected no sound.

How did I begin? I thought of my mother: I searched for the words she would have spoken. 'A kind Baptist minister and his wife are keeping an eye on her. They have some money to make sure she eats well enough for her and for her baby. When her time comes, they can pay for a midwife. All of this is being done in secret. No one will betray her whereabouts, not even to you, unless she permits it. But I will make sure that if you want to send her a message, it will reach her.' I waited. 'I promise,' I added.

I might not have said a word. Was she deaf? Stupid? But then I saw the tears coursing down her face. She made no effort to wipe them away.

'If ever you have anything else you want to tell me, send a lad to my house and I will come as soon as I can. Mrs Billings, you can trust me. If you know the name of your daughter's seducer, tell me, and I can bring him to book: I can't force him to marry her, but I can make him pay for his child's upkeep.' And if not, I would do it myself. 'Now, I fear you are not eating enough,' I said more briskly, in a slightly louder voice. 'Here: please accept this.' I dug in my pockets for the packages of ham, cheese and cake. There was also a packet of tea. 'These are for you.'

Her tears still rolled; now her mouth worked. But she did not speak, and I had to lift her hands in order to press the gifts into them.

I raised my hat and said softly the words my father would have used, 'May God bless you, and keep you, and cause His light to shine upon you.'

*　*　*

Rather than head straight back to the House I turned Esau towards the village and Dr Page's establishment. His maid showed me straight into the garden, where, in his shirtsleeves, he was tending the roses.

We discussed greenfly for a while – more accurately he did, because dealing with pests was an art regarded by my gardener as a secret available only to the initiated. However, I took all Page said to heart, and felt that in future discussions I would be able to do more than nod in agreement to everything the expert suggested.

As the maid brought out a tea tray which she placed, at his request, on a table in an arbour, he put down his secateurs and led the way to the shade. 'Have you something to tell me about my patient's progress?'

'Yes – and to ask you to treat another woman on the estate.' It was clearly understood that he would invoice his lordship, via me. 'Hortense was well enough to leave us, and has taken up employment with a lady in Warwick: only Mrs Faulkner knows her whereabouts.'

'Good. And who is the other lady in question? Another lady's maid?' he added meaningfully.

I thought of Florrie and the hairbrush. 'Not this time,' I said truthfully. 'Mrs Billings. She is thinner each time I see her.'

He sucked his teeth. 'I fear you will not see her at all by the end of the summer. Constant hunger, lack of proper nourishment – how can a woman like that shake off illnesses that would do no more than inconvenience someone in her ladyship's position? Of course I will talk to her, and give her some pills she will believe will do her good – the mind is a powerful tool, Rowsley, you mark my words!'

'Pills – good. And I will ask Mrs Arden to ensure a constant supply of food reaches the lodge.'

'No. Make sure it reaches her, and no one else. It is the way of the poor, Rowsley, to share food in a way you or I would find incomprehensible. The man of the house must eat, even if he is a drunken layabout. Paralysed, in Billings' case! The sons must eat. So if there happened to be any meat in the meal, that is the end of that. Then any girl likely to get into service must be briefly fattened up: no one would employ a waif, and the family needs both her space and the tiny wage she will send home, remember. Then, and only then, do the other females share the rest.'

When I got back, the staff were about to sit down in the hall: seeing a spare seat, I took it, nodding to Bowman, who was opposite me. Naturally we preserved the rule of silence, though there were questions I was desperate to ask. However, as the four of us adjourned to the Room, I spoke quietly to George, who had been sitting diagonally across from me. 'My office, good and early tomorrow, please, George – whatever the weather.'

'This time I'll bring a change of clothes if needs be, gaffer!'

XVII

This is a different sort of pain. Someone is squeezing my insides. Twist. Squeeze. Twist. Yellow blobs float in front of my eyes. My stomach heaves. Nurse has a bucket ready. There is nothing of me but pain.
I am on fire.
Nurse lifts my nightgown. 'I think we've won!'
Someone kisses my forehead. 'Something else to drink.'
I float away on the pain.

EIGHTEEN

'Said nothing! How can the policemen have said nothing?' I demanded, as the four of us adjourned to the Room for tea and coffee. Harriet and Beatrice had decided that although Florrie was acting as her ladyship's maid, she was not yet her properly appointed lady's maid and would not expect temporary admission to the Room. 'They simply left without telling us what her ladyship had revealed? I cannot believe it!' I strode about the room in frustration. At last I realized how childish I must appear, pacing in such a tiny space, to the imminent risk of a pile of books and a pretty work-box, and put my energy to better use by handing round the cups. For penance I sat in the least comfortable chair.

Harriet smiled. 'It is not impossible that a conversation with Elias might reveal something, Mr Rowsley. What a shame that Mr Baines does not open the pub on Sunday evenings . . .'

'A shame indeed,' I agreed. 'But some of the team practise in the nets on Monday evenings – I might just drift down. Meanwhile, some of you will have seen me break the rule and talk to George. When we were surveying the House for rain damage, we found a locked room.'

Harriet nodded. 'The one near his lordship's accommodation. A room adjoining one he always insists is allocated to one of his friends.'

'Does he indeed? I know – as I am sure you all do – that his lordship keeps pornographic books in his dressing room. I am – let us say, I am just being nosy. Unless any of you has a key that I don't, I will ask George to remove the lock so we can see what lies within.'

Bowman's eyes widened to their fullest extent. 'Mr Rowsley, consider what you are doing!'

'I should imagine Mr Rowsley will find a water leak to justify the exercise,' Harriet said. 'I could even create the leak: I could make sure a maid leaves a bucket unemptied, couldn't I?'

I shook my head. 'If anyone is going to get into trouble, it will be me. Yes to the water leak, no to anyone else being involved in the subterfuge.'

'The lie!' Bowman exploded. 'I will have no part of this!'

'I quite understand, Mr Bowman. And in any other circumstances I would not dream of anything so low. I will keep it as undetectable as possible, entering not through the corridor but through the door to the adjoining room. And George will repair any damage immediately. I just wish I had a key and didn't have to ask him.'

Harriet got up, walking swiftly to her bedroom. She returned with a wooden box, perhaps twelve inches by six, and four deep. She set it on the table, before unclasping the bunch of household keys from her chatelaine. 'This,' she said, flourishing one of the bunch, 'unlocks about half the chambers, this the other half. Let us see if there is anything in here that is similar in size and shape to them: it might save a great deal of trouble.' Picking up yesterday's newspaper, she spread it on the table and upended the box.

We searched with as much glee as if we were children, even Bowman joining in with a will. At last we had a choice of three possibilities.

Bowman smiled slowly. 'Only because I wish to exclude George from the proceedings, I assure you, I suggest you test these this evening, Rowsley, when her ladyship is taking sherry. It being such a fine evening, I will encourage her to take it in the red drawing room, with its fine views across the county. And then it will be but as a step for her to adjourn to the dining room. She is accustomed,' he said, in an aside to me, 'to eat there occasionally even when his lordship is not at home. I shall *forget* to ask her if she would rather be served there or in her own suite. I suppose a dish or two the aroma of which lingers would not be impossible, Mrs Arden? The sort of thing one would not wish to awaken to the next morning?'

'Fish? And she does like a curry of meat and vegetables.'

'Excellent! In fact, Mrs Arden, I really enjoy your curries myself. Might it be possible . . .?'

Mrs Arden patted his hand indulgently. 'Of course it might.' But I could see from the expression on her face that she was busily tearing up all her plans and working out how much of the evening's menu she might salvage.

By chance Harriet turned towards me, her fine eyes full of laughter. Though we both averted our gaze immediately, I did not believe that no one had seen the bolt of love between us.

And I did not care a jot.

I did care that I must not invite Harriet to accompany me on my expedition. I suspect from her wistful expression – the one she wore when I talked about my cricket exploits – that she would have liked to participate. She did offer, in the presence of the others, to walk up and down the corridor in question to warn me of anyone's approach, but Bowman was very much against the idea.

'Would you usually be on duty at such a time? Walking in the Family corridor? Well, then, Mrs Faulkner, it will simply draw attention to our conspiracy if you did today. No, you and Mrs Arden must maintain a convincing pretence of normal Sabbath behaviour. You might even sit in the evening sun on that seat of yours by the herb garden, might you not, and read? Off you go. And Mrs Arden, given the change in the menu, you might wish to be seen in the kitchen. Very well, Mr Rowsley, give me fifteen minutes. It may take me that long to ensconce her ladyship in the red drawing room. If I am not back in that period, I think it might be safe for you to take an idle stroll.' Having disposed of his cast like a theatre producer, he turned back to me and clasped my hand. 'Godspeed, Matthew.'

After all the latent drama, my adventure was very banal. The door opening on to the corridor swung open sweetly in response to the key Bowman had picked out. It locked equally sweetly behind me. My candles – I could hide them in a pocket, unlike the lantern I would have preferred – would have lit up, had there not been a small window affording enough light, a plain dressing room, equipped with all the appropriate furniture. The cupboards were all locked, but the tiny keys remained in the locks, and it was the work of moments to scan their shelves. Most were completely bare. For some reason a pile of sheets lay loosely folded on one. Some, equally empty, seemed shorter from back to front than the others, but I searched in vain for a reason. There were no pornographic books, nothing to suggest why anyone should wish to lock the room. The drawers? Yes, they were firmly locked, with no key in evidence, and the cupboard ones were the wrong shape. There was a slightly musty smell, although the window swung open easily enough when I tried it. Mystified, I made sure I had left no sign of my visit behind me, and slipped out of the room. If I looked hesitant I would only occasion remark, so I strode along as if I owned the place – not meeting anyone, of course.

I wanted to return to my house to change for supper – the light summer suit which Mr Bowman recommended for weather like this. Perhaps guilt took my footsteps the backstairs route, which naturally led me to the Room and – when there was no response to my light tap – to the servants' hall and the kitchen. Mrs Arden was sitting at her ease by the open door, perhaps to escape the strong smell of spices. She turned when she heard my footsteps.

'Ah, Mr Rowsley, could you do me the most enormous favour? I find I've forgotten to bring in any coriander, and the maid always picks parsley by mistake. Mrs Faulkner knows exactly where it is.' With a huge twinkle in her eye she pointed to the figure seated by the herb-garden gate.

'It seems as if we may not need George after all,' I concluded. Tim appeared bearing two tureens of curry; I waited while he fetched the rice and condiments.

Bowman shook his head. 'If you have already sent for him, find him some other urgent job, I beg you – one that will not arouse any suspicions on his part, of course. Mrs Faulkner, surely you can feign a check of the linen room and discover that some sheets are missing?'

'Of course. But would that be sufficient for me to demand admission to a locked room as part of my search?'

'If you attached the key Mr Rowsley used to your chatelaine, then no one would know it was not usually there, would they?' Mrs Arden asked. 'And none of the maids or footmen would dare question you. Unless they already knew something we don't.'

'What a good idea! And then, perhaps, quite by chance, of

course, I might notice something wrong with the shelves? Or is that a step too far?'

'Let us see if the errant sheets offer us any reason to worry,' Bowman said.

'And let us see if you have any keys in that wonderful collection that might open some of the locked drawers,' I added.

'Very well. I will add them to the chatelaine too – hiding them in plain sight. And if they work, I will open the drawers, locking them again afterwards, of course.'

Bowman seemed inclined to argue, but raised a forkful of our supper to his lips. He smiled beatifically. 'Mrs Arden, we are eating like kings! Or rather, of course, like nabobs!'

The table cleared, Harriet produced her key-box again, and we scrabbled amongst its contents like children fighting for pennies. Eventually we selected a fair sample. Then a bell rang: Mr Bowman's.

'Heavens, is that the time? I should be serving her ladyship's dessert.' He almost sprinted from the room.

'Clearly that pick-me-up you devised this morning, Beatrice, has amazing properties,' Harriet observed. 'Young Thatcher said he looked like death warmed up.' She mimicked, but not unkindly, his accent, remarkably similar to Florrie's. 'And now look at him, dashing round like a two-year-old.'

Her friend smiled. 'Perhaps I should accept his invitation to be his partner at the Harvest Home dance.'

'He's already asked you?'

'No, but he will soon. He does every year. And this year I might just call his bluff and agree.'

I could not help it: my eyes sought out Harriet's. Would she and I be going together? I tried to frame a question out loud. 'Does the estate host one big affair, or does each tenant farmer have his own?'

'Both. There is a lot of dancing, and quite a number of weddings three months later, if truth be told,' Mrs Arden said. 'Poor Mr Pounceman. He blames that demon drink that Florrie's given up.'

'And poor Mr Pounceman for another reason,' I said. 'I've been meaning to tell you: Mr Pounceman—'

'Has mumps!' they concluded my sentence as one, giggling like girls. 'Oh, we probably knew before Dr Page did,' Mrs Arden added. 'There are no secrets in a village.'

'In that case,' I said, suddenly serious, 'the villagers probably have as good an idea as anyone what has happened to his lordship.'

'I'm sure they do,' she agreed. 'But there's a difference between asking, Matthew, and letting someone tell you. We three – we four! – are too closely allied to the Family for anyone to make a laughing matter of his lordship's habits, to our faces at least. Behind our backs, now, that's another matter.'

'Would they laugh if they thought his lordship was anything worse than a wild and silly young man finally escaping his mother's grasp?' Harriet asked. 'I think not.'

I stared. 'Is he anything worse?'

'Who knows? But if the button that you found did come off his dress suit, then it might have been he you heard arguing in the shrubbery. And who was he arguing with? A young woman. I can think of two young women who suffered something at male hands. You are sent away on a crazy errand. I too am despatched on a feeble excuse. Maggie flees. He departs post-haste. Her ladyship departs to a spa – to a poor hotel, according to Hortense, not the sort of place where she would be accustomed to stay. And now,' she added, in a very sombre voice, 'he has disappeared from the face of the earth.'

'With Luke,' Beatrice added.

I took a deep breath. 'Harriet. Beatrice. I do not think we should mention this theory to Mr Bowman yet. He has loyalties to the Family I cannot match. That we should even think such a thing would upset him, very deeply. He might even . . . who knows. If there is evidence to be found, let us present it to him. Otherwise, for the sake of our friendship, let us keep quiet.'

The women stared, then, seeming to have reached a silent agreement, nodded in concert. 'Very well,' Beatrice said. 'We must all be each other's eyes and ears. But discretion must be our watchword.'

'Absolute discretion,' Harriet agreed. 'Now, he will be back within minutes: he must interrupt us in an entirely innocent conversation.'

'The Harvest Home dance, perhaps,' Beatrice said.

As Harriet had predicted, Bowman returned from his duties without knocking – and why should he knock? He was the senior man in the House.

He inhaled deeply. 'I am afraid that the curry which was designed to make her ladyship reluctant to eat in her chamber has left its lingering fumes to bother you, Mrs Faulkner. May I open a window?' He leant with his arms on the sill for several moments. When he turned back to us he was smiling, almost coyly. 'It is such a beautiful evening, I do not see why my colleagues and I should not walk with you part of the way back to your house, Matthew. Her ladyship is unlikely to need my services much longer once I have served her tea.'

'I will have the tray prepared this instant,' Mrs Arden declared.

Our dawdling stroll took us towards the shrubbery, where I was able to point out the spot where I found the button. Then, as if by magic, the talk became more casual, then lapsed altogether. Somehow four together became two groups of two. We were never quite out of sight of each other in the bright moonlight, never quite out of earshot, so there was mutual chaperonage. But it was not until we had reached my front door and said our goodnights that Beatrice and Samuel caught up with us. They were now a respectable distance apart, and absorbed Harriet into their company as if she had never left it. It was only then that I remembered I had left Esau in the main stables and had to chase after them. I was subject to a great deal of mocking banter, but it gave all four of us a few more minutes of happiness.

Esau seemed pleased to see me, but clearly did not know what to make of my singing – I think it might have been Mozart – on our journey home.

*   *   *

XVIII

I *have been in bed for a month now, out of harm's way, Nurse says. She has brought me books from the nursery, and I make myself read a little each day, though often I do not want to. What is the matter with me – all this time to read, but no inclination?*

NINETEEN

E arly next morning I retired to my office to find a plausible reason for having summoned George so urgently. After a struggle, I managed to jam one of the drawers of the rent-table sufficiently tightly, trying to ignore the fact he looked askance at me as he reached amongst his tools.

As he worked I was profoundly aware of the pace – no, the rhythm – that the House demanded of its denizens. All around young men and women were driven by the requirements of others, whether their demands were justified or not. With only her lady-ship in residence, why should all the main rooms be dusted and swept and polished? Why should such a fine array of produce be transformed into miraculous treats that her ladyship might simply dismiss? In fact, of course, Beatrice Arden broke many unspoken rules in giving the delicacies to the servants; many also went to ailing pensioners dotted around the estate, or to sick employees. The charitable errands around the estate were, of course, usually the province of the lady of the house, but here were entirely Harriet's responsibility – at first I had resented them on her behalf, but now I saw them as a golden opportunity to spend time with her, as our paths accidentally crossed.

I knew that she herself was slightly going against the daily rhythm: she was conducting a quite spurious check of the linen room, and then would sally round the various bedchambers in search of the items she had 'discovered' were missing. Much as I ached to go and protect her, I knew that while no one should be alarmed by the prosaic sight of a quiet woman going about her daily round, my very presence might indeed alert someone to her presence. I suspected too that the very thought that she might need to be looked after would be anathema to her.

After five minutes, no more, George was packing his tools away. Even before I could offer possibly shamefaced thanks, there was a knock on the door. It was Thatcher, to say that coffee was ready.

'Excellent. In here, Thatcher. Enough for George, too, if you please.' I might smile at him, but I was beginning to wonder if the young man might not be becoming slightly too assiduous in his attentions. Was he just being a good servant or was he too interested in garnering information. If so, for whom?

George didn't relish the coffee, adding spoon upon spoon of sugar to it, and making it as milky as possible. He seemed very preoccupied as he stirred the pale sweet mixture. 'Gaffer, I hope you won't take it amiss, but I had a strange fancy you might want me to break into that locked room when you summoned me so promptly.'

Another smile, though I was inwardly cursing. 'You have my word, George, that if I did I would not ask you in front of a whole table of interested ears.'

I swear he rubbed his hands in glee. 'So would we be using a code, like, gaffer?'

'If and when it becomes necessary, I'll try to devise one. Now, how is the work on the roof going in this lovely weather?'

'I could take you up now if you've a mind to see.'

I did have a mind to see. It was important for me to be seen wherever important work was taking place. Furthermore, it would keep my mind from Harriet's activities.

The sheer bulk of the building meant that the activity above their heads was hardly noticeable to most of the inhabitants. When the roof above the servants' bedrooms was repaired, it would be different – but then, the people making the noise worked far shorter hours than their domestic counterparts. Yes, even when only one of the Family was in residence.

George was pointing. 'We've patched here, but you can see the whole of that section has to be replaced. Look at those cracks: if we skimp now it'll last a winter, maybe two, but no longer. Best bite on the bullet, I'd say.'

'I'm sure you're right. Let me have an estimate and I'll discuss it with his lordship,' I said automatically.

'If he ever turns up,' George grunted. 'I hear Elias and his gaffer were sniffing round looking for him – is that right?'

'They certainly came to talk to her ladyship, but I wasn't privy to their conversation. Come on, George, you know I can't comment.'

My change of tone was rewarded with a comradely grin. 'Now, how long do you think this wonderful weather will last? It'd be good to make the place waterproof while we have the chance.'

'So do you want an estimate or not?'

'Of course. An estimate. In round terms. On my desk by the end of the day.'

He looked at me sideways. 'Very round, then. And when will I get your round answer?'

I used my most pompous voice: 'I am a very busy man, George – so probably not until eight tomorrow morning,' I added, clapping him on the shoulder.

Much as I would have liked to go down for coffee in the servants' hall and thence, of course, the Room, I had already arranged meetings with some of our tenant farmers to discuss improvements I thought were vital and they were inclined to dismiss as new-fangled. I could see from the last few years of their returns that they could well afford them, and could simply have told them to follow my instructions. But in my experience no farmer liked being bullocked into changes: somehow I needed to gain their support. With luck they would all leave my office convinced that they had had the innovatory ideas themselves – even if it took me the rest of the morning. I also needed to send a note down to the rectory to ask if Mr Pounceman was well enough for the meeting I proposed for this afternoon on the plans for Stammerton.

At last it was time to foregather for the midday meal. I found the Trappist regime irksome, but could not, in any case, have spoken to Mrs Faulkner about her morning. In the heat no one wanted to eat much, but seemed to dawdle all the more as they picked at their plates. Eventually, however, Mrs Faulkner gave the signal that the meal was over.

Bowman shut the door behind us with exaggerated care. He even looked askance at the window, opened to its widest point to encourage at least a breath of air, but Harriet shook her head. 'I don't want anyone else fainting,' she said. 'We've had our fill of that this morning, haven't we, Beatrice!'

Bowman said quickly, 'Not another child like Maggie in the family way!'

Beatrice shook her head. 'I don't think so. Dorcas has always been a fainter. And she assures me, quite vehemently, that she wouldn't let any young man touch her. On the other hand, as I was quick to remind her, sometimes young men don't wait for permission, and I'd want to know if anyone had . . . interfered . . . with her. And that he'd be dealt with. No matter who. Am I right, Matthew?'

What about our little pact about secrecy? It seemed the women had changed their minds. If they had, it was not for me to argue. 'If it is in my power, of course,' I said.

'What if it isn't?' Harriet asked, a strange tone in her voice. 'What then?'

'Then one hopes it's in the law's power,' Beatrice said.

Samuel nodded, but his face was troubled. 'What makes you ask that, Harriet?'

'Something I found this morning.' She took a deep breath. 'Perhaps you should close the window after all, Matthew. Just for a few moments. I'm sorry.' There was a long pause, even after I'd completed the trivial task. 'As you know, I was looking for an excuse this morning to unlock that dressing room. I did indeed find that sheets were missing from the linen room, quite a number, in fact, so my errand was legitimate.' She paused, swallowing hard. 'It seems that the linen was not put in a laundry basket, but left in that room. I have no explanation. I've left everything where it was. There is blood on three or four of them, and . . . stains . . . on all of them.' Her face burned. 'Our chambermaids, our laundrymaids, would easily identify the origin of these stains. They deal with them regularly when we have a house party. Married couples.'

'So why would these not have reached the laundry?' Bowman asked, apparently deciding that the best way to deal with her obvious embarrassment was to draw attention to the cause.

'Because we had no married couples in residence, of course,' Beatrice Arden said tartly.

'The blood would indicate . . .?' I too was embarrassed. 'That the woman sharing the bed was . . . might be losing her virginity?'

'Or might simply be enduring her monthly cycle,' Beatrice said.

I tried to lift the atmosphere. 'But let us not get trapped in unlovely details. The fact that these sheets were concealed suggests that someone did not want their activity to be discovered.'

'Or,' said Harriet, lifting her head and straightening her shoulders, 'they were kept for another reason. You see, I found something else. That shelf that wasn't as deep as the others: I prised the back panel away.' She patted the scissors on her chatelaine. 'I apologize in advance to you all. This is deeply embarrassing. You know the specimen cases that some ladies and gentlemen use for small items in their cabinets of treasures? Precious stones? Butterflies? There is a box like that behind the panel I removed. I cannot believe I am saying this in mixed company. But if I asked you all to go and look for yourselves, it might . . . draw attention.' She swallowed hard.

I moved to support her, but Beatrice was there before me, taking her hand.

She smiled her thanks, and, though crimson from the neck upwards, continued. 'Many of the sections of the specimen case are empty. But some are occupied by curls . . . by hair.' It was clear she could not continue.

How could I help? 'Can it be,' I heard myself asking, 'that this hair is not from the head?'

'Exactly. Which is why,' she said, 'I wondered if the sheets were . . . were trophies – of sexual conquest.' She got up and opened the window, leaning her forehead against the frame. Then she closed it again. 'One of the victims of such an . . . one of the victims might be Maggie.'

Bowman spluttered, his face so suffused with blood I feared he was ill. He reached in his pocket, producing a hip flask. But he didn't drink himself – instead he poured a generous measure into Harriet's cup. Her hand shook so much that Beatrice had to help her raise it to her lips.

Appalled that the women had had to utter such words, let alone be privy to the shocking and scandalous information, I said quietly, 'Perhaps you would prefer to resume this conversation when you are feeling better, Harriet. We shall all be better, I fancy, for a period of quiet reflection.'

She lifted her head, smiling bravely. 'Perhaps you are right. I need to order my thoughts, which are whirling like dervishes. Why, oh why, did none of the girls confide in me?'

I thought of the expression I had seen in Mrs Billings' eyes when I had questioned her. 'Fear,' I said. 'Fear of someone with power.'

XIX

'*I will not ask,*' the man with the tiny spectacles is saying, '*how you did it, but I would say that there is no pregnancy.*' It is not the new apothecary. I do believe it is Dr Hughes, who treats the family. He feels my belly through my shift, a nice clean one Nurse has found for me. '*But there must be no more treatment. The child is young and her constitution still delicate. Any further remedies and she might not be able to have children of her own. And that would not do, would it, Missy?*' he asks, touching my cheek with the back of a finger, the way Mrs Baird fusses the kitchen cat that sleeps with her, not Cook, at night. But that is our secret.

What happened in the library was our secret, he said, and already people know about it.

What will become of me now?

TWENTY

A terse note awaited me on my desk, informing me that the Reverend Mr Pounceman was not At Home – like Elias I wondered if that was in the social or literal sense – and that the meeting must be postponed. Neither alternative date nor apology was offered.

I was furious. But outside the sun was still shining, so I did the obvious thing: I vented my spleen in the fields, helping with the last of the hay-making. Who could have provided those intimate souvenirs? Could they have done it voluntarily? And were they willing volunteers in the coupling we all assumed had gone before? Trophies, Harriet had called them – and with such bitterness. If I had thought she would welcome it, I would have run back to her, laying down my rake on the spot. Rake! Even the innocent word made me catch my breath in horror because of its other meaning! Men in an earlier age had used the term with something approaching envious approval, not the profound distaste for such sexual adventure my friends and colleagues felt. And yet at university and since I had become aware of the double-standards of my contemporaries. They might cherish the pure women they dreamed of marrying, as I now dreamed of marrying Harriet, but they thought nothing of consorting with women selling their bodies: fallen women. My father always considered them not 'fallen' but 'brought low' by the terrible circumstances of their lives: he had outraged many of his circle by insisting on giving gainful employment to several in our family home, which hosted many an ecclesiastical gathering.

My body falling into the rhythm needful for the job, I could let my brain work. It would have been cruel to ask Harriet earlier: it had been brave of her to speak of such matters at all, especially in mixed company. But I believed I must ask her whether any dates attached to the trophies – anything at all that might point to women I could only ever think of as victims. If indeed they had been willing participants, that was one thing; if coercion, even by the fact that one party was powerful, the other entirely powerless, then somehow . . . should recompense be involved? If the result of the union was pregnancy, how might that be dealt with?

Soon I found myself working alongside Silas Kenton. I had enough breath to ask him how his wife and my soon-to-be godson were progressing: he gave as detailed report as I could wish; the gist was that both were doing well, and that my namesake was already sleeping through the night. This seemed to a mere bachelor to be a lowly enough achievement, but it occasioned great pride in his father.

'When will the christening take place?' I asked.

'Soon as we can talk to Rector.'

'You'll let me know the date?'

The question seemed to floor him. 'You wouldn't be coming – not coming to church along of us – would you?'

'Of course, Silas. Godparents make solemn vows on the baby's behalf. I can't not be there. And – if you are to have any celebration with your family and friends afterwards – I will fulfil another duty: I will provide the ale and cider for it. I should imagine Mrs Faulkner will provide some refreshments, too.'

He gave something like a snigger. 'Maybe you could ask her, gaffer?' Somehow the question contrived to nudge me playfully in the ribs.

'If you wish, I will.' I kept my voice as neutral as possible. It was one thing to be the predictable subject of gossip, another to be teased by someone to whom I had to give orders. But perhaps I should simply turn the subject. 'Will you be at cricket practice tonight, Silas? And what about that brother-in-law of yours? Harry?'

'Ah, you won't have heard, maybe. They reckon he broke some bone in his hand. Like a great ham, it came up. Says he can bat with one hand – he always was pig-headed. So he'll be there, but mostly watching, I dare say.'

'I hope the hand heals soon. We can't spare fielders like him. That last catch he took off my bowling was miraculous . . . Any other news I've missed?' I asked idly. 'What the newspapers call hatches, matches and despatches?'

He snorted. 'We're running bets on when Billy Portman's new wife will pop. Supposed to be as pure as the driven snow when they got wed; but she's mighty big for a wench only five months gone.'

Dr Page had joked about brides' fertility being tested before the wedding vows. I risked my own.

'Anyone else, of course it'd be likely!' Silas agreed. 'But he's strict Chapel. Seems he made some sort of promise when he signed the pledge. Anyway, let's hope that all's well that ends well. As for despatches, old man Burton's not long for this life they say. And what was the other one? Matches? Isn't that for you to say? Beg pardon, gaffer, but the whole village knows you're walking out with Mrs Faulkner, and they wish you well, too.'

'I'm glad to hear it. But not Harry, I imagine: he and Mrs Faulkner . . .?' I made a little rocking gesture. 'Or is all that history?'

'You saying he's forgotten about her and Maggie? Because I can tell you straight he hasn't, not ever will. He'd marry her tomorrow, someone else's babe and all, if he could find her.'

My heart leapt. Could that be the solution to all our theorising? 'Everyone knows, I should imagine, that I have done my best to find her. Yes? Well, I know roughly where she might be, and there is money to care for her and her baby. If you think he would like to send her a message, I can't take it myself, because she says she won't see anyone. But I know someone – a good woman – who could.'

He looked me straight in the eye. 'You mean that, don't you, gaffer?'

'Absolutely. I can't guarantee he gets a reply, of course. But I'll ask . . . the good woman . . . to pass it on.'

'And would this "good woman" be Mrs Faulkner?'

'No. She knows as little as I do. But I tell you this, Silas, man to man: if Harry still bears a grudge against her, still threatens her, then I will not help him at all. Not one jot. And before you object, remember that a man who wants to raise a hand against one woman may hit the next – his wife. And for all Harry says, having another man's child foisted on any young man often provokes him to violence against mother or child – am I right?'

'You are indeed, gaffer. Look'ee – could you get a message to her without him knowing? Then if she turns him down flat, he can't blame *anyone*, can he?' Again he looked me in the eye. 'No cause for him to use those fists on anyone then.'

I clapped him on the shoulder. 'I take your point. Thanks, Silas. And remember to let me know when that christening will be.'

He nodded, then looked at me impishly. 'You've not heard what they've been saying in the village then? That Rector's got' – he dropped his voice to a whisper – 'a dose of the clap.' He threw his head back and laughed. 'Not that I believe it, gaffer. That man lie with a woman? Never in a thousand years!'

The cricketers slipped away early from the hay-making; with me at their head, the foreman could hardly object. Since he'd once been a formidable bowler himself, he even took me on one side to give me some tips. Since they included a pint of cider and a pipeful of shag before every game, I didn't think I'd be taking his advice, but was grateful for it anyway.

I was in time to intercept Elias before anyone else spotted him, picking up a ball and leading him away from the others. 'We'll give the impression we're talking about where I want you to stand when I'm bowling – and yes, why couldn't you tell me how to improve? We're a good partnership but could be better.'

'You didn't take me on one side to talk about tactics, did you, Mr Rowsley? You want to know how our investigation is proceeding.'

'Of course.' I tossed the ball from one hand to the other. 'I know there will be things you mustn't tell me, but there may come a time when we need to co-operate in our jobs as well as on the field.'

'There may indeed.' Without the vividly-bearded Sergeant Burrows, Elias seemed much more confident. 'If I was you, I'd spread your fingers a bit wider, like.' He moved my digits. 'See how that feels. Thing is, I can't say her ladyship was much help yesterday. But I thought – though Sergeant Burrows didn't – that she was taken aback, you might say, when we said there was no sign of him at all. And eventually she did condescend to give us

a list of the great houses where he'd been planning to stay. We
have village constables from all over the county checking each
one – remarkable things, these telegraphs, aren't they? Now, if
you straighten that wrist . . . Between ourselves, I reckon he's
gone off with some wench or other.'

'Surely a young man with a title and with his wealth could
have his pick of society ladies without having to do anything
havey-cavey. And breaking up your own vehicle!'

'As to the first, I know ladies are supposed to be the weaker
sex, but I reckon they've got a lot more sense than they're cred-
ited with – can pick a wrong 'un half a mile off. My sister – sorry,
forget I said that.'

I held up the ball a tad awkwardly. 'Your sister was – shall I
say propositioned – by him?'

'Yes. And reminded him her sweetheart was a butcher by
profession, with a sideline in beating the boxers at country fairs.'
He smiled grimly. 'But I guess – no, I really must not tell 'ee
more, though I will say that with your hand like that and your
fingers like that you might be a yard quicker.'

'We'd best go and see,' I said, patting him on the shoulder.
'Thank you.'

It took four or five attempts to get used to my new action,
but after that I was certainly not so much quicker as more
accurate.

Eventually the captain called time. 'But only if you can show
me how well you can catch, lads.'

Harry should have been in his element, of course, as if he had
glue on his fingers. I expected him to lurk, watching sullenly as
the others proved how inept they could be. Instead to my amazement he joined in, plucking balls out of the air as if they were
ripe plums, only using his left hand. As the team headed in the
direction of the Royal Oak I fell into step with him, commiser-
ating with him but remarking on his amazing talent.

''Tain't nothing but keeping your eyes on the ball, gaffer. You
don't do so bad yourself, do you?'

I managed a laugh. I suspected we'd never like each other,
even if he knew I was about to try to do him a favour, but I
wanted peace amongst the estate workers and above all I wanted
a safe future for Harriet.

'I saw you talking to Elias,' he said, a touch truculently. But then, I reminded myself, he always spoke as if he was angry.

'You did indeed. He was trying to adjust my grip on the ball.' One hand over the other, I demonstrated. 'It seemed to work. And your fielding's as brilliant as ever. If only we could persuade a few more lads to come along on evenings like this – to learn the ropes and take over as older men drop out.' We continued in silence for a few yards. 'Would you tell me something? Between ourselves? Sometime ago you said that the House wasn't a safe place – for young women? Was this because you knew something or just suspected it?'

'What is it to you? Going to have me sacked for slandering them, are you?'

'Not at all. I'm genuinely interested.'

'So you didn't sack young Hortense and send her off with a flea in her ear?'

'Why on earth would you think that?'

'Stands to reason.'

'Come off it.' We were standing facing each other. 'Why on earth would I want to sack a woman I never employed? Hortense was her ladyship's maid, not a housemaid. And I have nothing to do with the hiring or firing of anyone in the House, as I suspect you know full well. Nor, directly, can I dismiss the outdoor staff, before you accuse me of that. Now, a straight answer, if you please. Why was the House not safe?'

'Ask Luke Hargreaves.'

'He is travelling with his lordship so I can't. I'm asking you. Very well, I'll ask you another question: are you telling me that it was Hargreaves who made the House a dangerous place for women or that he knows who did?'

He balled his fists and squared his jaw. I braced myself. Finally he dropped his eyes. 'I'm not supposed to talk. Not to anyone, though it comes hard. I just can't put folk in harm's way, can I? So if it's all the same to you I'll just button my lip.' He looked half the man he was before.

I dropped my voice. 'You are telling me it will put people's lives at risk if you betray information? Very well, I think that has answered my question without, I swear, endangering you. If you should change your mind, you know where to find me.

Or you might get your sister to pass on a name. That's all I ask. A name. Because I shall believe you and no one will have an inkling who gave me that name. No one. Ever. Now, let us speak no more of this. We are just two weary men needing our ale.'

I paid for the first round, as was proper, and then drifted to the back of the group as they drank. What I wanted was a word with Marty – and it seemed as if he wanted one with me. While my teammates chattered amongst themselves, he drew me into his private parlour. After enquiries about my health and, with a twinkle in his eye, that of Mrs Faulkner, he gestured me to a seat. He sat opposite me.

'I've just had a letter from my old friend Ianto,' he said.

'From your face it's not good news.'

'I don't think it is. But he assures me there's no immediate cause for concern. He tells me that little Maggie is ill – the vile town air, according to her aunt. So only the aunt turns up to the manse for the money. In effect, he's asking our opinion – yours, really – about whether he should keep paying her.'

'What is your instinct?' I asked, suspicion flooding my veins.

'Same as yours, to judge by your face. No Maggie, no money. But what if she is ill, genuinely ill?'

'I'd say there is no reason why Mrs Davies, who struck me as a most redoubtable woman, shouldn't visit her. It's what vicars' wives, parsons' wives, do, and God bless them for it.'

'My own sentiments entirely. I'll write back tomorrow. But I'm going to call time, now, Matthew: the hay-making and the cricket seem to have produced a thirst in some of those lads that I'd rather not have them slake here.'

XX

Nurse tells me that she and Mrs Baird are looking for another situation for me: I will not have to wait till the next mop fair to look for one.

'It's just not safe for her here,' Nurse says, as if I can't hear. 'And after . . . all this . . . I can't see her ever getting married, can you? What about that place where your sister works? Are they kind to children there?'

Mrs Baird says, 'I have another idea. But I won't say anything yet in case it raises her hopes.'

TWENTY-ONE

hardly expected to see my friends so late, but, taking my summer suit, I headed to the House in hopes. As before I found a hip bath awaiting me, and, though supper was obviously over, Tim appeared with a covered tray as soon as I entered the Room. I was to have a cold collation while the others took their dessert. Samuel Bowman was just returning from serving her ladyship hers.

Between mouthfuls of one of Beatrice's wonderful pies and a miniature salmagundi, I recounted the various conversations I had had, trying to edit out any references to the relationship between Harriet and me, as perceived by the estate workers and villagers.

Beatrice picked up on the element of fear I mentioned. '"Fear of someone with power" were the words you used at luncheon. That must point the finger at his lordship – or, given her behaviour, at her ladyship.'

Samuel in particular looked outraged. 'Do you realize what you are saying?'

But Beatrice continued quietly, 'I think we've all realized that this might be a possibility. But you mentioned Luke, too – and we all know he has a hasty temper. Could he be . . . no, surely his lordship would not protect him.'

'I worry about this speculation,' Harriet said. 'Surely we should wait to hear what Elias can tell us as he and the sergeant pursue their enquiries.' She looked around the table with a pleasing authority. 'Now, I am troubled by the news from Wolverhampton, and I have a proposition on which I would welcome your views. I can understand that Maggie does not want to be seen by Matthew or by Mr Davies. But I wonder if a visit from a woman would create the same sense of shame – from Mrs Davies, of course, and from Beatrice or me.'

'I would be happy to go, Harriet, but as a housemaid she answered to you.'

'Neither lady can go unaccompanied, of course,' Samuel said. 'And I am not sure that the landlord of the Royal Oak would be the right sort of chaperone.'

I could have shaken his hand there and then. 'Marty is one of the finest men I've ever met, in his own quiet way. But if it would make you more comfortable, Harriet, of course I would be more than happy to offer my services – and if you would prefer Marty's too I'm sure he would oblige.'

She nodded. 'What do you think, Samuel? Beatrice?'

Beatrice simply offered an impish smile. Samuel spread his hands. 'Sadly, for the sake of utmost propriety, I do believe Mr Baines ought to be one of the party.' As if aware he was casting a shadow over the company, he added, 'And did you learn anything else, Matthew?'

'Two things. That Mr Pounceman cancelled our meeting—'

'So would I, were I suffering from his condition,' Samuel exclaimed. He dropped his voice confidentially; the effect was to make him sound quite ghoulish. 'It is hardly any trouble in the young but in an adult male both painful and, I understand, potentially serious. He has' – he paused for effect – 'he has the mumps.'

Did he mean to sound so comic? I certainly thought he was taken aback by the gleeful laughter that greeted the revelation – but then he joined in with a will, even providing his immaculate pocket handkerchief for Beatrice to mop her tears.

'Poor man: I must try to remember him in my prayers,' Harriet said, though with no marked degree of sincerity. 'Very well, Matthew, what was the second thing you learned – though I am not at all sure that the first counts. It was, after all, Samuel who provided the important information.'

'True. Now, would one of you be kind enough to pass me that peach? This is better demonstrated than explained.' I took the fruit, placing it with my fingers spread where Elias had suggested.

Unsurprisingly my friends looked bemused.

Harriet, however, lit up with laughter. 'Of course. But you may need to adjust the angle of your thumb. Oh,' she said, 'if only we could all go outside – then we'd see if you've mastered it!' What was wrong? She had clapped her hands to her mouth as if trying to reclaim the words.

She had almost given away one of her cherished secrets. She had shared it with me once, and I glowed to realize how privileged I was. As such, it was my duty to rescue her. If only I knew how. 'I have been boasting to Harriet of my bowling skills,' I began, not inaccurately. 'I showed her how I held the ball – but Elias, now in his role of wicketkeeper, of course, thinks I can improve the flight. But I fear the flight of a peach would not be very straight, and when it bounced it would spoil a lovely summer treat. I once worked on an estate where the maser grudged every penny he had to spend on his land and even on his succession houses. Yet he constantly complained when his neighbours had earlier fruit or vegetables than he. And his pineapple pits were a disgrace.'

'Our masters are not always wise,' Samuel said, in view of our earlier conversation rather stating the obvious. But I was grateful as he embarked on a long anecdote involving an earl, no less, who used to instruct his butler to water the wine. The thought of wine sent him to the sideboard, where he had put a lovely dessert wine we could not resist.

The following morning found me bright and early at the Royal Oak, where Marty was supervising his outdoor lad swilling down the yard. When it was clean enough to satisfy him, he sent the boy, aged about ten, on his way.

Once his back was turned, Marty shook his head. 'If only he knew his letters, Matthew. Anything I ask he can do, except he gets bored because he's so quick to master it.'

'We need a village school,' I said firmly. 'So does every village. Meanwhile, why don't you teach him?'

'Patience – or rather lack of patience.'

'Very well, a school it must be! But it won't happen tomorrow, sadly. Now, Marty, I wonder if I might pick your brain about another youngster – little Maggie. Mrs Faulkner suggests that she and Mrs Davies should go together to speak to Mrs Batham and demand to see the child. I cannot imagine Mrs Batham rebuffing the two of them, especially as Mrs Faulkner was almost *in loco parentis* to Maggie. If you have no objection to the notion, and haven't yet written to Ianto, might you suggest it?'

He nodded slowly. 'But how would the good lady get to Wolverhampton?'

'She'd need an escort, of course – and for various reasons it would be good if you were one of them and I the other.'

'What's her ladyship say about it? Your walking out together, man, not this journey.'

'We have not informed her yet. But logically she should have no objection. I could name any number of butlers and house-keepers who are married yet continue with their employment—'

'Married! It's gone that far?'

I shook my head. 'By no means. But she is the first woman I have ever met who inspires such sentiments and . . .' I broke off, ashamed by my hackneyed words.

He held up his hand. 'Matthew, my friend, if she is the one, don't delay, I beg you. I am glad that I had at least a few years with my beloved . . .' He swallowed. 'I promise I will say nothing, and, if you wish, I will pooh-pooh any rumours, though they're so rife no one will believe me.' He looked at me sideways. 'If an engagement is in the air, then I wonder if it might be politic to speak to her ladyship. Upfront and honest, if you see what I mean. I know it's risky, but if she just happened to find out . . .? Anyway, of course I will suggest to Ianto the possibility of a little outing for the three of us. Especially if we could improve it by having lunch at that hotel near the railway.'

'You don't think Mrs Davies would be offended?'

'It's a temperance hotel, and we'd invite her husband too. I'm sure Ianto would agree to a change from her cooking. Everyone deserves a bit of a treat, if they can get it.'

'They do. It will be my treat and no arguments, Marty. As for your advice about Mrs Faulkner and me – you're sure it's not a bit premature?'

'Is it? Only you two can say that.'

Why had I never grasped until now that, should she deign to, her ladyship could watch what was going on in the grounds of her son's estate? It wasn't just the lake that she could see. A bizarre desire to wave at the blinds of her boudoir shook me. They were still closed, of course, even though the morning sun was shining warmly and it was a treat to be out in it.

Clearly I needed a very private conversation with Harriet – but one I must not rush. I recalled her shock when I first kissed her – not a physical one, so much as a profound fear of . . . something. Until I knew what that something was, I did not want to push her into anything for fear of losing her altogether. For that reason I must not seek her out, not offer any more pressing attentions than I had so far – all of which seemed to be happily received, I had to admit. Apart from that first, impulsive denial. Instead I knocked on Samuel's pantry door, where, using a magnifying glass, he was engaged in checking the state of the huge silver epergne which usually dominated the state dining room.

'It takes three footmen to carry this safely,' he said. 'But three is an awkward number. I'm always afraid I shall see a dent on it when it comes in here for cleaning.'

I scratched my head. 'George is very busy with work on the roof just now,' I said. 'But surely when there's a wet day he could make a little trolley for that.'

'I believe you're right!' He gestured various dimensions. 'Yes! You could let down one side to ease the epergne in place, then fasten it up . . . What a good idea, Matthew. But that wasn't what brought you here, not at this hour of the day.'

'In fact it was an entirely private matter, one that I hardly like to broach. Samuel, some time ago you mentioned your interest in Beatrice. It's clear that you take as much pleasure in each other's company as Harriet and I do in ours. The whole village is apparently expecting to hear our banns read any Sunday now; I dare say they gossip just as much about you two. The problem is, what if this comes to her ladyship's ears? You know her so much better than anyone else in the House. Knowing how loyal you are to her, to the whole family, I understand that you might not want to answer this question, but I must ask anyway: how would she respond – in either case?'

Sighing deeply, he put the magnifying glass back in its velvet lined box before he answered. 'I do not care to speculate. Even ten years ago, there was always courtesy in her treatment of me. Offhand, dismissive – because I am, when all is said and done, a servant. But even at her coldest, she maintained her dignity. Since the death of his lordship's father . . .' He broke off, shaking his head – in a way the Bard described, more in sorrow than in anger. 'In answer to your question, I might escape the worst of her temper, because there is, of course, almost a tradition of the family butler marrying the cook or the housekeeper. But I have been in her service for enough years to point out, with some humility, that she would not like the effect on her comfort, on the smooth running of the entire house, if I left, taking my bride with me.'

'I, on the other hand, am a newcomer with whom she has already crossed swords. Sadly for her, she can't dismiss me: only his lordship can do that. But she could get rid of Harriet, couldn't she? Which would thrust her into a . . . it might mean she feels obliged to enter a marriage she does not want.'

'My friend,' he said, putting his hand on my shoulder, 'there is no doubt in my mind that she loves you. But I can understand that you would like the relationship entered into absolutely freely. And there is something in her past – no, I've no idea what it is . . . She won't even tell Beatrice.'

I nodded slowly. Before I could speak, the clock, a particularly intrusive one, struck the half hour. 'Heavens! I shall be late at my desk.'

'Don't worry: if anyone asked I should say you were advising me about the epergne.'

XXI

Nurse has brought down a rush basket, which she puts on the table.

'Just right,' Mrs Baird says. 'Not that the poor mite has much to put in it.'

They exchange a smile.

'Let's see. There's her shifts; stays; drawers; stockings; indoor boots; a shawl.' But now Nurse is smiling at me. 'It gets very quiet in the nursery sometimes, and it's nice to have something for my hands to do. Here: I know you're growing like a young plant, but I've made sure there's a good deep hem on these so you can let them down.' She holds up two of the prettiest print dresses I've ever seen.

'And you'll need some ribbons to go with them.' Mrs Baird produces a tissue-wrapped packet. 'I saw how you loved those blue ones and these are the nearest I could get.'

There are blue ribbons on the bonnet she holds up; they match the blue of the cloak she carries over her arm. 'Come on: put them on. We don't want to keep Carter Joe waiting, do we?' She ties the ribbons under my chin.

'But the most important thing is this,' Nurse says, holding out another package. 'No, open it when you get there, not a minute before. And no tears, Missy – you're going on an adventure, that's what.' She hugs me to her, as tight as she can. I cling to her. She is safe and I love her. I feel her sobs match mine.

Mrs Baird eases us apart. Her embrace is shorter, but just as kind. She kisses my forehead. 'Off you go. Do us credit.'

Nurse says, 'And do yourself justice, my love.'

All of us are in tears, but Carter Joe is lifting up my basket and now he's lifting me.

TWENTY-TWO

M ost of my married contemporaries had known the women who were now their wives for a year or more before they became engaged. Then there was an equally long period before the marriage took place: compared with my relationship with Harriet they were love affairs in slow motion. There were many other differences: the men were young enough to have to secure their future careers before committing themselves to maintaining a wife and family. None of them, to my knowledge, had married a woman with a career of her own, even though it paid pitifully little and involved long hours and very little free time, with the notion of taking a holiday while her employer was in residence anathema – especially to the employer. Nor had their future wife carried the secrets of a past she was not yet ready to share – possibly could never share. And much as I hated myself for it, I wanted there to be complete openness between us on all things, great and small.

And then I had something else to hate: those words echoed the poem quoted by Mr Pounceman, justifying the great divide between people like my employer and the Mrs Billingses of this world, and for the rest of the day the banal little rhyme ran round and round my head, no matter how I tried to replace it with something else. It bounced through the credit and the debit columns of the accounts; it scurried along the lines of final demands and the minutes of meetings. It gnawed at the problem of my missing employer and his valet. Finally, towards evening, it drove me out of my office towards the home farm, where perhaps communing with a pig might finally dispatch it.

Hargreaves was involved in a serious argument with one of the labourers, not, I fancy, staged for my benefit, though I had known other occasions when they were. Until it was over I confined myself to discussing life, perhaps one-sidedly, with a sow suckling no fewer than ten piglets. Ten! The number seemed overwhelming. Yet how many human families were as big or even bigger: indeed, many of my uxorious friends liked to describe themselves as polyphiloprogenitive, as if begetting a huge brood was to be admired, possibly as much as having an erudite vocabulary. Having seen the exhausted state of their constantly pregnant wives I was less sure; emphatically I wished to save Harriet from such a life. And then I drew up short. This was something we must discuss; I did not even know her exact age yet, much less whether she was able to bear children any longer. If she was already past the age, did I care? My immediate response was that I wanted to share my life with her, not any putative heir. But could I look her in the eye and swear that was the case if she questioned me?

'Looks good, don't she?'

'Goodness, Alf, I nearly jumped out of my skin! Is everything all right?' I nodded over my shoulder at the man slouching away.

'It is and it isn't – which is the way of the world, I suppose. He's been helping himself to pigswill once too often. Once in a while you turn a blind eye, but sometimes you have to have a bit of a word. The lads – they know where they stand. But Wilf, he gave me a bit of back-chat I didn't like and I told him so. Calling my Luke a murderer indeed!'

'Heavens! That's dreadful! Will you let him keep his job?'

He sucked a piece of straw. 'Thing is, gaffer, he's got a new baby, well, a few months old now. A bit sickly, it is. And if I sack him, well, it's not just him as'll suffer, is it – it's not cricket, you might say. Same as if I stop his wages. Truth is I don't know what to do. So I just gave him a mouthful back, and I can't say I'm proud of myself.'

I scratched the sow, only to have her rear up, squealing. I backed away sharply.

'Have to be careful, gaffer, when they're with their litter. I've seen them knock down grown men. I even heard tell of one tearing a man's leg off. Half-eaten he was when they got to him. If they'd left it any longer I reckon there'd have been nothing left of him.'

'A pig eat a whole man? Never!'

'Maybe not all at once. I reckon they could drag what they couldn't manage into their shelter – I'd not want to be the one to go and look – and finish the rest as and when.'

We watched her in silence. Finally I felt able to ask, 'Why on earth should Wilf make such a terrible accusation against Luke?'

'Well, I've never denied the lad's got a temper. But he knows he has to watch himself – and Mr Bowman himself told me the lad was a credit to me.'

'He is indeed,' I agreed heartily. I added, from experience, 'But every man has a breaking point, and his lordship might not be the easiest master. Has he ever done anything that might infuriate Luke beyond endurance?'

'Such as what?'

'Young men often fight over a young woman, for instance. Did Luke have a sweetheart?'

Did Alf's reply come too quickly? Too huffily? 'Not that I know to. You'd know more than me, working in the House.'

I nodded. 'Unless they both met someone on this tour of theirs . . .'

'Some servant wench his lordship had a taste for, you mean. No, I reckon Luke'd know when to steer clear. He wants to get on in life, gaffer, even if that means swallowing his pride. No, someone must have harmed them both, stands to reason, or surely they'd both be home by now. Unless his lordship's done a bunk, of course, which I can't see he'd have reason to, or maybe been kidnapped and any day someone'll come asking for a whatever -you-call-it.'

'Ransom,' I said automatically. 'Alf, I know you don't know your letters as well as you'd like. Could it be you've had a letter from Luke you can't quite read? You know I'd always be happy to read it to you, and that the contents would be quite private between us.'

'Not a word, as God's my witness. It's the business of this smashed-up carriage of his that worries me, gaffer. The horses – well, a team of gypsies could make them vanish into thin air in two shakes of a bee's ankle, and they'd turn up at a horse fair a different colour and no questions asked or answered. The luggage: a nice lot of things to clothe a poor family there. The cases or valises, whatever Elias called them, they'd be tucked away at a pawnbroker's or even a fence's before you could say knife.'

'Leaving two strong fit young men dead?' I wrinkled my nose as I shook my head. 'What does Elias think of your theory?'

'He huffs and he puffs and won't say anything – and I daresay he's right: he's got to do his job the best he can. But I don't think all those fancy telegraphs he's been sending have got the answers he wants yet. I reckon he and his gaffer will be back soon, wanting to talk to her ladyship some more. When they do, ask about Luke, will you? As a favour to me? A man wants to know if his son's in trouble. Or dead.'

'I give you my word. If you give me your word you'll pass on any letter he should send you.'

We shook hands on the deal. He looked at me sideways. 'Of course, 'twas your Mrs Faulkner who got him to learn his letters and read like a gentleman.'

'Alf, you must not call her "my" Mrs Faulkner. I admire her greatly, but it's . . . everything is at a delicate stage, as you must recall from your courtship.'

He snorted. 'Well, so it ought to have been. But we both had too much cider at the Harvest Home and after that there wasn't much courtship as a bit of explaining to do. And her dad a sidesman at church, too . . . I've got no regrets, mind, never have had. Never so much as looked at another woman since. And if you don't think your eyes will ever wander, then what are you waiting for?'

Now Alf's question replaced the hymn as the words echoing round my head. I suppose I was waiting for a chance to talk to her alone and uninterrupted. As it was, the after-supper discussion circled predictably round the missing lord and the all-too-present trophies, all of which remained in the locked room. The question, increasingly urgent, was what we should do with them.

Samuel made a credible suggestion about the specimen box of hair. 'Provided you make a signed affidavit, Harriet, as to where you found it and when, I propose we move it to the safe in my pantry. Perhaps you, Matthew, would accompany me. I should imagine we might need something to carry it in? Do we have any suggestions?'

'Oh, I'll bundle it in with the sheets,' Harriet said. 'And I'll lock those in the lean-to outside the laundry.'

'Not now,' Beatrice said. 'Not with her ladyship in the dining room tonight.' She looked meaningfully at the clock.

Suppressing what I'm sure was a genteel oath, Samuel excused himself and left.

'I'll do it during breakfast tomorrow, when we know all the servants are together. We can count heads. If anyone is missing, I will have to abandon the project, however. But even when we have the . . . the material . . . locked up safely, what on earth do we do with it?'

'Pass it on to the police, I suppose,' I said naively.

'To Elias!'

'Ah. Indeed. And diligent though Sergeant Burrows appears to be, I'm not sure he would know what to do with it either. Or even, come to think of it, with the information that we have something that . . . It clearly incriminates someone, and to my mind that can only be his lordship.'

'And it would give one of us – someone from the House or the estate – a motive for killing him. Someone whose sweetheart had been seduced, or, worse still, taken by force,' Beatrice said.

All the blood seemed to drain from Harriet's face. Before I knew it, I was pressing her head between her knees, calling to Beatrice for smelling salts. She was back in a trice.

'Now, you take yourself off, Matthew. A whiff of this and a drop of brandy and she'll be as right as ninepence, I promise you.' The expression on her face did not match the confidence of her words, however.

For answer, I gathered her up in my arms. 'Open the door to her chamber and I'll lay her on the bed,' I said, suiting the deed to my words. I stroked back her hair, gently kissing her forehead as I left her to Beatrice's care. 'I'll be in my office or with Samuel waiting for news of how she does.' Certainly I would not leave the building till I knew she had recovered.

I encountered Samuel on his way back from serving her ladyship. Seeing my face he ushered me straight into his sitting room, and had a decanter and tumbler in his hand. Yes, a drink was what I wanted more than anything else. No. I put the glass down untouched. What if I had to ride for Dr Page?

As if I would ever have to ride on such an errand! A finger on the staff bell would bring someone running more quickly than I could scribble an explanatory note.

'Speak to me, man. Has she turned you down?'

'She is . . . she is unwell, that's all. Faint. Beatrice is with her.'

He patted my shoulder as if he was my uncle. 'No one better. I'm sure she'll be well in a trice. Drat! Why is her ladyship ringing for me at this hour?' He straightened his tie, checked his hair in the mirror, and set off, wiping the scowl from his face as he opened the door. I followed on his heels. 'I'll be in my office,' I told him, 'lest I drink all that brandy.'

Fifteen minutes of prayer did very little to calm me, I am ashamed to confess. My father would have reassured me that even without my incoherent pleas the Almighty would know what I wanted, the simple news of Harriet's return to good health. But I also wanted something more subtle, guidance on what to do once she was better; I could not bear to contemplate the possibility that she might not recover. At last I felt a little stronger, and I was actually seated with some appearance of calm when Beatrice tapped at my door and entered. She shut the door carefully behind her.

'She is doing well,' she said immediately. 'I have tucked her into bed and pressed some brandy on her. She will be asleep soon. I would tell you not to worry only I expect you would laugh in my face if I offered such impossible advice.'

'Might I see her?'

She looked at me with more compassion than I liked. 'I think she would prefer you not to.' She turned to the door.

'Beatrice! This thing in her past that so worries her – I can scarcely frame what I fear it must be. But she fainted tonight when we were talking about seduction and rape. As if she could scarcely bear to hear the words. Did something terrible happen to her when she was a young woman?'

To my surprise she came and sat opposite me. 'If it did, and I'm not saying it did, mind, what would people think of her? Think of the language Mr Pounceman used about little Maggie! However pure and blameless she's been since . . . whatever it was . . . happened, folk think that the woman is always the one that has brought the man low.' She snorted. 'All the time I have known Harriet, she has never looked at another man. Not the way she looks at you. But . . . Matthew, I don't think she'll have you, not in the end. And – no, I shouldn't say, but I'm going to, I am . . . I'm really worried she'll do something amiss.'

'To harm herself? My God! Beatrice, it sounds as if she'd prefer my room to my company, as the saying goes. Yes? So I'm going to do something – tell anyone who asks I've been called away on family business. Could you spare a couple of maids of all work, without Harriet knowing, of course, to clean and tidy my house? I hope to be having visitors before the week is out. I shall leave very early tomorrow, but I should be back by supper-time. If not, I want you to give her a note for me. I'll write it before I leave and then . . . shall I slide it under your door?'

'And give rise to even more gossip? Indeed you will not. Write it now, man, with all the feeling still bubbling away, instead of making a meal of it, as if you were writing a great novel.' She folded her arms and leant back in the chair.

I did as I was told.

My dearest Harriet

My heart bled to see you so unwell. I wish I could talk to you but Beatrice fears you are not yet ready for visitors. I am called away on very urgent business, but hope and pray you will be able to speak to me when I return.

Believe me when I tell you that I love you with all my heart and will do so till my dying day.

Your devoted

Matthew

To my amazement Beatrice opened the note and read it. 'Good lad,' she said, giving me a hug, as if she was my sister. 'Godspeed, Matthew, whatever your business tomorrow.'

XXII

Carter Joe drives away. He was kind, and talked to me about his pretty granddaughter.

I must not cry, must I?

Carter Joe left me by the front door, with its grand steps, and I am afraid I must walk up them and lift that huge brass knocker. But a girl not much older than me comes crunching across the gravel, and summons me with a wave of her arm. I am to follow her.

The kitchen is smaller than Cook's – but this is Cook, too, a tiny woman with a face all wrinkled up like an apple saved till spring. She takes my face between her hands and kisses me on the forehead. She calls: a tall thin lady appears.

This must be her ladyship. I curtsy.

The thin lady laughs. 'I am Mrs Cox, the housekeeper, child. Ooh, your poor hands are so cold. Come to the fire and Cook will find you some hot milk.' She wants me to sit down! 'And you will need a box for those treasures.' She points to the package. 'What's inside?'

I kept it clasped to my chest the whole journey. I can hardly uncurl my hands. At last I can take off the string and the brown paper. There are four things, more than I have ever had in my life. I show her: a Bible; a Prayer Book; a book with marbled covers and nothing inside; a bundle of pencils, tied with more string.

She nods solemnly, but her eyes are still kind. 'Put everything in your rush basket so you can carry it upstairs to your room.' My room? My own room. But I have learned not to hope. 'But hot milk first. And yes, one of Cook's special cakes. Now, I have promised Mrs Baird I will teach you everything I know about housekeeping,' she says. 'This is not as large an establishment as the one you are used to, but the same principles apply whatever the house.'

TWENTY-THREE

I embarked on my rail journey back from Lichfield almost fully satisfied with what I had achieved – though the visit I had sought would not happen immediately, it was promised. However, the evening newspaper that I bought was full of an account of a grievous murder. A young man had been slain out of hand by a woman – stabbed over twenty times as he lay with her. She was now rightly on trial. It seemed the whole train was tutting in disgust. I was myself. I read further. This vile, foul harlot's victim, an Oxford student, had been walking with a group of fellow-undergraduates who had encouraged him to befriend her. They had adjourned to a back alley, and intercourse had taken place. When it was over, she had produced a knife from her pocket and attacked him, with fatal results. What a foul crime. But I had missed one salient detail, had I not? The fallen woman – was a girl of eleven. She swore she had never been with a man before. Prosecuting counsel mocked the notion, as if it was normal for a child of that age to make a living from prostitution. The editorial stigmatized her as a vile Jezebel – yes, Mr Pounceman's language.

All I could imagine was a little girl, raped for a rich young man's pleasure, retaliating in the only way she knew. And almost certainly, without the very best of defence lawyers, she would hang.

I had walked to the estate station for the early train, and now strode back to my house, in such a fury that I noticed nothing of my surroundings. I believe I even forgot about Harriet. Still wearing my hat, I believe, I wrote an urgent letter to my cousin, the lawyer with the eye for a good contract: he must know criminal lawyers. Could he mobilize help for the child on trial? I would pay for anything necessary. Will stared at the envelope, dumbfounded by my insistence that it must reach the post tonight: he must ride into the village if necessary. The last collection was at nine o'clock.

Still flooded with energy, what might I do now? All I wanted
to do was rush to the House and beg to see Harriet, but I had to
accept the counsel Beatrice had left me in a short – and not
well-spelt – note: Harriet was much better, but had agreed to
spend another day in bed. It would be best to partake in my own
house of a meal Beatrice had sent there. If Harriet asked, Beatrice
would say my business had no doubt detained me.

I hoped her advice was good. What if she were somehow
trying to split us apart? I had imagined once that she was developing a *tendresse* for me.

Heavens! I was thinking like a lovelorn youth, an arrogant one
to boot. I burned with shame for even thinking like a foolish cad.
I only had to look around my house. Beatrice had been as good
as her word: whoever she had sent had made the whole place
gleam, from the back kitchen to the top corridor no one ever
used. Clean linen graced all the beds, with fresh-cut lavender
hung in bunches from the curtains and laid in pretty sprays on
all the pillows. The windows, newly-cleaned, had been left ajar:
since clouds were building, hinting at rain, I closed most of them,
but spent some time in my own bedchamber, gazing out on the
scene before me, elbows resting on the window sill, and my head
in my hands.

My supper was laid on a table in the morning room. I lit the
lamps, forgetting to draw the curtains. Soon a big moth – when
I was a child my nurse had called it a bob-howler and I couldn't
recall ever having learnt the proper name – tried to immolate
itself in the flame. I caught it, clasping it loosely in my cupped
hands, and released it, closing the window firmly behind it and
then drawing the curtains lest it start bringing reinforcements to
try again.

It did not take me long to finish my supper; I could not recall
afterwards what I had eaten. I found it impossible to concentrate
on reading the latest novel by George Eliot – I was sure on
another occasion I would be entranced by it, but not tonight.
Would I be able to discuss it one day with Harriet? It was she
who had recommended it after all.

It was much too early to retire for the night.

After a while staring at nothing, I headed for my study,
reached for a sheaf of paper, and sharpened some pencils.

There must be some way of collating the random pieces of information we had gathered and making coherent sense. But if there was, I could not find it, and retired to bed, seeking consolation, as my parents would have suggested, in the Bible and in prayer.

My heart was still heavy the following morning after an uneasy night's sleep. How had Harriet fared? Probably worse than I. And I was not there to comfort her – had no right to be. But handwringing would get me nowhere. I had work to do and responsibilities to assume.

The overnight rain having cleared, I walked up to the House, knowing that even if my appeal to my cousin would not affect the Oxford child's fate I had done something. Then I forced myself to start my working day, by simply looking around me. Yes, I was pleased with what I saw of the estate. The lake was almost ready for his lordship's pleasure boats to row on – all the foul silt had now been tipped out of sight and, more important, out of smell. Where the grass had been damaged by the carts transporting the muck, it was now growing nicely again, with only the deeper ruts still showing. The storm-damaged trees were being cut back. Scaffolding on the roof showed that progress was being made there. Somewhere on the far edge of the estate someone was burning rubbish. Gardeners were trimming the edges of the beds; one was obviously gathering flowers for the House. Two trugs were already overburdened. Traditionally the lady of the house would arrange them; would her ladyship bestir herself? If she declined, would Harriet be well enough to add them to her other duties?

As I got within sight of the House a lad hurtled towards me, so out of breath from his exertion that it was a full minute before he could gabble words about gentlemen one of whom wasn't a gentleman but he shouldn't say that . . . Cut to its core, the message was that Sergeant Burrows and Elias were waiting for me in the entrance hall. At least they would be thoroughly intimidated by the time Thatcher escorted them to my office.

I took care to check my attire before dispatching Thatcher. Then I sent him off to fetch us tea. I was tempted to check that he had closed the door firmly but told myself that the time to

ensure privacy was when I suspected that things other than polite
preliminaries were being said.

At last, tea cups in their hands, the officers leant forward as
if they too wanted to ensure confidentiality.

'It's about her ladyship, Mr Rowsley,' Sergeant Burrows said
in a stage whisper.

I raised a hand, and, treading quietly, opened the study door.
'Thatcher, when I want you I will ring for you. There is no need
for you to wait there.'

His back, as he imitated Samuel's stately gait down the corridor,
told me he was much offended.

I returned to the far side of my desk, a move which seemed
to subdue my visitors, an effect which deepened as I put paper
and pencil before me. 'Her ladyship,' I prompted.

'Is she . . . all there?' Burrows touched his forehead.

'You would have to ask her medical man, Dr Page,' I said. 'I
am so little acquainted with her ladyship I cannot offer an opinion
either way.'

'And where would we find this Dr Page?'

'I'm sure Elias can help. It's a pleasant stroll on a day like
this. He's had to treat a cricket injury or two, hasn't he, Elias?'

'Put my shoulder back in after I dislocated it,' he said.

Burrows looked at me sharply. 'You mix with the villagers?'

'I am proud to call some of them teammates, and one or two
my friends.'

'What about your employees, here on the estate: how well
would you say you know them?'

I should have seen this coming. 'Some very well. Others less
so.'

'Would you know any of them well enough to think they might
have murdered his lordship?'

'What?' I was on my feet. 'He is dead and you have not yet
told me?'

'I didn't say he was, and I can't say he isn't. There's still no
sign of him, Mr Rowsley. And I can tell you, in confidence, that
having left Nutsall Place he did not arrive at Kemberly House,
where Lord Palfrey was expecting him.'

'Neither is very close to where his vehicle was found,' Elias
pointed out.

'But then, if one were minded,' I mused, 'one might kill – or kidnap! – his lordship and drive off in the vehicle before disposing of it. Kill or kidnap Luke too, of course.'

Burrows raised a finger. 'Assuming Luke – that would be Luke Hargreaves? – assuming he wasn't the killer or kidnapper.'

Considering that I had been floating the possibility only the previous day, I believe I simulated loyal anger quite well. 'Luke? A good employee, with a very bright future.' And a father with a prize sow capable of killing and eating a man. 'And how would he dispose of not just his employer but a quantity of luggage, too?' The irony of this conversation was not lost on me. I hoped Alf would not have to endure a similar one. 'Surely this argues . . .' I nearly said, *collusion.* After what dear Harriet had found, it might well be that others from the estate were involved. I thought of the neat beanrows flourishing in cottage gardens – a man's body would fit neatly under the canes. Of the huge piles of sludge that might cover even four fine horses. 'Surely this argues that his lordship and his valet were attacked by a gang – of horse thieves, perhaps, since his lordship always bought the very best team. Have the horses been traced?'

'The horses – well, I suppose a gang of gypsies could make them vanish into thin air. Just like that!' he snapped his fingers.

'Exactly. And they'd turn up at a horse fair a different colour and no questions asked or answered.' Should I float the idea of fences and valises? On the whole I thought not. But there were other things that in all conscience they ought to know – the trophies. Since Harriet was unwell, they were presumably exactly where she'd left them. Presumably. But what if, having made an undertaking, she insisted on keeping her word, illness or no? I must simply keep quiet until I had spoken to her, even if technically I was concealing evidence. Possible evidence. I would simply have to speak to her.

The conversation continued for several more minutes; it became harder and harder to conceal my impatience. But I must smile and smile, even if I feared I was being a villain. But lie I could not, not when Burrows said, 'You are clearly a model employee, Mr Rowsley. Everywhere I look I see evidence of your diligence. Surely you must have had many meetings with his lordship – if any man could make a judgement of his character, you could.'

'Between these four walls? How would any young man be who had been indulged from birth and suddenly found himself in possession of a great deal of money react? In my time I have worked for landowners with a profound sense of responsibility, both for their families and for all those in their spheres, servants, tenants, local villagers. I found none of this in his lordship. Other people – like Elias here – have been acquainted with him longer than I have: you should seek their opinions too.'

'Please do not tell me what I should and should not do, Mr Rowsley. Why are you laughing, may I ask?'

'Because that was what his lordship said to me, if only in as many words. You are doing your job, sergeant; he never had a job to do, and like many others is the worse for it. He was a spendthrift, as we know. Maybe he had gambling debts and it was better for him to disappear.' I spread my hands. 'Or, since he liked the company of ladies, perhaps he annoyed one husband too many. I just wish I knew, Burrows – there are some urgent tasks that I really need his authorisation for before I start them.'

At long last they left, but I had a strong feeling that they would be back. Now it was not a matter of the tenderness of my affections, it was imperative I spoke to Harriet, with or without a chaperone.

Perhaps I was more abrupt than usual when I asked one of her housemaids where Mrs Faulkner might be. Certainly she looked very scared as she bobbed her answer. 'In the Room, I suppose, Mr Rowsley.'

I strode down the corridor, knocking before I entered. And found her, hat on, valise in hand.

'My dearest Harriet!' Had I shut the door? I didn't care. 'What are you doing?'

XXIII

I *catch some of the other servants gossiping.*
    'She's a fallen woman, you know. She shouldn't be allowed to mix with the likes of us, if you ask me.'
    'And why is she Mrs Cox's pet? Should be in the workhouse, surely.'
    'Or on a street corner, with others like her.'

TWENTY-FOUR

held her gaze; when she tried to bury her face in her hands, I took them and held them to my face, as I had done before.

'Whatever is wrong, you are not a woman to run away,' I said gently but firmly. 'My dear, you promised me that you would do nothing precipitate till you had spoken to my parents. And running away seems rather precipitate to me.'

I hoped to calm her, but she pulled away. 'You do not understand, Matthew – the guilt!'

'Guilt! Are you . . .? You cannot be telling me that you killed his lordship and Luke and disposed of their bodies!'

'No! Of course not! Why should I? But . . . Matthew, you cannot forgive me if I tell you . . . You cannot. And I would rather be dead than endure that.'

'Then do not tell me. Not yet. Apart from anything else,' I added, helping her sit down and removing her hat, 'the household would collapse without you. Whatever secret you have, you have lived with it for a long time: live with it a little longer, I beg you.'

'It won't change things; I can't marry you. One of us must leave the House. I can't bear to see you every day knowing I am living a lie.'

'In that case, one of us will have to give due notice and find other employment.' I smiled. 'But neither of us can leave until we know what happened to his lordship: we want to know the end of the story, do we not? Let me get us some tea.' I opened the door and called a maid. Closing the door, I said, 'If I could live with you I would be happy in a labourer's cottage – though I would miss someone taking care of my every whim.'

She managed a wan smile.

A knock at the door. Imagining it was the maid with the tea tray I went to open it – only to find myself admitting Samuel, looking pale.

'Have the police spoken to you yet?' he demanded, as if it

was the most natural thing in the world for two unmarried people to be closeted together in private.

'Yes. That's why I came to speak to Harriet: were you well enough to move the evidence yesterday?' I asked her.

She shook her head. But she straightened her shoulders and lifted her chin, as if declaring her weakness was over.

'Good,' I continued, 'because I think you have to "find" it today. Obviously you were looking for the missing sheets. Leave them where they are. Make sure the specimen box is behind the false shelf-back. They know that his lordship is no saint. They will soon find more people to tell him so. If we don't tell them what we've found, we're withholding evidence, which is a criminal offence.'

'When they question us, how much should we admit?' Samuel asked. 'For question us they surely will.'

'Surely we just tell the truth, apart from the change of date,' Harriet said. 'It's easier to tell the truth than to lie. Except – why should I need to unlock a door in my search?'

'Because you know doors here are never locked and were disconcerted enough to want to enter?'

'For disconcerted read nosy,' she said with an ironic smile. 'I suppose if the policeman have never lived or worked in a great house they won't know about the details of our everyday life. But we do need to sing the same psalm, all of us. Was it locked, gentlemen, or wasn't it? Was I sufficiently worried about a dozen sheets to go against my employer's obvious wishes? Do I regularly go snooping around?'

'No. But I had to, remember, because of the dry rot in the window frames. With George . . .'

'So we need to involve him in this little plot? I don't like it,' Samuel said.

'Let me think . . . He knew it was locked – even offered to break into it, if necessary . . . Then there was news of storm damage . . . So he never returned.'

Samuel mopped his forehead in relief.

'Samuel, would you accompany Harriet just to check? It would be terrible if someone had indeed moved things. Now, there is no reason at all why the two of you should not walk along a corridor together. I will go and tell Beatrice what is happening.'

Automatically, Harriet reached for her apron and popped on the cap I was beginning to detest. Opening the door for her and Samuel to precede me, I stayed long enough to replace her case and hat in her bedchamber, stowing the former under the bed.

Only then did I stroll to the kitchen as if I had all the time in the world, drawing Beatrice into the warm sun outside for our conversation.

I made sure it was I who eventually escorted Burrows and Elias to the locked room, offering the account I had agreed with the others – that Harriet, noticing that linen was missing, had checked all bedrooms and found the items inside. Naturally she had reported the matter to me immediately, hence the urgent summons.

The sheets were where I had last seen them, if perhaps better folded. Soon I was able to give a theatrical start – as if noticing for the first time that there was an extra panel at the back of the shelving.

Burrows obligingly prised it off. Yes, there was the specimen box.

'What a mercy that none of the fair sex has had to lay eyes on this!' Burrows observed, staring at the little curls. 'Have you any idea who . . . who provided these?'

My voice was like ice. 'What an extraordinary question!' At least I had the satisfaction of seeing his face flush to a deep brick-red. 'And, given the blood still evident on those sheets, are you assuming that there was anything voluntary about the circumstances in which they were acquired?'

Elias rushed in, perhaps trying to improve the situation. 'That'd be because they was virgins, more like.'

'And that is supposed to excuse something, is it?' He winced under my gaze. 'Sergeant, not so long ago, Maggie Billings, a young maid, disappeared from the House. She was pregnant, and on no account would reveal who the father was. Her mother is too scared to. Am I right, Elias?'

'If you say so.' He quailed. 'Anyway, yes, that's what folks say.'

'I suggest that you, with the authority of the law to back you, try asking her,' I said.

'It's a terrible accusation you're making, Mr Rowsley! Suggesting it might be his lordship—'

'I am not suggesting anything, sergeant. You are making a deduction – which is quite different. And, in the circumstances, quite a reasonable one, I fear. He is my employer, gentlemen; all this pains me deeply.'

'It pains you because you're like to lose your job, I suppose,' he sneered.

'It pains me because I should have grasped that there was a problem and tackled his lordship appropriately. Dear me, I wonder how many victims he had – if, of course, it is he!'

'Victims? You're calling those trollops victims!' Elias gasped.

'How else would you describe them? I should imagine they had very little choice in the matter. They may have been flattered, true, to be picked out like that. They may even have been seduced. But Elias, imagine your little sister was working here – twelve or fourteen. Imagine if she found her way into his lordship's bed: would she be a trollop?'

'She'd feel the back of my hand, that's for sure – for being stupid enough to fall for a rich man's tales.'

Burrows shifted. 'If my daughter was to . . . if she let a ploughman . . . then maybe I'd say she ought to know better. But saying no to a man who pays your wages, Elias, and maybe those of the rest of your family, all living in a tied cottage – how can you do that? And how would we know even then these . . . these girls . . . went voluntary, like. Walking along this corridor; a door opens; "Come here, and dust this!" his lordship says; there's this bed; next thing . . .' He gestured at the bloodstained sheets. 'Nasty business, this, Mr Rowsley. Because it gives me cause to wonder if his lordship was killed by someone working here – revenge, you might say.'

'Assuming he has indeed been killed.' I had had enough; I led the way out, locking the door behind me.

Burrows watched. 'It's unusual to lock a door in a place like this, isn't it?'

'I assumed you would want to keep the evidence safe, and would not want an over-enthusiastic maid to launder the sheets. As for the hair – as you said, one would not want innocent eyes to see it,' I said reasonably. 'There is just one thing you should be aware of, though I would not think of telling you except that it is common knowledge amongst the maids. There is a collection of . . . graphic . . . pornography in his lordship's dressing room. I cannot imagine you would want to inspect it – I would hate to disturb her ladyship. Remember, her boudoir is not far away. Now, may I suggest we proceed down the back stairs.'

They almost bolted.

The servants' entrance or the main hall? I opted for daunting grandeur. As before, Elias looked overawed. Neither spoke until the footman on duty opened the front doors with an intimidating flourish. I escorted them on to the broad sweep of steps.

Only then, rolling his eyes, did Elias speak. 'Sergeant, I've never been involved in a murder case in a place like this before.'

'You may not be now,' I said crisply. 'You haven't got a body, have you?'

As I returned indoors, the duty footman (Charles?) presented me with a pile of letters on a silver salver. As I rifled through them on my way back to my office only one caught my eye – a hand-delivered note from Marty, asking if I might spare him a few minutes of my time. He proposed to wait on me at the House at four thirty unless he heard from me to the contrary. Curious, I dispatched a note confirming that he would be most welcome.

The other correspondence could wait until I had drunk a cup of strong coffee and told Harriet and the others how I had got on with the policemen.

'They suspected nothing?' Harriet asked, narrowing her eyes in anxiety.

'So far were they from suspecting anything that Sergeant Burrows thanked God that no woman had had to lay eyes on the curls,' I said, with a wry smile at her. 'They did wonder why I should lock the door after me – a foolish slip, perhaps. But I scared them away with the threat of her ladyship. Tell me,' I continued, helping myself to one of Beatrice's superlative biscuits, 'is this complete uninterest in the goings on here in the House typical of her? In winter, yes, I could understand that, as if she were hibernating like a squirrel – but in this glorious weather? In fact, in the face of his lordship's – shall we call it a protracted? – absence I am truly surprised she does not involve herself more with the running of the estate. Lady Graceleigh, my previous employer's wife, always had her finger on the pulse of their properties. Regardless of their status, workers felt they could approach her with their troubles when she went on her daily ride. Some even asked to see her in the castle itself, where she welcomed them freely. Yet when I asked her ladyship here about the Stammerton plans, she was very dismissive of my request for permission to act. She simply told me to get on with the job I was paid to do. I can't understand such inertia – it seems quite unnatural.'

'If you ask me, her ladyship is consuming more laudanum than she should. Much more,' Harriet said. 'Samuel: have you seen anything else?'

'Her consumption of wine has risen too. I have suggested that she take the dogcart and tools round the estate as she often does in summer, or takes the air in the parterre. But most of the time, as you will know from Florrie, she rises late, often does not dress till suppertime, and stares, apparently unseeing, at the lake. Do you suppose – no, I am being foolish – that she knows that something has happened to his lordship and is in mourning for him?'

'She's not pining as you or I would pine, that's for sure,' Beatrice observed. 'She seems to eat everything put before her. Yet Florrie tells me she never gets any plumper – in fact, she's having to put extra tucks and darts in some of her dresses.'

I had not sought a chance to speak to Harriet alone: she would know I would not allude to her plans to escape in public, any more than she would reproach me in front of the others for returning her property to her bedchamber. What I did hope was that I could justifiably invite her to meet Marty.

XXIV

*T*he passages Mrs Cox chooses for me to read aloud to her while she sews gets harder and harder. Occasionally she will ask me to repeat a whole sentence – sometimes even an entire paragraph – because I have not made its meaning clear. Now she reaches for a volume of verse. I am to read poetry. Keats. I may take it to my room to study it there.

'You are doing well, my dear. Very well. Ignore those silly girls who are being so unkind to you. Yes, I know all about them, but if I intervene it will only make it worse for you. Be strong. Remember, "Sticks and stones may break my bones, but names will never harm me." They will marry labourers and cowherds. You will run a castle. Now, to do that you will need to understand money. Can you add up and take away? Show me. Oh, dear. But when I have finished, you will be able to deal with columns of figures as easily as you read Pamela just now.'

TWENTY-FIVE

'Left Mrs Batham's!' I groaned. 'Marty, was Maggie ever there?'

'Not for as long as Mrs Batham claims she was, I'll warrant,' Marty said. 'Ianto tells me that he and Mrs Davies pressed her as hard as they could for details, at one time threatening to call a constable, but she clung to her story: that one day, as Mrs Batham was out shopping, Maggie stole the remainder of the money her aunt had collected from the manse and left, without a note. Now Ianto is just one of many clergymen in the area: he has written to each one asking them to be on the lookout for a woman of Maggie's age, pregnant and surely by now destitute.'

'Apart from offering a reward, is there anything I can do?' I asked.

He shook his head gravely. 'Not until she is found. It's a sad business, isn't it, Matthew. Now, I'd best be on my way. No, not the gentry's door, my friend – I'll go the backstairs route, if it's all the same to you.'

'It's the one I prefer to use myself,' I said, truthfully but disingenuously.

And by some miracle Harriet was leaving her room as we passed it. Naturally I stopped and performed the introductions. To my delight, as they shook hands, she pressed Marty to take tea in the Room. 'You will find Mr Bowman and Mrs Arden there – not to mention a plate of freshly-made scones and a sponge cake as light as a feather. We are all as concerned about Maggie as Ma– as Mr Rowsley is.'

He retained her hand for a few more seconds, as if to show he understood more than he would share with anyone else. 'Matthew is the name I like to call him too, Mrs Faulkner. I hoped we would become better acquainted,' he continued, 'on a trip to Wolverhampton, but it seems that must be postponed, at the very least.' As he spoke, to my shame, I knew that somewhere in my genuinely profound anxiety for Maggie lurked a pang of deep, yes, painful, disappointment that our innocent outing was not to be. 'Shall I wait until I can apprise all of you of the latest developments? That cake smells wonderful,' he added, comically rubbing his stomach.

Samuel was inclined to stand on ceremony, but both women warmed to a side of Marty I'd not seen before: an enviable ability to make a new acquaintance into an old friend.

Soon the pleasant exchanges turned to the grim news he had brought us. Tears welled in Harriet's eyes and, to my surprise, in Samuel's.

He turned to me. 'Surely, Matthew, the estate can offer a reward for anyone finding her safe and sound? Surely!'

'Of course. I will contact the constabularies of all the towns around Wolverhampton and ask them to organize it forthwith.'

'There must be,' Harriet said, her voice thick with emotion, 'the chance that she will be found . . . dead. And we are not the only ones concerned. Someone must break the news to Mrs Billings. Marty, are you well enough acquainted with her?'

'Only with her menfolk, I'm afraid. But if you wish—'

'That must be my job,' I said decisively. 'But I would be so grateful, Marty, if you would go with me.'

'Bless you, I have to pass by the gatehouse to get back to the village. We could walk together.'

Beatrice said, 'You must have a woman with you. I would offer but I hardly know her.'

'No, I will go,' Harriet said, gently but firmly. 'Could you prepare a basket of essentials, Bea? She may not wish to eat, but feed her family she must.'

Mrs Billings seemed less interested in the news of Maggie than in telling me about the bright blue pills Dr Page had prescribed her, which she swore were doing her the world of good, all thanks to me and my generosity. The words tumbled out of her toothless mouth almost at random, becoming a torrent as she saw what Harriet was carrying. Marty, lurking behind us in case she had demanded details of her daughter's departure, stayed silent until she went in, closing the impressive door behind her. He shrugged eloquently. His face told of his sadness: he must be contrasting his own grief for a girl with whom he'd done no more than pass the time of day, if that, with her own mother's apparent lack of feeling.

His departure for the Royal Oak left Harriet and me in an embarrassed silence. To break it I told her about the fate of his wife and child.

'That's why he's moved here: to get away from the scene of his tragedy. You've probably heard what a good influence he is in the village. He won't let anyone drink more than they should – which in his reckoning is more than they can afford. He doesn't begrudge them the warmth of the snug for no more than half a pint of ale carefully nursed for a whole evening.' I could chatter no more. I turned to her, hands outstretched. 'Oh, Harriet!'

She reached for them, but snatched them back, as if they might be burnt.

We had not moved from where Marty had left us.

She set us in motion, keeping a respectable distance from me and obviously trying to find something to say, but failing. I honoured her all the more for offering to come on an errand which must necessarily involve us in an unchaperoned and probably embarrassing walk together.

'I am sorry about this morning,' she said at last. 'I broke my promise to you. I was wrong.'

'I was wrong to extract a promise you didn't want to keep,' I countered. 'I am sorry to have caused you so much pain.'

'It is pain – but mixed with so much happiness. I can't bear to leave here, and I couldn't bear the House without you. What shall we do, Matthew?'

'For the time being we will do nothing. *You* know that I love you and would marry you tomorrow if I could. *I* know – I *believe* that you love me, but I know something holds you back.'

'It's because I love you that . . . No, I have to be able to confess everything to you before I agree to marry you.'

'Let us consider ourselves engaged, then – with a couple of provisos! Oh, Harriet, there has to be joy in this world. Think of Ianto, grateful for even the very few years he had with his beloved wife and their daughter. It is wrong not to accept joy in whatever form.'

To my amazement – and yes, joy! – she put her hand in mine.
'Yes. Let us consider ourselves engaged – with provisos. And,
oh Matthew, I promise that I will not try to give you the slip
again.' She took a deep breath, as if to return us to some form
of normality, and withdrew her hand. 'Tell me, are you going to
practise your new bowling grip in time for Saturday's match?'

'This very evening, if you will supervise.' We were both
shaking with emotion, but stayed apart, rather than let the embrace
we both so desired provide entertainment for a group of labourers
making their slow progress to their next task.

'I believe you must find a moment to tell her ladyship,' Samuel
said, 'despite all the evidence leading me to suppose that she
will not take kindly to the news.'

'One of her own servants brought so low!' Beatrice said. 'No,
my advice is you should continue to do good by stealth, Matthew.
She's told you to run the estate: run it. And make sure your plans
for Stammerton are in place before the Reverend Kill-joy gets
better – which he won't for some time, I hear. He's suffering
from – no, modesty forbids me to mention the parts affected.'

'Orchitis,' Samuel said loftily. 'A result of the mumps.'

Serious indeed, in a man not yet old.

'Oh, don't talk to me about mumps!' Beatrice said. 'Another
kitchen maid's got a face out here.' She gestured. 'Elsie.'

'Three of my girls have already had it or are getting over it.
What about your young men, Samuel?'

He narrowed his eyes. 'Thomas – but then he's sweet on young
Elsie, isn't he? He's probably caught it from her. Oh, dear. I hope
he doesn't suffer what Mr Pounceman has.'

'At least the wretched man's not the marrying sort,' Beatrice
snorted. 'But Thomas and Elsie – a nice, normal, young couple.
You don't want the bedroom side stopped before it's even started.
Oh, drat! There it goes.'

In response to his bell, Samuel heaved himself up, donned his
most impassive face and set off upstairs.

Having an uneasy suspicion that Beatrice might try to leave
us unchaperoned, I grinned. 'Ladies: I have borrowed a cricket
ball from young Will. It would be so helpful if you could assess
for yourselves whether I have made any progress.'

Beatrice was on her feet in a flash. 'What fun! So long as we stick to the south side of the building, mind. We don't want to annoy her ladyship.'

'We'd better stick to the north side then: if she craned her neck she'd be able to check on us from her boudoir otherwise. Do you mean to recruit a footman or two to join the game?' Harriet's eyes danced.

'I think Samuel's presence will suffice,' I declared.

XXV

'*I*know that entertaining Master Augustus is not what some might see as your job, my dear,' Mrs Cox says, 'but I'd advise you to do it with good grace. The more you meet with the aristocracy, even their schoolboy sons, the easier you'll be in their company. So tomorrow, when her ladyship gives me her orders for the day, I will tell her that I can excuse you your duties. It's such a shame the other young gentlemen are so full of measles they can't leave their rooms, and it's as likely as not the unaffected guests will depart as soon as maybe. But this will be yet another opportunity for you to prove how useful you are.'*

'*Wouldn't a footman be better company for him?*' I venture.

'*His mama fears they would be too rough with him or lead him into bad ways. So tomorrow there will be no dusting, no sweeping: you will be out in the fresh air. And apart from enjoying yourself, you may earn a nice fat tip. Off you go now – but remember, you need to have learnt that sonnet by heart for tomorrow evening.*'

TWENTY-SIX

G iven the heightened state of our emotion, it was probably for the best that the following day involved visiting Shrewsbury to discuss with an architect my plans for Stammerton. Sadly the surveys in progress encompassing the whole of the United Kingdom had not taken in Shropshire yet, so I found the most detailed maps I could and all my sketches. We had a most productive day, including an excellent luncheon at the Lion. I also found time to do a little shopping, desperate, as you can imagine, to find a present for Harriet to celebrate our unofficial and unannounced betrothal. A ring or brooch would have been too obvious, in a sense perhaps premature in any case. But a gift she must have.

A bookshop called me – but I suspected she had books I'd never dreamed of. Nonetheless, I bought a beautiful edition of *Northanger Abbey*. I was tempted by a volume of poetry by Matthew Arnold. Would she find him too gloomy? How would she deal with the sentiments of 'Dover Beach'? It went back on the shelf at once. What was I doing, looking in a haberdasher's, of all things? I emerged the purchaser of a length of blue ribbon, the colour of her eyes; surely it might find a place on her best hat? And some fine chamois gloves.

Thence to a gentlemen's outfitters for new shirts and two splendid bow ties; and a bootmaker – my riding boots were a disgrace. On impulse, I added Samuel and Beatrice to my shopping list. Gloves for Samuel to match some I might need myself, and a return to the haberdasher's for gloves like Harriet's for Beatrice. They were not imaginative, I had to admit, but at least none of us would suffer from cold hands later in the year.

I returned like a happy schoolboy. The fact that I did not know when I might find a moment of privacy to present the gifts added an almost enjoyable frisson.

Supper was devoted to a discussion of my plans for Stammerton, which I conceded could not go ahead until George declared the roof watertight and I had accorded Pounceman the courtesy of breaking the news myself.

'Don't hurry with that!' Beatrice said with a huge and decidedly unladylike wink.

Harriet flushed deeply.

I was spared the necessity of replying by the bell summoning Samuel.

'She's in a funny mood today,' he said, as he hauled himself to his feet. 'I might have to water the dessert wine.'

'Maybe it's the change in the weather,' Harriet said. 'Look at it!'

'All the better for testing George's repairs,' I said, watching the drops hurtle down the window. But my heart sank. There would be no gentle walk for the four of us – the two twos – tonight. 'It looks as if it's here to stay. It reminds me of when I was a child, praying it would be dry in time for the next day's cricket match – and I find that child in me again! What if I can't try out my new grip tomorrow?'

The rain drenched down all morning. George and I conducted a tour of the attics, finding only one leak in all the work he had organized.

To celebrate – and to save him another soaking – I invited him back to my office to share coffee and Eccles cakes, some of Beatrice's best handiwork. When we were done, I reached out the plans I had taken to Shrewsbury. 'I would rather not start without his lordship's approval,' I admitted, 'and meanwhile there is plenty of work left to occupy you and your team in the House.'

'Ah, it'd be good to catch some of that dry rot before it spreads through the plaster and brick. Have you thought any more about all those paintings and such in the attics?'

'They're not mine to think about – nor, in fact, her ladyship's.'

'But some are really nice – and it can't be good to keep them up there, getting hot or cold according to the season. They'd be better off in some of the bedrooms, surely. Which reminds me, gaffer, do you still need me to tackle the door in that locked room? It's just the weather for an indoor job today.'

'So it is. But we found the key for it. There are just odds and ends in there.' I hoped he wouldn't have occasion to find it was still locked. 'Anyway, here are the plans.' I unrolled them. 'The church here, a school here . . .'

He peered. 'It's a bit too dark to see, isn't it?'

I rang for Thatcher, asking for more lamps. 'And could you ask Mr Bowman for a considerable favour, please – the loan of his spectacles?'

I could not understand the tension. Something was simmering, I knew not what: it had been throughout the silent meal in the servants' hall. At first I put it down to my imagination; I was as sulky as a bear at losing my game of cricket; I could not argue with the captains' joint decision, conveyed to me in a brief note, but I could wish it had not been necessary.

At last, adjourning to the Room, I saw yesterday's beautifully ironed newspapers in a pile on the table usually occupied by Harriet's reading matter. Why would anyone put them there?

Samuel's voice was unusually solemn – the point of pomposity, in fact. 'It is a matter of great good fortune that I managed to prevent her ladyship from seeing these,' he said, touching the pile before we sat down. 'My dear Matthew, what are you doing?'

'Forgive me if I tell you I do not have any idea what you're talking about.'

'Your name involved in a murder case. The Oxford Murder Case.'

Flummoxed, I stared. At last I clicked my fingers. 'Oh, the trial of the little girl alleged to have murdered her lover. But what does it have to do with me?'

'What indeed? Your name is here, clear as day.' He jabbed a finger at me. 'I have to tell you that you are sailing very close to the wind, Matthew.'

'Let me see,' I said. 'Oh, my apologies and thanks for these.' I returned his spectacles. 'Poor George is sadly in need of his own pair.' Taking the top newspaper, I made my way to the window, to catch the little light available. 'Thank goodness! My cousin has agreed to defend her! Mark Rowsley, Samuel, not Matthew! He is my cousin.' The clever cousin, who drew up my contract. Criminal law was not his forte, but even I would have been able to make inroads into the prosecution case.

'It *is* your doing, then?' Samuel spluttered.

'My doing? I wrote to him alerting him to the case, of course I did, when I saw it.'

'But he shares your name. Consider the affront to the Family that he should take on such a case!'

Had he gone mad? Mark was a lawyer. What would anyone expect him to do but take on a case? 'Let us sit down and talk like the friends we are,' I said, desperate not to lose my temper.

Harriet said firmly, 'The tea will be stewed if we do not drink it. Beatrice? Samuel? Matthew?' The smile she awarded me as she passed my cup was so intense it seemed her face glowed. 'Perhaps, Matthew, you could tell Beatrice and me why the case so outrages Samuel?'

What a strange way of putting it. But I thought I understood.

'The case is likely to become a *cause celebre*.' Samuel and Beatrice would just have to keep up. 'I read about it in a paper the other day, and' – I must choose my words carefully – 'and I knew at once it would be hard for the defendant to get a fair trial. In brief, a girl had sexual relations with him in a back alley of the town. She stabbed him. The defence is that . . . I don't know what angle Mark is taking. Ah! Here we are: he's spoken to the press about his plans for Monday. "Eleven years old . . . small for her age . . . evidence that she was a virgin . . . drunken jape . . . night out with six friends, all witnesses . . . eight o'clock the following morning . . ." Well done, Mark. Just the line I'd have taken!'

Samuel was still blustering. 'You are proud that your cousin is defending a murderer!'

'I am very proud that he is acting as a defence lawyer. At such short notice, too.' I spoke with the most naïve enthusiasm I could, as if I knew that they all really shared my beliefs, and that Samuel was merely acting as devil's advocate. 'I couldn't believe that the poor little girl had no proper legal representation so I brought the trial to Mark's attention. I told him I'd only pay his fee if he won, too,' I added with a smile.

'You are paying for this – this scandalous behaviour!'

'I am paying for a child of eleven to have a defence lawyer. In the interests of fairness, since I should imagine the witnesses, the sort of young men I came across at university, will have prepared their story beforehand to make themselves look good.

You see, not all students behave like the gentlemen they eventually become. Not when they are drunk. I have seen – no, I will spare you since many of their little amusements are not fit for any sober person's ears, man's or woman's. One of the least bad – and even telling you this disgusts me – was playing football in their college quadrangle. The football was a hedgehog.'

'A hedgehog? In my last place we had to invite the sweet little things into the kitchen to deal with the beetles!' Beatrice said. 'Shame on them.'

'Did these students inflict similar harm on humans?' Harriet asked quietly.

For answer I touched the newspaper. 'Can you imagine otherwise? I am sorry – the men I knew were foolish boys thinking they were unfettered by the law and even by the laws of common decency. Yet at least three are now barristers, and two are clergymen. When those louts grow up,' I added, touching the newspaper, 'they will blush with shame for their part in this.'

'If they have committed perjury, they may blush before that,' Harriet said.

'Sadly I doubt if it will come to that. It's one thing to find what a lot of people will still see as a guttersnipe walk free, quite another to send a group of "young gentlemen" to jail for lying.'

'Of course.' Her anger sizzled.

'And quite wrong, I agree. Remember, the law is made and enforced by the same sort of person.' I stopped abruptly. I was in the right, of course, but there was no point in upsetting Samuel further, when I knew I had the one person who truly mattered on my side. Truly, I think that everything I said had been directed at her.

'So had Maggie taken a knife to her villainous seducer, would you have condoned that?' Samuel persisted.

'I do not wish anyone ever to take another's life. "Thou shalt not kill." But sometimes, just sometimes, there may be extenuating circumstances. And justice must always be combined with mercy.'

'Would that mean letting her get off scot-free?'

'A young man seduces a very young woman and gets her with child. She will walk to Wolverhampton on her own. She will give birth in absolute poverty. If she had struck him with a weapon and hurt him, would she not have been justified? I am not a judge, thank goodness.' I took a deep breath. 'I have shocked you, my friends, and I am sorry. But sometimes friends have to agree to differ on certain subjects, for the sake of their other friends, if for no other reason. To be frank with you, when I read about the trial, I saw not an anonymous child in the dock, but yes, I saw little Maggie. That's why I acted as I did.'

'And I honour you for it,' Beatrice declared. 'Kicking a hedgehog, indeed . . . I think we could all do with another cup of tea, don't you?' She bustled off.

'Can we shake hands and remain the friends we are?' I asked Samuel.

He hesitated – a moment too long, I feared. But Harriet stepped forward and put our hands together.

I knew that something of immense importance was happening, and that anything that followed would be bathos. If only I could be alone with her, for even a few minutes.

Beatrice opened the door, holding it for the maid carrying the tea tray, which she set on the table. She bobbed her way out.

'Would you all excuse me for a moment?' I was about to retrieve the little gifts from my office in the hope that they would lighten the mood. But even as I stood, we heard raised voices outside.

The door flew open.

XXVI

I am running and jumping and throwing – no, bowling! – a ball. Master Augustus is laughing too. He is very serious when he bats and I bowl. It is very important he learns to bat well, which means I have to bowl well. Sometimes he hits the ball a long way away. Twice I catch it. Twice I hit the pieces of wood called wickets.

The sun shines in the bluest of skies. The grass we crush as we run and jump smells sweet. I am laughing.

Is this what they call happiness?

TWENTY-SEVEN

'We have found Luke Hargreaves!' Sergeant Burrows declared.

'At least we think we have,' Elias added quietly.

'And we'd like someone to come and identify him,' Burrows continued, as if ignoring the chirp of a bird.

'Now? On the wettest Saturday afternoon you're likely to see?' Beatrice asked. 'If the poor man's dead, won't Monday do?'

'This is a murder enquiry,' Burrows said, adding, insultingly, 'in case you hadn't realized it, miss. Mr Bowman?'

Samuel and I exchanged a glance. 'Mr Bowman will soon be tied up with his duties here,' I said. 'If Alf, Luke's father, can't do it, which I think he would want to do, I can take Mr Bowman's place.'

'But you've only been working here five minutes, haven't you, sir? You're hardly the man to do it.' The news seemed truly to have gone to Burrows's head.

'If it's length of acquaintance you need, I have known Luke since he was as a boy,' Harriet said, getting to her feet.

Burrows recoiled. 'It's not woman's work. Look, we'll take his father and you, Mr Rowsley, if that's all right. Get your hat, then: we're off to Wellington.'

The journey was long, uncomfortable and pointless: the corpse laid out before us was not Luke. It was nothing even like Luke – twenty years older and by the length of his hair and fingernails a gentleman of the road.

Alf was more emotional after the examination than before. He had managed a truly heroic stoicism on our outward journey, but spent the jolting cold gloom of our return alternately fulminating about the policemen's folly and bemoaning the fact that his son was still missing. I could only agree with both sentiments, and wished we had been able to express them to Burrows – clearly

Elias had never wanted us to embark on such a fool's errand. But the policemen had remained in Wellington.

Though it was after ten when the cab dropped us back at my house, I made Alf wait a moment or two – the cab too. I knew I would have a more than adequate collation waiting for me on my dining table: Beatrice and Will between them would have seen to that. Protocol – and Alf's own need to tell his wife the news – meant I could not ask him to join me as I ate, but I could provide him with a basket of food for his own late supper.

I waved him off, travelling, as he said with a wry smile, like royalty.

I didn't feel like smiling. I felt soiled by the whole experience. Soiled – and enraged to the point where I knew only one remedy for my fury. Scribbling a note to bring my friends up to date, I ran up to the House to leave it with the night-duty footman and then ran back again, by then soaked to the skin. Why not get wetter still and wash away my anger? I stripped in the scullery and dowsed myself under the pump in the yard.

What a vile end to such an interesting day. It didn't end there, of course: my sleep was riven with nightmares of Maggie's face atop the mortal remains of the poor tramp, time and time again. And then it got worse. It was Harriet's face I saw.

At least dawn was now breaking, and the birds were in full voice. Throwing open my window I breathed deeply. With Mr Pounceman still safely on his sick-bed, perhaps I could persuade Harriet to walk to church with me – or perhaps, simply, to walk, though clinging, penetrating drizzle had replaced the rain.

It was only as I went down to my study that I found a note on the salver Will liked to use, part of his aspiration to higher things, no doubt. It was from Marty, enclosing another, this one from Ianto. The news, said the minister, was bad. None of his fellow pastors had seen Maggie except one, a fellow Welshman as it happened, whose ministry was in a nearby village. He had tried to speak to a country girl obviously near her time but when he started to question her she had slipped into an alley and he had lost her. Ianto would keep me informed.

It was too early to go up to the House. Even assuming my friends were up and about, the servants' hall would be full of purposeful chaos. The servants whom Harriet had granted days off – most of them, with only her ladyship in residence – would be desperate to have their breakfast and leave. The others, knowing it was their turn the next week, were buzzing round preparing the food betimes. So I sat down to write to my parents, telling them, belatedly, of my unofficial and still secret engagement and asking their blessing. Since I had already asked them to support and comfort Harriet in whatever her secret trouble might be, I had no doubt of their delight and enthusiasm. I walked down to the village myself to post the letter, and another to Mark, thanking him and urging him on.

On my way back I was accosted by Dr Page, who slowed the trap to a halt and offered me a lift to Thorncroft House.

'The House?' I repeated in panic, thinking of only one person.

'Yes, her ladyship has had one of her turns.'

'It sounds as if these are a regular event. But I don't recall her having any illness beyond extreme bad temper – we are speaking confidentially here, aren't we, Page? – since I arrived.'

'You sum it up very succinctly. In a child I would call them tantrums, and prescribe a day of bread and water to cool the patient. In her – she used to have them when his late lordship wouldn't accede to one of her demands. After his death, she found their son malleable – as I am sure you have. But now I see I must keep an eye on her – perhaps daily – as something seems to have triggered another attack.'

'The word you use is interesting. Attack. Think about Hortense – my God!'

He raised a warning finger. 'Who declined to say who had hurt her, of course.'

'Of course. Has her ladyship hurt anyone?'

'Don't worry: your Mrs Faulkner was not involved. Not at the start, at least. Bowman was the victim. A crystal vase to the face. He looks as if he's taken part in a prize-fight.'

I was desperate to blurt out an enquiry about Harriet – not involved at the start, at least – could mean anything. But I managed to ask, 'How serious are his injuries? On a level with Hortense's?'

'No fractures, I think. But he's not a young man, and he will heal more slowly. Fortunately other servants were at hand to rescue him. Mrs Faulkner sent for me straight away; she'd already procured steak and applied it to the worst of the swelling.'

'And – you said she was involved with her ladyship too?' I could not keep the anxiety from my voice.

'She insisted that she should keep an eye on things when young Florrie put her ladyship to bed, on my instructions. I believe her presence was not welcome, and even from the corridor where I waited I could hear harsh words being said. I have to say that your name was mentioned. And I understand that congratulations are in order.'

'Page – could you stop just one moment? What did you say just then?'

'Whoa! To both of you, man and horse. Her ladyship was making a great song and dance about seeing the two of you walking together; Mrs Faulkner retorted that there was a lot to talk about in the running of an estate and house like this, so it was natural for the two of you to converse whenever you ran into each other. "Well, I forbid it!" her ladyship says. "You are not to speak to him at all. It's a bad example to the other servants." "With due respect," says Mrs Faulkner, "Mr Rowsley is not a servant. And if even a servant woman may not speak to her affianced husband I do not know to whom she may speak!" Do you know, I applauded – from the safety of the corridor. To make such a statement and in such grammatically correct form, too. And, I confess, for I hope you are not a jealous man, Rowsley, I offered her my felicitations with a fraternal kiss as she emerged, quite magnificent in her anger.'

I was so overcome I could barely speak. 'All I ask,' I said, with a shaky laugh, 'is a congratulatory handshake, my friend. I am the happiest man on earth.'

He obliged, with great warmth and vigour. 'But you are one in a quandary. How can Mrs Faulkner possibly stay on at the House? I should imagine a woman in her position must be given notice, or payment in lieu.'

I laughed. 'And I have to be the one to authorize it! But I suspect she will want to work on, to hand over to her replacement. In a building as big as the House, it is quite possible to avoid running into someone you wish to avoid. I've not seen hide or hair of her ladyship for a few days now, and not because I was skulking in the shadows. On the other hand, Samuel is in an even trickier position, as is Mrs Arden. I'm sorry: I shouldn't—'

'Don't worry: I gather their futures are linked, one might say. Mrs Arden was very much in evidence last night, though it was officially Mrs Faulkner who sat with him through the night, for propriety's sake. Where were you, by the way? I quite expected to see you there, talking control.'

'With my dear Harriet there, there was no need for anyone else to take the reins. No, I was on a wild-goose chase with Alf Hargreaves, making it plain to the police that a five-foot-six elderly tramp was never going to be confused with Luke, six foot in his socks if he's an inch. Page, you have your finger on the village pulse in more than one way: what is the consensus about Luke and his lordship amongst your patients?'

He set the reluctant horse slowly in motion. 'There isn't one. Theories abound, as I'm sure you know. And some people are more than happy to point an accusing finger at a neighbour they've fallen out with. Oh, they all think both men are dead – or that his lordship, thinking Luke knew too much about his goings on, has killed Luke. Or that Luke, disgusted by his employer's goings on, has killed him to prevent more harm being done. One man has fled abroad. Or both have. Or both have been kidnapped and are being held to ransom by a murderous gang of gypsies. And you must have a theory too?'

'You've summed up mine. Most of them. Actually, I wouldn't rule out ordinary robbery as a motive, and maybe murder, if the two men fought back, as I'd expect them to.' The less said about all the possible burial sites on the estate the better, not to mention all the reasons for local men and women alike to want to get rid of their landlord. 'Now, as to her ladyship – is she fit to stay where she is, or does she need . . . more specialized facilities?'

'She's not ready to be carted off to a lunatic asylum, if that's what you're asking. But I have told Mrs Faulkner I think a nurse or two should be discreetly added to the staff.'

'And poor Samuel? He is the most loyal, most devoted man!'

'He is undoubtedly safe in the hands of those most capable women. I have removed the steak from his face, and asked instead for pure clean ice – and bother any fancy ice cream desserts that

that puts at risk. He declines any laudanum, by the way: all three blame her ladyship's troubles on it, though I have assured them that the drug calms and does not excite.'

Even so early a stable boy was at hand to deal with the horse and trap, and for no more than a shilling or so a week. I flipped him a sixpence as I walked with Page through the servants' entrance. We were greeted by a group of pale kitchen- and housemaids; some tears had obviously been shed. But Page breezed through them, entering Samuel's room with the most cursory of nods. Beatrice was now sitting with Samuel, bathing his poor swollen face with a bowl of iced water.

'I can't stop him talking, doctor,' she said, getting up to curtsy. I took her hand, gathering her to me as if she were my sister. 'Giving instructions about the day's tasks.'

'Lucid instructions?' Page asked softly.

She nodded. I felt a rush of relief.

Page took her place on the chair by the bed, taking Samuel's pulse, and gently touching the bruises. 'Excellent – better out than in,' he declared breezily, 'and your pulse is much calmer and more regular. But I'll not have you worrying about what you should be doing, my old friend: a day of calm, lying in the dark for you. Sips of tea, a nibble of toast dipped in the tea if you get hungry. I'm sure your friends will keep you company by reading the Bible to you. Or some particularly soporific sermons. Yes, sleep is the best healer. And I will see if it's doing its job this evening.' He turned to Beatrice. 'But you nurses must get your sleep too. Watch in turns. Rowsley here can take a turn too, if he's minded. Now, I have a baby on its way, so I'll wish you all good day.'

Beatrice took her place again immediately. I escorted Page out into the corridor. He touched his finger to his lips.

Harriet intercepted us: we could step into the Room if we wanted privacy. I ushered her in too, before closing the door. 'Well?'

'As I told you, Rowsley, age is against him. But I believe if you tell someone they will get better, they will believe you. So no hushed tones, no creeping around with funereal faces.'

'I quite understand. But what I don't understand, Page, is how her ladyship can get away with doing that to one of her most devoted retainers.'

'Assuming we summon the police in the form of that hayseed Elias – what would he do? What could he do? Would Bowman ever testify against her?'

Harriet snorted with laughter. 'And her ladyship would make mincemeat of poor Elias if he even tried to speak to her. In any case, Matthew, even assuming there was a chance of justice, wouldn't it have to be at the hands of her peers? In the House of Lords?'

Page laughed. 'I'll leave you two lovers to discuss the finer points of law, shall I? Summon me if there's any sign of change in my patient. I shall be with Mrs Rivers down by the church – but I can't imagine I'll be there long. Pods quickly, she does.'

My fiancée and I found something other than the law to discuss.

XXVII

*S*ix short days we have, laughing, playing with the bat and
ball. But then Master Augustus' sister is well enough to
travel, and I must go back to my feather duster. Mrs Cox
says it will not do for me to cry when he goes; I think someone
has told him the same thing. But I can see tears in his eyes, as
I curtsy my farewell. Awkwardly he shakes my hand, folding my
fingers over my palm. 'When I am grown up, you . . . you must
come and be my housekeeper,' he says in a rush. 'Please.' Quickly
he taps my clasped hand. 'Buy some books!'

I know I mustn't call him Gussie in front of his mama. 'Yes,
sir. Thank you, sir.' I curtsy again and back away from the
barouche in which he is to travel. I stand with the other servants
to wave. The barouche is already moving when he calls, 'And
this is for you too! One-handed, Harry!'

So I obey. With my left hand. The ball is mine. Mine. I smile
and wave even harder. 'Goodbye, Gussie!'

The two golden guineas Gussie put into my right hand will
go into my box. And so will what I will treasure even more: the
ball I caught.

TWENTY-EIGHT

With much reluctance, Harriet and Beatrice went to Morning Service, accepting that it would be good for them to get some fresh air, while I sat with Samuel as he dozed, reading to him from his Prayer Book. From time to time I would check his pulse, and apply more iced water to his poor bruises. When he roused, he sipped a little tea from an invalid feeding cup, and managed a painful smile. Suddenly he put a finger and thumb into his mouth, grimaced, and flourished a tooth, its root still bloody. 'Like Dr Page said, better out than in,' he mouthed. I found a rag for him to bite on to stem the blood, not that there was much. On impulse I poured a tot of brandy, telling him on pain of death – mine, at the hands of Beatrice – if he drank any. It was merely mouthwash, and must be spat out. 'Seems a waste – but I'm sure you're right.'

His docility alarmed me. But I could scarcely consider it grounds for summoning Page.

He was asleep when Harriet and Beatrice returned, flushed after their brisk walk in what was now watery sunshine, but opened his eyes and raised a hand – even that was bruised – in greeting.

'I fancy his breathing is more even,' I said quietly. 'But he is not the man he was, are you, my friend?' I showed them the tooth, wrapped in a beautifully laundered handkerchief. Beatrice seized the little bundle, as if it was a gift.

'Give me your bonnet, Beatrice, and I will bring you your tea in here,' Harriet said, with quiet authority. She nodded quietly when I offered to assist.

There was no need, of course, for either of us to do such a mundane task as boiling a kettle and pouring water on to tea leaves. But in the quiet of the kitchen – the young men and women were still dawdling back from church – it was good to feel the ease of each other's company.

'How is he?' she asked quietly. 'Really?'

'No worse, or I would have summoned Page. How is Beatrice?'

'How would you imagine? But she is puzzled: why is he not angrier? In his position, in Hortense's indeed, I would be fulminating against the perpetrator! Even a model employee like Beatrice declares she would. Loyalty and devotion are all well and good, but that sort of behaviour, even from the most generous employer, is surely . . . unacceptable.'

'Absolutely.'

Neither of us wanted our conversation to end, but we could hear the voices of the churchgoers as they returned across the yard. I picked up the tray and followed her back to the sickroom.

By now Samuel was awake and getting fretful, insisting that he must get up and dress. 'I must serve her ladyship's luncheon,' he declared. 'I must. No one else can do it.'

'Nonsense,' Harriet said decisively. 'Although it is Sunday, there are still plenty of footmen who could do it quite admirably.'

'No! No!' He pushed at the bedclothes. 'It must be me! It must!'

I looked at Harriet and then at Beatrice. 'Laudanum?' I mouthed.

They nodded as one.

'Come, my friend,' I said gently, 'you have trained your young men to perfection: what about Tim and Thatcher working together?'

'Them enter her ladyship's room? Never!'

'Let us talk about it when we've had our tea,' I said quickly. 'Today Harriet entrusted to me the difficult and skilful task of making it. I hope you will approve and forgive my efforts if they don't match Beatrice's.' As I spoke I supported him so that Beatrice could put the feeding cup to his lips.

Letting her voice drop gently, Harriet gave a detailed account of the morning's sermon. I cannot imagine that whoever gave it would be flattered by the result as he drifted into sleep.

Beatrice insisted on staying with him for a few more minutes, though soon she would have to supervise luncheon.

My office was a less compromising place for Harriet and me to talk, so we adjourned there – separately, of course, to maintain a vestige of decorum. She even seated herself at the far side of my desk: we were there to talk seriously, firstly about what should have been an entirely trivial matter – her ladyship's lunch.

'There must be two servants,' she said firmly. 'A maid, yes, but a footman in case her ladyship becomes violent again and needs to restrain her. Tim is excellent at serving, but he is still too young and anxious to take on the task.'

'I might have just the person.' I flung open the door. 'Thatcher, step inside and close the door behind you.' He did as he was told. 'Now, you really must get out of the habit of lurking so close to doors where important matters are being discussed. I am sure Mr Bowman has trained you all to be as silent as the grave, but it might well seem that you are spying.'

Red to the ears, he spluttered his apologies.

'Very good,' I said. 'But this simply will not do. I think you have choices here. Continue as you are, and I will have you dismissed. Or learn to do as you are told.'

'Sir! Please sir—'

'Do I deduce you are doing what you are told? But by someone other than me? Well, that is another choice: tell whoever gave you your orders that you have been found out and cannot – in the words of the Bible – serve two masters. If you serve the other person, you cannot do it outside my room.'

'But sir – please sir!' I had not once raised my voice but he was near to tears.

Harriet glanced at me: might she take over? 'Dick Thatcher, we have known each other a long time. Since you were so high.' She put her hand, palm down, about four feet from the floor. 'Yes? You have never been very brave, have you, because you were afraid that if you got into a fight or even answered back you might lose your job, and your family would go hungry. Now, to someone who does not know you, you might seem strong and powerful. But I remember the scared little boy. I think you're scared now, even though your family now work for Farmer Twiss's cousin. So there's no need to be frightened: you can be brave. And the bravest thing you can do is simply tell me the truth: who is telling you to spy on Mr Rowsley?'

'I swore on the Bible, Mrs Faulkner.'

'Very well. How did she persuade you to swear?' Her voice was very reasonable – gentle, concerned. But the question elicited the response we needed.

'She—' He broke off, scarlet again.

'Very well. Now, you need not tell her ladyship about this conversation when you prepare her luncheon table and serve her.'

'But I'm not a butler. I'm just a footman!'

'And as you probably know, our dear butler is too badly hurt to do this task himself. You are young and healthy, Dick. You will report to the Hall at eleven forty-five exactly. Do I make myself clear? Oh, and just to remind you: no more putting that ear of yours to Mr Rowsley's door, for her ladyship or anyone else.' At no point did she raise her voice above a quiet conversational level. She even smiled kindly as he bowed himself out.

Once I made sure he was obeying her orders, I closed the door and kissed her hands. 'You were magnificent, Harriet, far more effective than I would have been with all my bluster.'

She accepted my tribute with a laugh. But then her quiet, watchful expression returned. 'Something rotten is going on here, isn't it? This violence. This spying. Spying on someone you would have thought had the Family's absolute trust. You are totally beyond reproach—'

'You may be biased in your judgement!'

'I was not . . . as prejudiced in your favour . . . when I understood that you were trying to put heart back into the estate and tenant farms, not just milk them for his lordship's hedonistic schemes. Perhaps,' she added, her eyes twinkling again, 'it was your decency to the poor and powerless that made me . . .' She tailed off, cheeks aflame. She took a deep breath. 'As I was saying, you are as honest as the day is long, so it cannot be that she suspects you of any misdemeanour. Which means, in my book, that she is afraid of you. Do you know why?'

'No. That is the long and short of it. I wish I did: it might make things clearer. You don't think, do you, that she believes I know what happened to his lordship? That I might have killed him? After all, I know of his – shall we call them peccadillos? – and had I a mind for revenge I know the estate well enough to be able to dispose of his body. All those heaps of leaf mould and mud from the lake, for instance. Or cottage gardens with flourishing bean rows. We spoke once of using lime-washed wallpaper to improve fertility: a body might do just as well. Or pigs like Alf's with a taste for flesh.'

'What?' she gasped.

'Apparently an enraged sow in farrow is a perfect executioner.'

'Heavens, Matthew, all my time living in the country and I never knew that. So you could dispose of a body – his and Luke's, of course! – with ease. That's always a consideration when committing murder. Do you have a motive?'

I spread my hands. 'We have argued about money? He has forbidden me to develop Stammerton?'

'That sounds a little academic. Would you kill for such a reason?'

'Not personally, no. After all, I am at liberty to terminate my contract and find a more enlightened landlord if I wish. I *was*,' I corrected myself, 'until my circumstances, *our* circumstances, changed. I might kill if – say – I had been sweet on Maggie, or one of his other victims. Harriet, that is truly what I fear most. That some enraged young man has had his revenge and availed himself of one of those many hiding places.'

'Would you condone it if one had?' There was no laughter in her eyes now.

'I would understand it. I would sympathize with the perpetrator. But despite that, I would want justice done and seen to be done.'

'And what would that justice be? Being hanged by the neck till dead?'

I shook my head slowly. 'The perpetrator might be said to have been bringing justice on his beloved's behalf. I would understand. I could forgive. The French have a less cut and dried law than ours . . .'

'*Crime passionel*?' She could still surprise me.

'Exactly. I suppose the law's inflexibility is what prevented me from emulating Mark. But even he knows the law's limitations – the biggest being that it was designed and enacted by rich men largely for their own benefit. I shall be so glad to introduce you to Mark: our after-dinner discussions will be a joy. Even if they bring us no closer to any conclusion than we are to determining why – if! – her ladyship is afraid of me.'

The topic was discussed exhaustively over our *tête à tête* luncheon, though still no conclusion was drawn, except that perhaps that, given her newfound propensity for violence, her ladyship had gone mad and fancied I might be spying on her.

Given the fact she had given me *carte blanche* to run the estate, I found this hard to credit – unless she wanted to make sure I was doing just that. But that didn't ring true even to my own ears. 'But, call me fanciful if you will, I am worried about Samuel's safety in this building. If her ladyship has lost her reason – even intermittently – then perhaps she might come and finish what she started. If Dr Page was in agreement, he could be removed to my house, with the two of you to nurse him. She would not follow him there.'

'But yours is a bachelor establishment, Matthew. Do you even have sheets for the bed?'

'Indeed. And the beds are in fact made up. I was hoping for some visitors and – this was while you were so unwell, my love – Beatrice despatched some maids to spring clean the place, did you not?'

Harriet narrowed her eyes in puzzlement.

'My visitors did not materialize after all. So there would be no problem in accommodating you.'

'And you?'

'Samuel would have to have my bedchamber. Meanwhile, I would occupy his.'

'On the grounds her ladyship could assault you as well!' There was alarm as well as mockery in her voice.

'On the grounds that I would be both locked in and have a chair wedged against the handle,' I said, omitting to point out the fact that I might well be patrolling the building at a time when all might be presumed to be asleep.

I did not need to. 'You are planning something foolish, aren't you? Remember,' Harriet pointed out dryly, 'it's not just her ladyship you have to deal with – it's Thatcher, who makes up in brawn what he lacks in brain.'

'I might invite Elias to accompany me,' I said, improvising. In fact, it seemed a good idea.

'On what grounds? It would be a brave man indeed who admitted to being afraid of a woman!'

It was the patient himself who scotched the notion.

'Move me out of my own bed? I tell you straight, Matthew, I will not go. In fact, I'm getting up now to go and serve her ladyship's dinner, and that's final.' He heaved himself unsteadily to his feet. 'But you might help me to get dressed. I would take that kindly. Ouch!' He sat down again, clutching his head. 'The world is turning.'

I laid him back gently. 'Samuel, you are a good loyal man, the very best. But someone hit you so hard you might have died. So if you will not go to a place of safety . . .'

He clutched my hand. 'I cannot! And, to be honest, I fear I could not even if I wanted to. I have hardly been ill all the time I have served here. But now . . .' He sank back with a sigh.

Putting my head round the door, I summoned a servant, and passed him a note I had in readiness. 'Take this to Dr Page now. Find him, wherever he may be. Now, I said!'

In the event, all my fine plans for heroism came to nought. Dr Page deemed Samuel too ill to move, despite my covertly expressed fears for his safety.

'I understand, and I am tempted to agree with you – not that I think anyone would have the gall to strike the poor man in his own bed. Perhaps I can suggest a solution: my apprentice, Job, is a strong young man. I will tell him that as part of his training he must watch over our patient, checking his vital signs and ministering to his other needs.'

'Thank you. I will make sure he is well rewarded,' I said.

'Excellent. Now, while I am here, I will go and see how her ladyship does.'

'Before you do, Page – the Rivers baby? Everyone will want to wet its head.'

'A sturdy girl.'

The women almost ignored the news about the baby beyond perfunctory hopes about her future. They were more concerned about Samuel's health, of course, but admitted they were pleased with the neat solution. Even so, Beatrice did no more than toy with her supper; neither Harriet nor I was much more enthusiastic. I was keen to draw the meal to a close so that I could speak to Thatcher. I was pleased to see that he had survived the ordeal.

'How is her ladyship? Did she enjoy a good meal?'

'Sir, she was angry to see me. But she was more angry that I'd been sent in the place of Mr Bowman.'

'Angry? I presume you told her how ill he was. Dr Page's apprentice is staying overnight to nurse him, incidentally. Job.'

Even the sturdy Thatcher looked impressed.

'Go and have your own supper now. But remember, if the bell rings for Mr Bowman, you are to answer it immediately – mid-mouthful if necessary. If she has not rung by the time you finish your meal, you present yourself to her to enquire what she would like for dessert, and return to serve it to her. This is all good training for you, Thatcher, though you may not think so just now. Off you go!'

He turned slowly, but then faced me again. 'Mr Bowman – he will be all right, won't he, sir? He's always been good to us footmen – straight as a die.'

'All we can do is pray,' I said gently.

Job arrived at about nine, quickly establishing himself in the sickroom. For their health's sake, I insisted that since the evening was fine, Harriet and Beatrice joined me in a turn round the rose garden, the scent of which was almost overpowering. We strolled in silence, all no doubt, contrasting the happy evening when we walked as a foursome with tonight.

'Some people,' I said quietly, as we turned back towards the House, 'believe that prayers are acceptable wherever they are raised. And I think a garden, in the cool of the evening, would be a good place, don't you?'

XXVIII

*C*hristiana Willes, the new master's son calls me. Willes for short, as they call boys at school, he says. I am as good as any fellow he knows. Better than most. I am now not just the upper housemaid, but also the chief cricket coach, and Sir Peregrine has personally raised my wages by two guineas a month. 'What is a little dust,' he asks rhetorically, 'compared to a son getting his cricket Blue?'

But I know my place. Master Alfred tried to kiss me. He knows that if he tries again, I shall not teach him how to deal with the new way I have devised to make the ball spin when it hits the ground.

I would like to kiss him.

But I know that what that man did means I cannot ever kiss anyone or be kissed. Ever.

When Master Alfred goes back to Cambridge, there are more guineas in my box, another ball, and a pile of books he tells me I shall enjoy.

Though I have already read some of them, I relish every page.

TWENTY-NINE

It was remarkable how quickly the household settled back into its routine after the trials of Saturday and Sunday. Samuel was no longer feverish, but Dr Page, on his regular visits, insisted he must keep to his bed for a few more days at least, though he permitted Beatrice to reduce and finally to discontinue the dose of laudanum. Thatcher continued to carry out his duties, his demeanour becoming more sober and stately by the hour. But it seemed to be with some trepidation that he accosted me outside my office towards the end of Wednesday afternoon, bowing in the stiff-hipped way that Samuel himself cultivated.

'Mr Rowsley, sir, I wonder if I might have a word in private?'

'Of course.' I unlocked my office door – it still seemed strange but now I deemed it necessary – closing it behind us. I gestured him to a seat, and retired behind my intimidating desk. In the face of his continuing embarrassed silence, I said, 'It seems to me that you have changed a great deal since our last conversation in this room. Yes?'

I was rewarded with a bashful smile, which took five years off him.

'But do I sense that something is troubling you? Are you worrying what will happen to you when Mr Bowman is well enough to return to his duties?'

He blushed. 'Well, of course, that does cross my mind. But that doesn't mean I don't wish him well, sir. He's been like a father to me, like I said. To all of us. I suppose, until he gets strong again, I might assist him, carrying trays and opening doors – that sort of thing.'

'I will suggest it to him – recommend it, in fact, because you know as well as I do that he will wish to return to his post before he is truly recovered. But there's something else?' I leaned forward. 'Thatcher, would you rather talk to Mrs Faulkner? You've known her a long time and it might be easier.'

He shook his head. 'I wouldn't want to worry a lady's head with anything like this. And you may wish to sack me for even thinking what I . . . I'm sorry.'

'Just tell me what is worrying you, young man. Dismissal could not be further from my mind.'

There was a long pause. He gnawed a hangnail. 'I wonder – sir, do you think her ladyship . . . this is why I can't speak to Mrs Faulkner . . . Sir, might she have – I don't like to use the word . . .'

'Man to man, Thatcher,' I said.

He looked around, as if someone had replaced him as a spy. '*Agentlemanadmirer*, sir.' He spoke so fast he blurred the words together.

I was flabbergasted by the notion. 'An admirer?'

'She's started to lock her door at all times – Florrie says she has to wait a long time on some occasions, and so do I. And I'd swear I heard a man's voice once. Just the once, mind you.'

All sorts of explanations, none I could share with him, chased each other round my brain. Personifying reason, I spread my hands. 'Thatcher, how could a man – how could anyone – get into the House unseen? Get up to her rooms unseen? There is always someone around.' But not in the Family wing, of course. The corridors had been deserted whenever I had been near the locked dressing room. Or had someone seen me? In an old house like this there might well be spy holes so that promiscuous husbands or equally adulterous wives might know if they were about to be caught out. Perhaps her ladyship had indeed got wind of my activities, and installing Thatcher as her informer had been her response. I thought Harriet would have a better chance of discovering that than I.

'I don't know, Mr Rowsley, and that's the truth. But there's all those connecting doors and staircases never used except when George was checking for dry rot – and her ladyship, having lived here so long, might know of them.'

I nodded. 'Of course. Have any of the other members of staff mentioned anything? The chambermaids, for instance? They, after all, strip beds and perform . . . tasks . . .' Tasks which the presence of bathrooms would eliminate.

He took a second to work that out. 'Ah. The chamber pots. I'll ask, shall I?'

'I think I'll spare you that! But if you were to hear gossiping or complaints, it wouldn't be disloyal to tell me. Or to tell the maid in question to speak to Mrs Faulkner. I will forewarn her so she will not be shocked.'

The chance to speak to Harriet did not arise till we all gathered in Samuel's room after luncheon. Predictably, she was not so much shocked as disbelieving, until Beatrice reminded her of the horses the night-time arrival of which she thought she had heard. 'What if . . .?'

'People of her class always used to have much looser morals than the rest of us,' Harriet pointed out. 'His late lordship now – he had a fearful reputation as a man about town.'

'A rake's how I'd put it. But now we're all supposed to be puritans, aren't we? At least according to Mr Pounceman, who is now, by the way, apparently convalescing in Malvern. I wonder how long we'll be without him. Not that I miss him, don't get the wrong impression, but what about hatchings, matchings and dispatchings? Life doesn't stop just because he's probably become a eunuch!'

Not for the first time I wondered how Samuel would cope with her when they were married.

It was time to divert everyone: there had never been an opportunity to produce the little gifts I had bought in Shrewsbury. Trivial though they were, they lightened the undoubted atmosphere.

The turmoil at the House, and my lingering and egotistical feeling that I should be there to protect the women against dangers unknown, meant I had missed cricket practice – and much local gossip of course. I should imagine Job's presence in the House occasioned a great deal.

Page continued his daily visits, those to Samuel getting shorter and shorter in comparison with those he spent Upstairs. Surely he was not the lover that Thatcher suspected? I dismissed the possibility immediately. But another, still inchoate, formed slowly but insistently in the back of my mind.

XXIX

I tell myself that the satisfaction of a job well done, that contentment and a calm mind constitute a longer-lasting emotion than happiness. It is the dogma I live by. Serene as a swan, I go about my daily tasks. I never raise my voice. I never lose my temper. I am a perfect employee.

Even my dreams are pleasant. No, I cannot deceive myself. My dreams let me down, as I relive those five minutes – was it as long as that? – in the library, that took my life away.

I love Matthew. He loves me. How much longer can I withstand the desire we both have to marry?

Provisos?

The biggest proviso is how I tell him – unless an even bigger one is how a good pure man like him will react.

THIRTY

S amuel was not well enough to have resumed his duties when I received a letter from Ianto Davies. It was short and to the point. Someone he knew had pulled a dead young woman from a canal near him, which he thought might well be Maggie, given other circumstances, he added mysteriously and irritatingly. Would I care to make a formal identification so the people who came to the rescue might claim the reward?

'He didn't say anything about the poor child's baby?' Harriet asked gently, watching me drink strong tea to steady me.

'No. Nothing. But there's this line about *other circumstances*: could that allude to a baby?'

'If it does and if the baby is alive it must come back here. I can find a wet nurse in the village until Mrs Billings is able to look after her. No, she never will be, will she, not with all the blue pills in the world? Ada? Her hands are already full, what with her children and doing her best for her mother. Yet I would not see the baby go into the workhouse or an orphanage: never!'

'And it may not be an orphan. His lordship may still be alive somewhere.'

She snorted. 'I can't see him recognising his by-blow, not in a month of Sundays. No, we must find a better solution. Enough of this speculation! When is the next train?'

'This is a whole new world!' she gasped as she peered through the railway carriage window. 'One I never knew existed. Oh, I have read about it – I believe I have read about everywhere from Norway to the South Seas. But all my journeys have been from one place of employment to the next.'

'I wish I could have made your first trip with me one through a better landscape,' I said. 'One with cleaner air and happier people. But we can pretend that over there are the Alps, not chimneys belching foul smoke. We can pretend that the turgid water of that canal is a lake so clear we can see the fish.'

Her response to my folly was the saddest smile I had ever seen. Perhaps she was shocked by my insensitivity – we were going to identify a body, after all. But a deep unease I did not want to recognize made me shiver. Dare I take her hand? I reached for it: it lay passively in mine.

If Ianto Davies was shocked to see an unmarried man and woman present themselves at the manse, he did not show it. He greeted me as if I was an old friend, and Harriet with almost as much enthusiasm. I suspected Marty had told him about us.

'Would you care for a cup of tea, or would you rather get the sad business over and done with first? Yes? We'll take my trap and head down to the Navigation down Bilston way – they've laid the poor girl there.'

'The Navigation? A public house?'

'Yes. In an outhouse.'

'Not a mortuary?'

'That's how they do it round here. Bleak as it is, it's like a social event – people go round to see the body and have a quick half while they're at it. One day it'll all change – there's already talk of building a proper mortuary. I'll just get my lad to get the trap.' He rang a bell. Someone shouted. He shouted back in Welsh. 'This way, now.' He led us into his tiny yard, where an aged horse stood resentfully between the shafts of an equally venerable vehicle. He continued as if five minutes had not passed, 'There will be an inquest, of course.'

'Suicide?' I asked quietly, hoping that Harriet did not hear.

'Why should it be? Someone saw the poor little wench – I'm sorry, you pick up the lingo if you live here long enough – the girl on the towpath and said she might have slipped. She was pretty well crawling, she was so weak, they said. A man on a narrowboat. Him and his wife. I know them a little. They don't come to chapel, but they have been to the parish church and had all their children baptised, as if the water carries some sort of extra luck, with them living on it. But they were more interested in fishing out the baby. Like Moses in the bulrushes, they say, only in a cut – that's what they call canals round here, Mrs Faulkner – not a river.'

'Did the baby survive?'

'Bless you, yes! Didn't I tell you? I'll be forgetting my own head next. A little girl.'

Digesting the news, neither of us spoke. Ianto urged the reluctant horse into a slightly faster pace.

'Ah, here we are!'

We fetched up at a depressed-looking public house, Ianto leading us down one side to a shed, which was not even locked.

'Are you sure, now, *cariad*?' he asked Harriet, who had stepped forward. 'I'd recommend waiting outside and letting Matthew—'

She said simply, 'It's I who was responsible for her in life: I owe her this in death.'

We walked in side by side.

As we emerged, she nodded, as if like me she was unable to speak. 'Yes. Poor Maggie,' she said at last, her voice a mere thread. Then she straightened her shoulders, and resumed her usual business-like tone. 'Is there an undertaker you can recommend, Mr Davies? I want her brought back immediately to the village where she was born, and given a proper funeral, not tipped into a pauper's grave.'

He nodded. 'I will see to that for you.'

'The living are even more important than the dead,' she said. 'You mentioned Moses in the bulrushes? Who took the baby in?'

'Not Pharaoh's daughter, I'm afraid! Jem Stride. He's a boatman. In charge of a narrowboat – actually, his wife is, I'd say. Not a barge: you must never call them that. And you're in luck. They're still moored, waiting for their next load. *Kingfisher.* Is that irony or optimism? I'll leave you to judge. Down over that humpbacked bridge.' He encouraged the horse to a dingy patch of greensward. It was happy to stop.

We looked around us. Amid all the vile smoke and fumes, a line of ragged washing fluttered defiantly from front to back of the brightly-painted vessel.

'And there behind her is a butty boat, which means they can carry extra cargo. That'll be their horse, there.' He jerked a curly thumb at the animal in question. 'Watch the ropes.' He banged on the side of the cabin, calling. A woman appeared, her sleeves rolled up, revealing arms as muscular as a prize-fighter's. Nestled within them was a small bundle, wailing. Ianto stepped away without performing introductions, as if wanting to see how we comported ourselves.

Harriet surged forward. 'Is that Maggie's baby? Mrs Stride, I'm Harriet Faulkner: I've come to take her home to her grandmama!'

'Over my dead body, you do! 'Er's my little one now, ain't you, my pretty? You're your ma's pretty Lizzie.' As the wails increased, she simply lowered her bodice and put the babe to her breast, just as one of Alf's sows would let a piglet suckle. Blushing, I averted my gaze, but Harriet managed to smile encouragingly. 'I lost me last babby after she picked up a fever. But the milk's coming nicely, ain't it, my pretty?'

Harriet nodded. 'Is she thriving?'

'Oh, ah. You can have a look if you like – but you'm not taking her nowhere, understand?'

A bent and wizened man appeared along the towpath, accompanied by a yellow-toothed brute of a dog which snarled at the sight of us.

'Charlie! Give the lady and gent a hand aboard, will yer? And keep that bloody dog quiet, or I'll tie a brick round its neck and drown it myself.'

Down a short, steep flight of steps, the cabin smelt of poverty and dirt, but was neat and tidy. 'The rest of the kids are at school,' Mrs Stride told us, as she sat on a what in fashionable circles would be a window seat, but here was not much more than a shelf, covered in a rag rug. She shifted the baby to the other breast. 'We might be poor, mister, but they goes when they can. They knows their numbers and their letters as good as anyone.'

Mr Stride nodded, pulling out a pipe as he sat down.

'And you can take that stinking pipe outside, too, like a Christian man. Ah, they've all been christened and all,' she added proudly as he sneaked off. 'As I'll swear on that Bible.' A huge tome, swathed in a shawl, lay on an upper shelf.

'And they can all read and write?' Harriet asked quietly. 'How old are they?'

She listened patiently to a recital of names and ages. I followed Mr Stride out on to the tiny area by the tiller, where I passed him my cigarette case. There was no sign of Ianto. We smoked in silence, the dog occasionally snarling in its sleep, with the women's voices murmuring inaudibly on. In silence? Just as there was constant smoke billowing from the manufactory chimneys, so there was incessant noise – from the iron wheels on the cobbles of the street, and also from what sounded like giants' hammers.

'Steam hammers, that's what they'll be,' Stride said. 'They need coal. That's where I come in. We'll fill the butty boat with coal, plus a bit more forward there. Hard for the missus to keep things clean. Nice when we go through a bit of country. Rabbits, pheasants and such. Nothing what belongs to anyone else,' he added hastily. 'Never a sheep, nothing like that. Smell that? Rabbit stew. Better a job like this than in a works. Seen a lot of me mates carried out of them in coffins. Them what they call chemicals – not getting anywhere near any of them. So I carries coal. They say as the coal gets into your lungs, but it's not so bad if you wet it first.'

'What will your children do?'

'The missus says if they learns well, the wenches might go into service or work in a shop. My lad – I'd like him to go for a soldier. We got hopes, mister. Hopes.'

'What about Lizzie?'

'Treat her the same, won't we? No better, no worse.' He spat into the green waters. 'That missus of yours – she might want the nipper but it'll break my old woman's heart to let her go. Look at her face.'

I nodded. And thought of the hopelessness of Mrs Billings. And of Ada and Silas, who might have a claim, though I could not imagine how they might manage with yet another child. Of course I could find them another, bigger cottage; of course I could increase Silas' wages. And yet . . . was I going to play God? I feared I was. 'Now we're on our own, tell me about the baby's mother.'

'Topped herself, no doubt about it. But I won't tell the Coroner that, bless you, no. Don't want Lizzie growing up knowing that. Moses, that's what we'll tell her about – like we found a little princess in the reeds, not a princess finding a lad, if you get my meaning.'

'What if we told you she was the daughter of a rich man?'

'Oh, not that old story! Some gentleman has her as his fancy woman and kicks her out when she gets in the family way. Bastards! Begging your pardon, sir. Funnily enough, the bab had something tucked up in the rags we found her in – amazing it stayed there, now I come to think of it. As if her mam wanted it kept safe. Come back down – I'll show you.'

The baby lay asleep in Harriet's arms, but Mrs Stride, although busy at her tiny stove, barely took her eyes off her. Stride shifted the shawl covering the Bible: 'There!'

I took what he was offering. A silver spoon, complete with the Family's coat of arms. I showed it to Harriet. Without touching it, she nodded.

'I think Maggie, Lizzie's mother, stole this,' I said gently, 'and it could get her family and maybe you into a great deal of trouble if it was found here. Mr Stride, you said you want to raise her as your own, no better and no worse. Maybe Mr Davies has told you I offered a reward for someone telling us where Maggie – the baby's mother – might be found. You shall have that. I have another offer for you: let me return this spoon secretly, and – no! listen to me! – and I will give you some money instead, more than any pawnbroker would give. You know Mr Ianto Davies, minister up at the Baptist Chapel in Wolverhampton, I believe?'

'Ah. He said as how he'd bring you here. I bet he's over yonder – trying to stop old Biddie supping her stout. He's straight, is Mr Davies, so they say.'

'As straight as any man I've known. Are you a drinking man, Mr Stride? Because if you are, I don't want to give you a lot of money that'll go straight down your throat.'

His wife said, 'He ain't signed the pledge, nor never would. Why do you ask?'

'Because you'd need a lot of money to raise Lizzie properly – and that would mean for your other children too, doesn't it? Exactly the same.'

Harriet, unprompted, took up my theme. 'Money for schooling. Money for a doctor if they – if you! – fall sick. Money for apprenticeships.'

'Safer than going to be a soldier,' I said aside to Stride. 'Better prospects.'

'You bribing us, or summat?' Mrs Stride snapped.

'Never!' she responded, tears in her eyes. 'I can see you are good people – Lizzie's name is already in the family Bible, Matthew!' She stopped, blushing, as she used my name for the first time in public. 'At home she has a grandmother – she has an aunt . . . But who am I to try and take away a child from a loving home?' Tears welled from her eyes. 'Promise me, never to let her go to the workhouse or an orphanage: you must trust Mr Davies if ever you fall on hard times. Promise me!' By now the tears were running freely.

Stride looked awkwardly on. 'You mean we can keep her? Maybe you could write that down in the Bible, missus.'

'I've told you, she's not mine to give away. But—'

'Let's call it finders keepers, then,' Mrs Stride said decisively. 'And we'll promise on the Good Book. We'll have that reward, Miss, but you can give Mr Davies the spoon money. Just in case. Know what I mean?' She proffered the spoon, which Harriet slipped into her bag.

I handed over the money.

Mrs Stride stared, and then peeled most of the notes off, handing them back to me. 'Much too much.' She considered a moment longer. 'Suppose you give that lot to Parson Davies too. Hey, I'll do it myself if he's anywhere around.' She went up on to the tiny deck and bellowed.

As we drove back to the manse, Ianto was so joyful he might have been a smile personified. 'Oh, you'll doubt this and worry about that, but in my view you have been extremely wise. Assuming her family did want her, what would a court of law do? What would your employer say, Matthew, if the by-blow he's gone to all that trouble to get rid of suddenly reappears? Answer me that, eh? Now, you shall see me lock this money, in a sealed envelope signed by all three of us, in my chapel safe. No – don't argue: it's what the Strides will expect. Make it all legal-looking – I know it's not, but who's to ask? And who's to say a woman like her won't love a child and bring her up as well as a duchess would. Not that a duchess has anything to do with her children, or so I've heard, it's all nurses and maids. Look you, here's the chapel: come along in. I can feel God here, for all it was only built five years ago. A proper organ, see . . .'

Harriet was generous in her thanks to Mrs Davies for the late luncheon she pressed on us. Chiefly she needed tea to revive her, saying that her appetite had died at the sight of the poverty of the area. Perhaps it was true: at least our poorest villagers had cleaner air to breathe and the chance of occasional fresh food. She expressed proper admiration of all our hostess's schemes to benefit the poor drudges of the area.

At last it was time for the journey home. Seeing a newspaper boy, I bought a paper. I suspected I might be his only customer.

Usually when I offered her my arm, she gaily dismissed the need for any assistance; today, as we walked to the station, I could feel her fatigue as occasionally I took her weight. Under her pretty hat, her head was bent. I couldn't see her face, but I could feel the depth of her sighs, as if she lamented more than the death of a simple servant girl. And we still had to break the news of Maggie's death, of course.

'I must change into mourning first,' she said, as if she read my mind. 'We will all wear black in the House, until after the funeral at least. Who will take the burial service?' she gasped, as if thinking of it for the first time.

A porter slammed the door on us. We were in motion.

'Not Mr Pounceman, not if I have anything to do with it! I wonder . . . I might ask my father, if the Church permits. He certainly would be willing, I would vouch for that. And you would be able to meet him and Mama when they stay in my house – you'll recall Beatrice had the house prepared for visitors—'

'For them?'

'Exactly. I wanted them to meet you – you to meet them! It was to be a surprise for you! But an aunt was unwell, and they had to postpone their visit. They are due any day.'

We were walking back from the station and had nearly reached the House, when we saw Silas, trudging towards the servants' entrance.

Harriet and I exchanged a glance: this would not be a comfortable conversation, but one which she would initiate.

'Silas!' She took his hand and retained it. 'I have just come from Wolverhampton. I fear I have sad news for Ada and for your mother-in-law.'

'Well, it's something Ma-in-law won't hear, Mrs Faulkner. I

was on my way to tell you she passed away this afternoon, God rest her soul – just when we hoped those blue pills were doing her some good, too.'

'I'm so sorry.'

It was my turn. 'My condolences, Silas – and to Ada. How is she?'

He shrugged sadly. 'I'd say she was glad her ma's suffering was over. But she can't stop the tears coming yet. But you said you have bad news too – young Maggie, is it?'

'It is indeed. She had a daughter, whom some kind people have taken in as their own. Unless you and Ada might want . . .?'

His face expressed purest panic. 'Six, and already – and yes, another on the way. Don't say it, Mr Rowsley. Dr Page already has. So – would those folk love her?'

'They already do, Silas: I tried to bring the baby away, but it would have broken their hearts. But you must tell Ada – consult her.'

The panic returned. 'If his lordship hears, won't he do what his ma threatened and turf us all out?'

'Not if I have anything to do with it!'

'But he's your boss, Mr Rowsley – he might sack you too. And where would we all be then? And the Stammerton folk too? If you ask me, you're the only one who seems to care about the land!'

Harriet stepped diplomatically into my horrified silence. 'In the meantime, is there anything you need, Silas? No? May I ask if you have any plans for the funeral? Because we've arranged for Maggie's body to be brought back here to be buried amongst her own, and it occurs to me that she and her mother might be reunited in death.'

He snorted. 'If I was Maggie I wouldn't want to be anywhere near her ma. You know why the poor mite ended up miles from home? Because her mother sent her, that's why!'

'Sent her!' I repeated.

'Ah, 'cos her ladyship said to. She said if there was any squeak about poor Maggie being with child by his lordship, which, by the way, she said wasn't true, though we all knew it was, not just Maggie but the whole family would have to go. So off the girl went, and Mrs Billings pointing everyone in the wrong direction, like. Come on, Mr Rowsley, sir – that search we had. All the time Ma-in-law knew you were wasting your time, and everyone else's too.'

I nodded gravely. 'Tell Ada what I have suggested. If she thinks separate graves are more appropriate, then naturally the estate will pay for two.'

'Now, all the women will be able to come here tomorrow afternoon for their mourning outfits which I will order myself,' Harriet said, cutting through the tension with a practical offer, 'and I will provide black armbands and hatbands for you men.'

'Thank'ee.' He shuffled with embarrassment. 'But where'll we get a preacher and who'll pay for him? There's not much in the funeral fund pot, Mrs Faulkner: not enough for a funeral supper.'

'Maggie was not treated well by the Family when she was alive. The least they can do is pay her expenses in death – and her mother's too, I believe. Don't you? As for the wake, as we have illness in the House, we could have the big harvest tents erected.'

'And the clergyman would take the service – or services – for very little, if any charge, Silas,' I added. 'My own father. He won't have known Maggie or your mother—'

'Neither did Pounceman, if he called the poor little wench all the things I heard tell he did!'

'No. He didn't, and Mr Rowsley told him he shouldn't have spoken as he did. But I knew her, Silas.'

His eyes popped. 'You'd speak in the church, ma'am?'

She shook her head. 'I've no wish to scandalize the village. But others knew her: Marty Baines did. And his friend the Reverend Ianto Davies did. She will be spoken well of.'

He nodded slowly. 'And I suppose, when push comes to shove, that's all anyone can hope for.'

As he walked away, I found the most banal question to fill the fraught silence. 'So many mourning clothes so quickly?'

'A warehouse in Shrewsbury,' she said briskly. 'And I formally request that the estate pay for them, Mr Rowsley.' She smiled, perhaps combatively. 'Why should people with nothing and with no choice in the matter have to pay for something they may never wear again?'

'Why should they even have to pay for their own uniforms?' I asked. 'And have to accept aprons as Christmas presents as they do in some households?'

She gasped as if in pain. What could she mean? But she simply returned to the matter in hand. 'Now, the funeral – or funerals. Are you absolutely sure that your father will officiate?'

'Yes. Papa is the obvious choice. A senior churchman – how could Pounceman or his bishop object? And he has a frighteningly kind heart.'

She shot me an amused glance. 'Excellent. Matthew, I am worried that . . . No, it is time to go in: Beatrice will be needing numbers for supper.'

'And I am sure she will be able to provide us with some afternoon tea: poor Mrs Ianto is no great cook, is she? But I need to talk over what were really not our decisions to make: would you join me in my office for a few moments?'

We went, as the local phrase had it, all round the Wrekin as we wrestled with our consciences. At last, I said, 'Ianto said it would be like this, didn't he? Let us call it quits, unless Ada is desperate to have the child – in which case there would be months if not years of wrangling, none to anyone's benefit except the lawyers'.'

As I spoke, my eyes dropped for the first time on the newspaper I had bought. 'Harriet! Harriet! He's done it! Mark's done it! Look!' I thrust the paper into her hands. 'That poor child! He's got her off! And there's talk of bringing perjury charges against the drunken men who lied about her! In many ways, this has been the worst of days. But there is always joy. Little Lizzie will grow up poor, but she will grow up loved. The child in Oxford has endured a terrible ordeal but – my darling, what have I said?'

She had fainted clean away.

XXX

It was easy to pretend I was overcome simply by a combination of hunger and the emotions of the day, but we both knew my fainting fit was caused by something else. He was simply puzzled and desperately anxious; I was riven by an anguish so great I would wish it on no one – and yet I know that Oxford child may one day face the same dilemma as I face.

To tell or not to tell? No matter how much I pace my room and try to argue my way out of it, the answer must be to tell. The next question is how: do I kneel before him, like a penitent to a father confessor, and spell it out, word by word, euphemism by euphemism? That way I would know his reaction was truthful in its spontaneity. If I wrote him a letter, I would not see his face as he read it.

If only I had someone to advise me. Beatrice! She would tell me to say nothing. But that would be to marry under false pretences.

The more I pace, the less I know.

And then I hear voices.

THIRTY-ONE

Dressed for supper in the Room, I found myself in the servants' hall staring at a battered Thatcher, currently surrounded by a mass of hysterical maids and angry footmen. Harriet was establishing calm, sending a young woman for cloths for the blood and dispatching one footman to summon me, another for Dr Page.

'I can save you one errand at least,' I said, catching her eye and smiling. 'Better?' I mouthed.

Her smile worried me, but this was not the time for delicate questions. I watched her deal with the whole situation, even deploying me once or twice on errands, once to check that the noise had not troubled Samuel, the next to assure Beatrice, flurried for the first time I had known her, that he was well. I was proud to work as part of her team. Accordingly, when it was time to ask questions and we adjourned to my office, I naturally looked to her as at very least my equal.

Dr Page sat opposite us at the table, rather than the huge desk. He looked uncomfortable, as well he might.

'I do not ask you to break your Hippocratic Oath, Page – but I do need to know what is going on in this house. Not just for my sake, but for the sake of all the staff going quietly about their work who might meet the same fate as Hortense, as Samuel and now young Thatcher.'

'Nothing but a few superficial cuts!' he blustered.

'Only because he is a tall, strong, young man,' Harriet said. 'What am I exposing my young women to? I have advertised, as you asked, for a nurse, but until one is engaged, I believe they are all at risk.'

Page took a long, deep breath. 'What do you think is going on?' Clearly he was desperate for a few more moments to work out how he should deal with the situation.

Indulging him, I said, 'I believe that the cause of all these injuries is not her ladyship. Male voices have been heard coming from her private rooms.' I looked at Harriet.

Nodding, she continued, 'The chambermaids tell me there is evidence of more than one occupant. Mrs Arden tells me food has started to disappear from the kitchen. I believe her ladyship is concealing his lordship. Am I right? I take your silence as an affirmative. So how do we now proceed?'

Widening his eyes at her calm authority, he said, 'You have alternatives. Some would say his lordship should be arrested, and feel the full force of the law. But when did the House of Lords last convict one of their own? Some of them would probably think that the beating of servants is acceptable! It is for wives, after all.'

A flick of her eyebrow told us what Harriet thought of that. 'Is it only those for whom I am responsible that have been hurt?'

'I understand . . . there are rumours . . . that vehicle of his – I believe someone at a house he had been staying at had his revenge. I treated his lordship and Luke when they returned here. They had to hand over their mounts to the man who accompanied them as part of their punishment. All very medieval.'

'So *Luke* is here too! Does his father know? He doesn't! Oh, how cruel.'

'Is Luke his valet or his guard?' I asked.

'Both – more the latter, I suppose. What you must understand, Rowsley – what you must both understand,' he corrected himself, with a small bow, 'is that this is not his fault. He is suffering from a sort of madness, the result, I fear, of his father's . . . indiscretions. You will note there was only one offspring of the marriage. I believe his lordship passed on the . . . the infection . . . to his wife. The version his current lordship has is almost certainly hereditary.'

'No wonder mamas with marriageable daughters made them avoid him,' Harriet said quietly. Then her face hardened. 'He knew about this – is it syphilis? – and still seduced or raped the servants? Knowing he could infect them? He should indeed be brought to trial. They, after all, have a life sentence.'

'But his legal advisers would argue insanity – and then he would be confined to an asylum where there would be no hope for him.' He spread his hands. 'This is not a decision to be taken lightly, is it? One thing we must all agree on, I know, is that he must lose his liberty. He will lose his mother too, by the way, soon enough – her symptoms are manifesting themselves now. The sins of the fathers, and of the husbands . . .' He shook his head as if, for the first time, in despair. Then he resumed his professional demeanour. 'What I propose is this—'

'Page, I may have some proposals of my own, but not till I have discussed them with the key players in the household – my fiancée, Mr Bowman, and Mrs Arden. Without them, this household is nothing. Their years of loyalty and dedication must not be thrown away by our high-handed decisions. They must and will play a part. In the meantime, it is understood that the places of the staff will be taken by professional nurses and guards. The usual channels have not provided them yet: I'm sure you have people you can summon in an emergency like this? Thank you.' I reached for the bell.

'I've not quite finished here yet,' he said. 'I'll make sure the sedatives I have administered to both are working, and then take one more look at young Thatcher. We don't want those cuts to scar and spoil his beauty, do we?'

'Indeed, we want no one to suffer long-term damage. I repeat, we need specialist attendants, Page, and some strong young men in case the sleeping draughts haven't worked. Thatcher's deputy will escort you to the servants' hall.' I rang.

I was not just being unwontedly officious. I wanted to have a few minutes with Harriet to see what she thought of my hasty plans. I drew my chair to hers, and took her hands in mine. 'It has been a hard day for you especially, my love, and it may get harder. I have a few ideas. But if you disapprove in any way, foresee a single difficulty, I will abandon them without another word, I promise. Today we proved we have a special understanding, but I was conscious that I said things without consulting you first. Can you forgive me for jumping in? It will never happen again, I promise: we may be of one mind, but we need to establish that first!'

'Yes. Yes, I forgive you and yes, we should work as a team.' A blush suffused her face. 'I—'

'That is how my parents have always worked. It is the basis of their happy marriage. I hope it will be the foundation of ours.'

'You may not – you cannot want me when . . .' She swallowed

hard. 'There is something you should read before you speak of marriage again. I will give it to you tonight.'

I feared she would faint again, she was so pale, but she gathered herself together. 'Meanwhile, these plans of yours . . .'

Our shared supper was a very sober affair, but at least Page had deemed it safe for Samuel to partake of the lightest of courses and a very little wine and water.

As we had agreed, I let Harriet explain the situation.

'Any ordinary person who has done what his lordship has done would stand trial and no doubt be put in prison. But as a peer of the realm, his lordship is entitled to very different justice – and it is unlikely that he would be jailed. On the other hand, he might be sent to a lunatic asylum, which might seem the best option.' She paused to look at the others' faces. 'He would be deprived of his liberty, which is just, but might be submitted to all sorts of indignities that people like you, Samuel, who have served the Family so long, would find unacceptable.'

'He was my master, and his father before him – God rest his soul!' There was no doubting his loyalty – which was about to be put to an even greater test.

Harriet continued, 'Having his lordship certified would have all sorts of consequences. There is the obvious pain to her ladyship, but I am sorry to say that Dr Page considers she may be suffering from the same disease as her son – and some of our estate workers and their children, of course, may be afflicted.'

Poor Samuel's face was a study in painful disbelief. 'No! His father was a kind employer – a decent man!'

'I agree. But even the best young men have . . . adventures . . . when they are young. "See Naples and die!" they say – because of the amount of disease spread by' – she groped for a euphemism – 'disease spread from man to woman and back to man. It seems to Dr Page that his lordship's father may have infected her ladyship – and that their son, our current lord, is suffering from congenital syphilis.' Her blush threatened to overwhelm her.

It was time for me to take over. 'Sadly he is not known for his sexual continence, is he? And the disease may shatter the lives of people who, as their employer and landlord, he should have been protecting. I believe the estate must offer discreet but genuine compensation.'

Beatrice spoke up. 'If his lordship – and maybe her ladyship too – are confined to an asylum, the House would have to be mothballed and even if the estate workers are kept on, all the domestic staff, maids and footmen – even Luke – would end up without work. Think how many families that would affect!' She exchanged a quick glance with Samuel, clearly concerned for their future.

'Exactly,' Harriet said, to both her words and her unspoken fear. 'As you may know, the only person who can dismiss Matthew is his lordship – and he probably has to be in his right mind to do it. So another suggestion comes to mind.' Carefully she did not say whose mind. 'The House is big, is it not? Most rooms are never occupied, nor were even when we had company. So it would be possible to seal off one wing – to make it as safe as an asylum. Dr Page would bring in specialist staff to care for him, and also, we could ensure, the very best doctors – not necessarily to stay here but to visit from time to time to make sure he is being treated properly and in the most up-to-date way. Of course we would not need nearly so many staff, but at least a few could keep their jobs – and with Matthew holding the purse-strings I think we can assume that no one would be dismissed out of hand. The estate could pay pensions to people feeling they were too old or set in their ways to find a new employer.' She took a breath, as if to steady her voice. 'Those afflicted with his lordship's disease would also find money and if necessary a refuge here.'

Samuel gave me a harder stare than I was expecting. 'Would this be legal? You might be feathering your nest for all the Law would know.'

'I might. Samuel, half of me would love to abandon the Family to its fate. But like you I feel the burden of responsibility on my shoulders. Responsibility not just to you, my friends, and everyone in the servants' hall, not just to the estate workers. You know I've long wanted to improve the estate houses and rebuild Stammerton. That way his lordship would leave a wonderful legacy of hope, not despair. And the building and furnishing would provide work for those who may have lost their jobs.'

'Save them from the workhouse, you mean?'

'Samuel, I would do almost anything to save anyone from the workhouse, having seen the conditions in even the best ones. We agree that all our colleagues here, great and small, are human? Let them not be treated inhumanely, then.'

'What about Mr Pounceman? Won't he shove his oar in?'

Harriet produced a sweetly malicious smile. 'I suspect that if Matthew's proposals are accepted, the family lawyer will suggest a board of overseers, such as workhouses have. If he were one of them he might be less inclined to gripe.'

If she had murdered four archbishops and seven babes in arms, I would still want that woman to be my wife. I said, 'We must also ask the lawyer to institute a search for the heir to the title and the estate – to the best of my knowledge, he is a second cousin, currently living abroad. He must be informed; with luck he'll be wise enough to return so that he may learn how an estate like this functions.'

At this point Tim knocked the door. 'Sir, the people the doctor asked to come have arrived.'

Samuel rose to his feet. 'Mrs Faulkner, I think you and I should escort them to the rooms concerned and discuss where they may be best accommodated.'

I nodded. 'And I must send a note to Elias to tell him that his lordship has returned home safely, with Luke, but is too unwell to explain any more. Harriet – that book you recommended. Might I borrow it now, and read it in my office? Then I can return it to you and perhaps see if we come to the same conclusions about it before I leave for my house.'

She bowed and smiled, though she was white to the lips. 'Of course. I have some accounts to complete before I retire for the night so please feel free to disturb me.'

XXXI

*H*e is knocking at the door. My hands shake so much I can barely lift the catch. When your whole world revolves on one man's decision, it is hard to be calm.
His face is pale. Haggard.
He kneels at my feet. 'My dear, I am sorry . . .'
He has read my diary and cannot . . .

I am lying on my bed. My pillow rises, and brandy slips between my lips. I open my eyes. Gradually I focus on his face. He smiles, supporting my shoulders, urging another sip upon me. Replacing the glass on the table, he strokes my hair from my brow.

'I should have run to you with joy, proclaiming my love from the roof-tops,' he is saying, 'and urging you to marry me tomorrow! Instead – you thought . . . How could you have doubted me? Men have been so wicked to you: that was what I was sorry for.'

'You can't apologize for someone else's actions,' I say gently. 'But—'

'Can you imagine, having known me run to the defence of that unknown child in Oxford, I would find it possible to feel anything except guilt for my sex and love for you, a child victim of an evil arrogant man?'

I take his hand, and shake my head.

'Have you seen him since, to shame him?'

'Never. But I have read about him, in the reports in the news-papers of trials at the Old Bailey. He is a distinguished judge, Matthew: I try to relish the irony, but I don't always succeed.' I make myself continue. 'Every bride is supposed to be a virgin, and now you know I am not.'

'If there had ever been a Mr Faulkner, who had conveniently died and left you an eligible widow, society would have cooed in delight had you consented to marry me. Please, please consent to marry now.'

'*What will people say?*'

'*What a strange question! Ah, you assume everyone will know that you have a secret. Let me see, how many people knew – when you were a child, that is? Four at most?*'

'*The girls who bullied me—*'

'*Oh, forget them! More important are the women who looked after you. Are they still alive? If they are dead, you need not worry about their gossip. And if they are alive – heavens, Harriet! – they cared for you so well I would like to kiss them on both cheeks and invite them to our wedding. When shall it be? Soon, please!*'

I have to say it: 'We have a funeral to arrange first, immediately in fact, since the men say it will be hot by the end of the week. Then there must be proper time allowed for mourning.' *I suppress – because it would make him laugh – a desire to quote from* Hamlet.

'*But a very quiet wedding ceremony—*'

'*Can you imagine that? Not if we held it here. And our friends have the right to celebrate with us – heavens, Matthew, there is not much joy for people here, not much innocent pleasure. Don't deny the women the chance to deck the church, the men to feast themselves silly – what have I said?*'

He actually blushes. '*I have this most inapposite allusion to* Hamlet *forcing itself upon me!*'

'*Not "The funeral baked meats!"*' *We collapse in childish giggles in each other's arms.*

So here I am, wishing he did not have to leave me and return to his house. In any other circumstances I would have had a bedchamber prepared for him. But there is so much joyous tension between us this perfect summer's night it would have been even harder to have him sleeping nearby than to wish him goodnight and send him on his way.

THIRTY-TWO

A very few weeks later, sleek in his city-smart clothes, Mark stood beside me as my best man. My father, granted permission to marry us in Pounceman's church, stood before us, smiling whenever our eyes met. He had discreetly rewritten the usual vows: not for anything would I ask Harriet to obey me. Behind me as many of the servants as possible were crammed into the pews alongside Ianto Davies, his wife and Marty Baines. Luke and Dr Page were sidesmen. Beatrice sat beside Samuel, her face alight with joy and fun, Samuel's a little disapproving – though that might have been an illusion caused by the remains of his bruising.

Soon she would come.

I heard Mama's voice in the porch: she insisted that Harriet having no father to give her away she would act as mother and father and friend and lend her her arm up the aisle.

There was a murmur – she was there. I heard everyone get to their feet.

I turn – and this extraordinary woman picks up her skirt and runs towards me.

Matthew Rowsley will return in

LEGACY OF DEATH

to be published in 2020

Turn the page to read an
exclusive first chapter.

ONE

My daily walk takes me to the site of the new model village: it always pleases me to see how fast the work is progressing, despite the shortness of the winter's day. But today something is wrong. The labourers are resting on the handles of their picks and shovels. Thomas, the foreman, is wiping sweat from his brow.

He scrambles out of the trench as I appear, and comes towards me, waving his hands as if I am a sheep that has gone the wrong way. I almost expect him to say, 'Shoo!'

But his eyes are full of fear. 'No, Mrs Faulkner. Mrs Rowsley, I mean. No, don't look, ma'am. 'Tis not fit for a lady's eyes. 'Tis a body, ma'am! A dead body!'

Mr Wilson cast his eyes around Thorncroft House's red dining room, where we had gathered round the long mahogany table, watched from the walls by his lordship's ancestors. None of them was welcoming, with two portrayed by Lely particularly disdainful. 'Welcome to this, the first meeting of the trustees of Lord Croft's estate, convened to oversee both its day-to-day and its long-term needs. I believe we are all here now, gentlemen – and ladies, of course,' he added with a patronising smile that could not fail to raise the hackles of at least two of those present, though they both responded with dignified nods.

Irritated though I was – had I not clearly explained to him that all, regardless of rank and sex, must be accorded the same respect? – rather than interrupt, I resolved to speak to him as he left.

'Perhaps,' Wilson continued, as unctuous as it was possible for a solicitor to be, 'in view of the solemnity of our business, before we are seated we might open with a prayer. Mr Pounceman?'

That was an invitation the Reverend Theophilus Pounceman would never decline. A severe attack of mumps in the summer had left him somewhat thinner, but had by no means dented his elegant carapace. In another milieu he might have been a dandy;

in the environs of the Church he dressed and lived like a prince, though he was simply the village rector, the generous living bestowed on him by the previous Lord Croft. In his late thirties, his good looks and excellent prospects might have made him seem very attractive as a potential husband, but I had not yet met a woman who even liked him. As for him, he disdained what he always referred to as 'the weaker sex'.

The long exhortation to the Almighty to restore Lord Croft to health was countered by a plea that we might enjoy a long and profitable association. Perhaps I was not the only one who registered a word that was decidedly suspect: as land agent I wished to be visibly meticulous in a role I had always performed with the clearest of consciences, never taking more than my contractual salary. Hence my discussions with the Family's solicitor, Montgomery Wilson, respected for his probity and probably even his pomposity throughout Shropshire, who had agreed my suggestions for people who were eligible by dint of their closeness to the Family or as noteworthy members of the village of Thorncroft. In addition to Pounceman were our village doctor, Ellis Page; Tertius Newcombe, a prosperous farmer; Samuel Bowman, the butler who had dedicated his life to the Family; Mrs Beatrice Arden, the cook; and my dear wife Harriet, once Mrs Faulkner, the housekeeper.

'I have received an apology for absence from Mr Martin Baines and my clerk has taken note of those attending,' Wilson said. 'So we can proceed to the first item on the agenda: conversion of the family wing to a lunatic asylum for his lordship and his mother.'

Samuel Bowman writhed. After some fifty years in service, he was, however, so used to waiting until he was spoken to that he could do no more than stare at me.

'I think most of us would prefer a term that carried less opprobrium,' I said. 'Her ladyship is not far from death, I believe?' Dr Page nodded his agreement. 'And his lordship's disorder might well be a result of not his own but his father's indiscretions—'

'Let us call them by their correct name,' Pounceman declared. 'Transgressions! Sins of the flesh!'

'His late lordship, Mr Chairman, is not here to defend himself,' Harriet said with such quiet assurance she might have been speaking at formal meetings like this all her life. 'But I agree, as I think we all do, that we should perhaps refer to the family wing by another term than lunatic asylum. Mr Bowman was speaking of this earlier.' She nodded across the table to her colleague, her beautiful hair, confined under a much less un-flattering cap these days, gleaming in the candlelight.

Wilson might have been as surprised to hear her speak as to hear her chair burst into song, but after a moment's hesitation he took his cue, and nodded towards Samuel. 'Mr Bowman?'

'All of us servants have always called it the family wing. We don't need to change its name, Mr W— Mr Chairman. There are new locks on the doors; there are bars at the windows. It is safe. It does not need to lose . . . to lose its dignity.'

Wilson nodded. His clerk, a sad-faced youth in a suit a size too large, scratched at his paper.

'Family wing it is,' Wilson declared. 'And the changes to the fabric, Mr Rowsley? I believe Mr Bowman has already alluded to some of them.'

'Indeed. The estate carpenter has also installed some extra doors for security. He has gone to great pains to ensure they are in keeping with the House. However, he assures me that as and when it is safe to remove them, it can be done with no major damage to the fabric.'

'So all is well on that front. Does anyone have anything else to add? Very well, let us proceed to the next item: guards – or do you prefer another name, Mr Bowman?'

How would he react to the sarcasm?

'The staff all refer to them as attendants or nurses,' Samuel responded with a slow dignity that matched his best attire. 'After all, many of them used to be in regular service here, as footmen or maids. Dr Page has had them trained.'

Page was not going to wait to be patronised. 'As a country doctor, Mr Chairman, I did not consider myself sufficiently au fait with current developments in the treatment of such illnesses, so I invited experts from the county asylum and Royal Salop Infirmary to instruct those who volunteered for new roles.'

Wilson, outgunned, nodded. 'And the rest of the staff?' He looked at me.

'I can tell you that all the outdoor staff have remained in place, with the exception of the Family's personal grooms, both of whom have sought and found employment elsewhere. They will be discreet,' I added. 'As to the others, Mrs Rowsley is responsible for the maids, Mrs Arden for the kitchen staff and Mr Bowman for the footmen.'

Harriet and Samuel, despite his initial anxieties, reported confidently on changes, only Beatrice Arden showing any sign of nervousness. She too sported a less ugly cap.

'So many staff still employed!' Pounceman jumped in. 'Really, Rowsley, how can you possibly justify that?'

This from a man who employed at least eight servants to nurture him! For answer I looked at Wilson, who peered over his spectacles. 'Mr Pounceman, I would be more than grateful if you would address all your comments through the chair. There would appear to be a large number of people still drawing wages, Mr Rowsley.'

For answer I passed him a copy of the wages bill for the last three years. 'As you will see, the servants, whatever work they are doing, are not highly paid. The fabric and fittings must be preserved in the best possible state, and to do this we must rely on their expertise. Such a building is not for the present occupier alone: it must be kept in trust for his heir. As and when staff find new employment elsewhere, the posts they leave vacant may or may not be filled – that will be at the discretion of those directly supervising them, or this committee if the members prefer.'

'My opinion, for what it is worth,' Wilson said, 'is that such decisions might well be left to those with the requisite knowledge and experience. Are we all agreed? Ah, Mr Pounceman.'

'We are trustees for a reason, sir. We are to oversee what is done so no one takes advantage of a delicate situation. How are we to know that there is no nepotism, no other sort of favouritism?'

Dr Page raised his pen. 'Mr Chairman, I should imagine that these loyal employees around the table with us have never had much in the way of supervision from anything except their consciences, with which, to the best of my knowledge, they have imbued their underlings. Perhaps, if any exceptional remuneration is to be made and they are in any doubt, they should report to Mr Rowsley as land agent?'

'Although that has always been the case, Mr Chairman, I am

more than happy to pass my powers of approval to those of us gathered here.'

'I still believe we should approve all the accounts, not just wages but other expenditure. We do not want the estates to become Rowsley's milch cow, do we? I see that he has appointed a clerk to assist him.'

I had. A bright lad once the stablehand at the village pub. Harriet had taught him to read, and though I paid him in shillings, not pound, at the moment, I was sure he would one day become a professional man in his own right.

'Mr Pounceman, I would remind you that it was at Mr Rowsley's personal suggestion that this board was formed. I think you might keep such insinuations to yourself in future.' Wilson rocketed in my estimation. 'You will note that he is required by our articles to submit his accounts to us, once they have been scrutinised by one of my more expert colleagues. Now, I fear we have wandered from the agenda.'

Pounceman raised a hand. 'I would like to table a motion.'

Wilson shook his head. 'Then you must raise the topic in Any Other Business, sir. There is something else to be raised then too, so let us turn our attention to the next item,

rebuilding Stammerton.' He contrived to ignore Pounceman's raised hand. 'Mr Rowsley: thank you for submitting these drawings and estimates to us all in advance. Our discussion can now be informed, not a matter of speculation. I am sure you would all like to comment, but I must remind you to comment through me, as chairman. My clerk will take note of everything you say. Dr Page?'

Page acknowledged the invitation with a nod. 'There are those who may consider such a wholesale change an extravagance. However, as a doctor who regularly sees the effects of living in such hovels as pass for cottages, the effects of not eating because there is no food available, I support Mr Rowsley's proposals wholeheartedly. If the foundations could be dug tomorrow it would not be too soon for me.'

'Thank you. Mr Newcombe?'

'I'm glad it's not my money being spent, that's all I can say. But I agree, many of those cottages are a disgrace. Mr Rowsley and I have had conversations in the past, and it can be admitted there are things over which we have not seen eye to eye. However, persuaded by his arguments, I have started to improve my own labourers' places, little by little, and given them plots for allotments, and I have to admit, they are more cheerful as a result. They work harder, too. So maybe there's an element of self-interest in Rowsley's plans. As for the school, they say that Parliament will soon be insisting on free education for all our children, and being a step ahead is never a bad thing. But I warn you, universal education will change things. And not always for the better.' He paused. 'It's a nice little church proposed there – you must be pleased as Punch, Pounceman. Sorry, Mr Chairman. I would imagine Mr Pounceman must be pleased as Punch.'

Whatever the vicar wanted to say, he would have to wait. Wilson invited Samuel, who had bravely raised a hand, to speak.

'Mrs Fau— Mrs Rowsley! – knows more about teaching and so on than I do, but I can tell you this. When we get the youngest servants into the House, they are poor, weedy specimens, weak and pretty well useless. But then they get three good meals a day, and they are transformed. So I say the allotments are a good idea, which means the cottages need a means of cooking this food. A kitchen. And it's not decent the way families are crammed together, boys and girls, children and grown-ups, so they need proper bedrooms.'

Pounceman was shaking his head. Eventually Wilson noticed, and invited him to speak.

'Our Lord said we would have the poor always with us. It is right to give them alms, to admit them to the workhouse if they are deserving. But these cottages will be given to the deserving and non-deserving alike! How can you— how can Mr Rowsley house a man who drinks away his earnings next to a sober God-fearing man who comes to church? A school? I agree with Mr Newcombe that it will give people ideas above their station, and cause unrest. A cricket pitch on the village green? That will encourage idle loitering!'

Harriet raised a finger, catching Wilson's eye. To Pounceman's clear chagrin, he was invited to make way for another speaker.

'With due respect, Mr Chairman, I believe a village green complete with cricket team will actually help prevent revolution. His late lordship, for all his faults – some of which have sadly recently come to light – was popular with his workers and his tenants because he had, as they would put it, no side, no self-importance, one might say. He played alongside people earning a pittance and came to care for them. He insisted food parcels were despatched when illness struck a family. He knew everyone by name. I won't say he was a model landlord, and that was partly because his agent was quietly feathering his own nest, I suspect. But because he knew his men and they knew him, if violence had ever arisen, he would never have permitted the militia to lay a hand on them, and I believe his men would have guarded him with their lives.'

Wilson nodded gravely. 'Mrs Arden?'

Although I thought I knew her well, she surprised me. 'Privies, sir. Why not have proper sanitation? Someone I know lost his wife and family to the cholera in Manchester. He says that with clean water from pipes and – forgive the term – water closets, such a dreadful disease could never flourish. And I know this is out of order, sir, but I'd like to see piped water and bathrooms and water closets here in the House, too. Those nurses Dr Page brought in: they say you have to be extra particular where you've got sick people. Beg pardon, sir.' She subsided, her blushes painful to behold.

Wilson produced a rare smile. 'Thank you, Mrs Arden. An excellent idea. We must discuss it further in Any Other Business. Mr Pounceman, I suspect you have not completed your contribution? What are your thoughts about the church, which I gather does not conform to your own ideas?'

They did not.

Finally we reached Any Other Business. By now I was sure I could see another little smile playing across Wilson's austere features. But he maintained his calm and judicious bearing throughout, even as Pounceman embarked on a diatribe against me.

'I cannot disapprove of the measures taken to secure the house during the term of his lordship's illness. But nothing will reconcile me to the wholesale changes proposed during our earlier discussions. His lordship may recover, after all.' He glanced at Page, who responded with a sad shake of the head. 'And when he does, he will no doubt expect to find a reasonable amount left in the family coffers. If the Almighty chooses to call him home, then his heir should find his inheritance intact. Oh, we have heard that it is a second cousin, probably living in the Antipodes. We have heard all about Mr Rowsley's fruitless attempts to find him. But until he does appear, I say we should veto all these pie in the sky notions!'

'How fortunate,' Wilson said quietly, 'that given the urgency of the projects, we will not have to wait long. Ladies and gentleman, his lordship's heir is already in the country!'